S0-BCW-183

SATAN'S SURROGATE

SATAN'S SURROGATE

Brian McNaughton

CARLYLE ● NEW YORK

Also by Brian McNaughton
from CARLYLE BOOKS

SATAN'S LOVE CHILD
SATAN'S MISTRESS
SATAN'S SEDUCTRESS

This is a work of fiction. All the characters and events
portrayed in this book are fictional, and any resemblance
to real people or incidents is purely coincidental.

Copyright © 1982 by Siena Publishing Corp.

All rights reserved

CARLYLE BOOKS are published by
Siena Publishing Corp.
New York, New York

ISBN: 0-503-07076-9

Printed in the United States of America

CHAPTER ONE

He handed his slip to the girl behind the desk and she giggled. It happened all the time, but this time was the last straw. Instead of scowling out the window as if he had far weightier things on his mind than the rudeness of a stupid girl, he said, "What's so funny?"

"Nothing. I was thinking—" she turned away, her shoulders shaking—"of something else."

Unable to maintain this rare show of aggressiveness, he turned to scowl out the window. When he dared to look back, she had gone to talk to another girl at the end of the desk. They were both giggling. He caught the first one's eye. She blushed and fled into the stacks.

He ought to change his name to something less incongruous with his appearance, like Dumbo Myopionio. O. Leo Bottom. Porky Mumford Pigge.

"Sterling Fairchild?"

It was the second girl, all business, because the first was now undoubtedly clutching her aching belly as she rolled around in the stacks with Kafka clenched between her teeth as a makeshift gag. *One morning Gregor Samsa awoke to find that he was Sterling Fairchild.*

"You may keep books from the Special Reserve only overnight." As she banged her rubber stamp, she tried to pretend he was a real person. "Are you taking Dr. Doyle's ballad course? That's unusual, for a freshman."

"I made it on my looks."

He believed she smiled, but he had used up his daily quota of the courage he needed to look girls in the eye. He seized his book and lumbered away. Her book. *The Myth of the Otherworld in the English and Scottish Ballads,* by Gwyneth Underhill: who was now unjustly, ludicrously, Dr. Doyle. Her husband was a sleazy PR man who wrote those brochures that ought to say, "Amworth College nestles in the rolling hills of western Connecticut like a happy little louse in an armpit." Matching the ineffable Doyle with Gwyneth Underhill was like casting Jack Lemmon at his sweatiest as the knight-at-arms whom *La Belle Dame Sans Merci* held in her thrall. The God of Injustice who lies like a spider in his web at the center of the universe must have chuckled at his nastiest joke when he ordained that Gwyneth should come into the world almost two decades before Sterling and give her hand to a blithering ninny.

He slumped his way down the broad steps of the Wilbur Whateley Memorial Library and confronted a fat moon hung in daylight over hills like heaps of multicolored gumdrops. *Even a man who says his prayers . . .* He had brightened her day when he'd found the nerve to blurt out a question about werewolves. She had been talking about the shape-shifters in the ballads, with specific reference to *Tam Lin*. Held captive in the Otherworld, Tam Lin tells his sweetheart that she can restore him to the world of men if she clings tightly to him no matter what form he takes: adder, lion, bear, red-hot bar of iron. (Gwyneth clung tight with lithe thighs and arms and lips as Tam shifted to a pear-shaped freshman.)

Gwyneth went on to explain that shape-shifting was a common talent of the Others. *Fairies,* even though that was their traditional name, was a word she avoided: perhaps because it provoked snickers from the jocks who sat in the back row, enrolled in British Balladry 102 under the misapprehension that it would permit them to sit around pickin' and grinnin' like Buck Owens, and who had bailed out before the first week was up. But she said she eschewed the word because it had gained improper connotations of cuteness and small stature from Shakespeare and from German folk tales. She told them of the Irish farmer who was convicted of burning his wife to death because he was convinced the Others had stolen her and left one of their own in her place. The woman he soaked with kerosene and set alight was "too fine" to be his own wife, he maintained, and she was unable to eat mortal food. The unfortunate woman's father and several neighbors backed up the husband; and curiously enough, all of them testified that the victim had been taller than the real wife by a good two inches. To this day, the children of Clonmel recall the tragedy by chanting the verse:

"Are you a witch, or are you a fairy,
Or are you the wife of Michael Cleary?"

The Others, she said, most often appeared as full-sized human beings, but they could change their shape to anything that suited them. "Like were-wolves?" Sterling had choked. "Exactly," she'd said, smiling—smiling at *him,* and with approval. "But the Ballads were collected long after the last wolf in the British Isles had been killed, and so we find few references to them. The quiddity of folk poetry is the quotidian. You don't find kangaroos in Appalachian ballads." And she went on to discuss the one about the seal who could turn into a man, leaving Sterling adrift in the past with the special smile she had given him.

Gwyneth wore gowns to class—not ordinary dresses, but gowns she made on medieval patterns—looking as if she'd just popped in on her way to a tourney. That was showmanship, of course, and his duller classes could have used some of it. She had a habit of stopping abruptly in mid-sentence and seeming to listen, as if she were getting the latest flash from the Otherworld. That was only absentmindedness, it was to be expected from a woman of genius. And when she would turn suddenly on a student with a question or comment, the intensity in her pale green eyes could seem maniacal. The first time Dr. Doyle had zapped Sherri Purvis with that look, Sherri had screamed and dropped her books. But Sterling could explain that aggressive intensity as simple enthusiasm for her subject, and a desire to infuse others with her zeal.

They called her the Wicked Witch of the West, not just because of her style of dress and her other mannerisms, but because of her reputation as one of the most demanding graders at Amworth. During the first week he had overheard a couple of girls (one of them the screaming Miss Purvis, of lacteous breasts and melliform bottom, whom he had made scream for *More! Sterling, more!* in his dampest fantasies) discussing Dr. Doyle's tough grades, and he hadn't been able to resist pushing into their conversation to say, "The last person to pass her course was Aleister

Crowley, in 1898." But they hadn't known who Aleister Crowley was, obviously, and they'd stared at him as if he were . . . as if he were Sterling Fairchild. When would he learn to stop barging in where he wasn't wanted? That area seemed to embrace the rest of the earth's population, with the not-invariable exception of his mother.

But things were improving, as his mother had said they would. "You'll find yourself in a bigger, freer sort of environment, Sterling, where people will accept you for your brilliance, for your kindness, for all the truly wonderful qualities that you have chosen to bury beneath all that acne-ravaged flesh." No, she hadn't said exactly that, but he'd inferred the last part from the look in her eyes.

As one instance of the improvement, Dr. Woodling seemed to enjoy talking to him—listening to him, mostly. But that was his job. And his roommate, Randy Scheuer, who sat around in his underwear all day trying to get three metal balls to roll into the holes of a baseball puzzle, didn't actively object to him. And the librarian—the second one—had smiled sympathetically (or he believed she had) at his self-directed joke. And Gwyneth . . ."

But to use her name in the same train of thought with Randy Scheuer and Dr. Woodling and some dumb girl at the library was blasphemous, so he waited until he had labored to the top of Beardsley's

Hill, overlooking the campus, before he paused to wheeze her name aloud: "Gwyneth!" From this height, after he had assiduously smeared the sweat on his glasses with his sweaty shirttail, he could see rising above the western hills the tower crowning the Gothic Revival house where she lived with that vacuum in the human race, Doyle; with Doyle's mother, the forbidding mountain that had given birth to the mouse; with the mother's companion, or whatever, a brassy old baggage named Cassilda Oliphant; and with the two undesirable Doyle children. Sterling had spent so much time lurking in the tangled undergrowth behind their house, hoping for a glimpse of Gwyneth, that he felt he knew—and hated—them all.

The campus lay in shadow. Yellow squares began to glow in the ivied walls, but the bright-speckled granite shelf where he sat still lay in broad daylight, and it would remain light enough to read for another hour. He pulled his late-afternoon snack, sandwiches and a thermos of milk, from his brown paper bag.

Sterling had never courted a tan, and such a courtship would have been spurned during a late September sunset in New England, but some impulse directed him to unbutton his shirt. He told himself that he was doing this only because it was too warm, but that wasn't exactly the reason. He felt a vague sensation of constriction, of imprisonment, as if his shirt had beome a straitjacket. He decided the impulse wasn't worth analyzing. He succumbed to it while thinking of more important things.

Like Gwyneth's skin, for instance. It reminded him of fine china, it was so pure and sleek and white, but blood glowed deep beneath the translucent surface. In his imagination he saw her blood not as a liquid but as purified fire, an inner radiance that pulsated as it wove through the fantastically intricate network of her slim body. He wanted it to explode around him and into him—

Confused, he shook himself out of his reverie. The thought of blood, anyone's blood, had always made him ill, and the sight of it, especially his own, had sometimes made him pass out. The very sound of the word, plopping on the eardrum with a liquid thud, was distasteful. But in an unguarded moment, his mind had wandered down a strange path where blood had seemed something quite different from what he had always supposed it to be. He had almost seen, for an instant, through the eyes of another creature entirely, a creature in whom blood could arouse an almost mystical—but nonetheless rather physical excitement.

Her hair was of a blackness beyond the ultimate destiny of Nothing, but at odd moments the sun struck bronze from its profoundly complex no-color. It clung rather than hung, coiling at her neck like a witch's familiar. Sometimes he saw her living with him in a moldering castle, where she would be seized by some illness whose wasting effect would burn away everything but her beauty and make her infinitely more desirable to him. While he brooded, lean and hawklike, she would read to him: *I have reached these lands but newly . . . from a wild, weird clime that lieth, sublime, out of space, out of time . . .*

He took off his shoes and socks and, after a guilty survey of the hilltop, retreated to a point where he believed he could not be seen from the campus and removed his trousers. He had no idea why he did this, except that he wanted to. He was afraid that someone might see him and laugh, but that fear, which normally ruled his life, seemed remote and irrelevant. When he crept back from the granite shelf into the shadow of the trees, he felt more comfortable, but the reduced chance of detection had nothing to do with that. It was simply more pleasant, that was all, to be in damp grass and cool shadow.

He sat down with the book and his sandwiches: sardines and onions on slabs of rye bread slathered with sour cream and liberally dosed with pepper. As he unwrapped the first one he was surprised to find that it held no appeal. His food was—he groped for the precise word, and when it came it baffled him—*dead*.

What nonsense! All food was dead, with the possible exception of raw clams or oysters. Thinking harder about it, he realized that this proposition wasn't true, not even of this sandwich: if he'd left the onion undisturbed, it might have sprouted, and the whole sandwich was swarming with lively bacteria and latent molds. He never would have thought it possible, but he had to force himself to take a bite, and the bite was so like tasteless ashes in his mouth that he spat it out and put the sandwich aside. The milk from his thermos was no better.

He sagged forward with his belly crowding his knees and worried that he was ill. Loss of appetite was the first symptom of many fearful diseases. He was working harder than he'd ever had to work in his high school days, and what little sleep he got was tormented by feverish visions of Gwyneth. It was also true that the unremitting whisper of Randy Scheuer's little metal balls was churning up in him a subterranean frenzy that was due to erupt any day now; and that frenzy (he sometimes thought of tearing open the plastic case and pounding the little balls into Randy's skull with a hammer) might be the symptom or even the cause of some psychological disturbance.

But when he tried to list other symptoms, he could think of none. On the contrary, he had never felt better in his life. Frustration, yes, anger, yes, loss of appetite . . . no, he couldn't really say that; he felt hunger, but the food he'd brought couldn't satisfy it. Also, most uncharacteristically, he felt like dancing or running. He couldn't say exactly which he wanted to do, but he felt a deep prompting to do some combination of both: an activity that he couldn't quite visualize. He resisted it. He felt like singing, too, and he didn't resist that impulse:

"And first came out the thick, thick blood,
And then came out the thin,
And then came out the bonny heart's blood;
There was no more within."

Blood again. He remembered feeling queasy when Gwyneth had quoted those lines in class, but they didn't affect him that way now. He felt positively exhilarated. He tried to shake off the feeling as he turned his attention to her book. His hands moved with unaccountable clumsiness as he opened it.

Gwyneth had told her class that the entrance to the Otherworld of the ballads was variously described as lying in the deep woods, on a remote mountaintop, or, most frequently, under some shunned hill. The Others could travel freely to and from our world, but mortals seldom saw theirs. Sometimes men and women would be spirited away to it. Sometimes they stumbled upon it by accident and were wined and dined extravagantly, only to discover that the food and drink served by the Eldritch King held an enchantment that forced them to remain in the Otherworld. They could also fall under such a spell by making love to one of the Others. Mortals sometimes slipped unawares into the perverse chronometry of the Otherworld; as in the case of the medieval monk who paused for a moment to listen to a singularly melodious bird-song and found, on resuming his journey, that three-hundred earthly years had elapsed.

He had been struck by a similarity of these myths to a staple of the science-fiction and fantasy tales he had always loved: the concept of parallel universes, occupying the same space as ours but vibrating on a different wavelength. He had thought at first that he ought to make his comparison the subject of a paper for Gwyneth's course. It would be amusing to prove that science fiction took one of its favorite gimmicks from the fireside entertainments or people who hadn't been able to read or write, much less theorize about the Fourth Dimension.

Then he began to wonder if he hadn't gotten it backwards. The concept had originated with modern scientists, not with the fiction writers; and why should people who had excluded wolves from their ballads because they weren't sufficiently banal have devoted so much attention to an idea suggested hundreds of years later as a far-out possibility by theoretical physicists? Could they have known something we don't? Suppose there really was an Otherworld whose shape-shifters could visit ours at will to work mischief, kidnap or seduce mortals, exchange their infants in the cradle for ours . . .

Moonshine, of course, but the sort of moonshine

that had always fascinated Sterling and made him wish that it might be true. Before writing his paper he wanted to determine where Gwyneth stood on the question of the objective truth of the ballads and to trim his sails accordingly. For all he knew (she had never committed herself in class), she believed in werewolves and seal-men, in changelings and unquiet graves and in wizards who could transform themselves into red-hot bars of iron; or maybe she viewed all these as symbols from the collective unconscious. To find out what she believed, he had borrowed her out-of-print book from the library.

But he found that he couldn't read it. He took off his glasses to wipe them, but they fell from his oddly inept hands. He didn't even try to pick them out of the grass because his full attention was seized by the page that lay open before him. He felt a cold touch of panic; not so much because he could see the characters on the printed page with a clarity he'd never known when wearing glasses; but because those characters made no sense to him whatever. Dimly, as one perceives a faint star at the edge of one's vision, he knew that they were letters of the English alphabet, but when he focused his attention directly on any one of them, it was meaningless. It might just as well have been a Chinese ideogram.

He was going mad. A nervous breakdown. Overwork, lack of sleep, the constant irritation of . . . of that creature which rattled the metal balls, the constant fear of . . . similar creatures—all had combined at last to . . . Words now seemed as hard for him to grasp as printed letters.

He sprang to his feet. The urge to get moving was not just an urge now, it was an irresistible compulsion. He flew across the granite apron and down the sheer side of the hill. He couldn't analyze his exact method of locomotion. More than anything else, it was like those dreams in which he would float a few inches above the ground, whisked from place to place by some force not entirely dependent on his own will.

This analogy reassured him. This was a dream. It was true that his senses had never functioned with such tingling vividness in any dream, or in waking life either. But that was merely a condition of the dream: he was dreaming that he had superhuman perceptions and powers.

He'd dreamed before of appearing naked on campus, and those dreams had provoked agonies of shame and fear. He wasn't at all concerned about it now. Nakedness was a simple fact of existence for the creature he had become, it was the only way he could be.

He knew exactly where all the creatures were. They made a frightful din, clumping along on their big feet cased in dead skins and stinking chemicals, while they shrieked and babbled their incomprehensible monkey-talk. He could identify the separate sounds made by each and every one of them. A huge, sensitive net seemed to spread out from him, a net composed of smell and hearing and sight, and he could read the distant trembling of each discrete strand.

He sang, giving way at last to the urge he had felt before without knowing what it had meant. This time he didn't chatter in their gibberish but sang his own song, the song of his massive chest and his blood and his breath yearning to the moon. Silence fell on the noisy creatures. Then some of them laughed, began again to babble, and their irksome racket rose to its former pitch.

He slithered among the shadowy underbrush on his belly. Two of the creatures clumped past him: tall, pale oblongs with grotesquely tiny mouths, flat faces, and round, protruding eyes. He hadn't remembered them as being so tall, but that had something to do with his marvelous new way of moving around. When he stood up, his eyes were no more than half as high off the ground as theirs. With blind eyes, stinking mouths, useless nostrils, pasty bodies sprayed and swathed in disgusting substances; they sickened him. But within the filthy wrappings he sensed the throbbing of the red nebulas of energy he lusted for.

He flew to one of their fetid warrens and whipped through a crack in the door. He knew that two of their females, plump and smooth and weak, were alone in the building. The rest of the creatures were gathered in another place to gorge themselves on their bland food. He shot up the stairs to the door of the occupied room. It stood ajar. Inside he heard the sound of running water.

"You gonna spend your fucking life in the fucking shower, Sherri?" The noises meant nothing. "Sheeest!"

Far though these creatures were from his standards of what was right and beautiful, he yearned for their pale bodies with something more than lust. He wanted to embrace them so as to blend them with himself, to absorb their essence, to . . . to devour them.

But his courage almost failed. The big, stone building screamed at his prickling neck that it was a mountain about to collapse on him. And the tiny hole within it, the cubicle where his prey chirped and squeaked in total ignorance of the terror that had come upon them, was a narrow trap that would never let him go. He lifted his eyes. Through the scary metal gallows that was their bunk-bed, he saw the open window and the moon beyond it.

"It's about time. It's—*my God! What is that?*"

He snapped the first one's fragile neck and struck the second, fresh from the shower and less rancid. He ripped off the towel that covered the plump flesh. He ripped off the hand that tried to retain the towel. He inhaled hot, quivering chunks of the creature as its red cloud of energy burst and sprayed around him.

CHAPTER TWO

"I myself got no objection to eating a broad, but this guy was ridiculous."

It took a great effort, but Stuart managed to laugh like one of the boys. He had been answering stupid questions, filling ghoulish requests for photos, and tolerating inappropriate jokes like that one all day long in his office, and now the vultures had come to perch on his telephone wires at home. He tried to shake off his own petty discontents. They were nothing to the fact that two bright young women had been torn up like last year's centerfolds.

"You have all you need now, right."

"Yeah. I'm sorry to've bothered you at home—"

"That's why I'm in the book."

His daughter Joan had been waiting impatiently

for him to hang up. She said, "What's *fea-falt,* Daddy?"

He could only stare at her. Fee-fault? Had some obscure fiscal sin caught up with the Doyles? Was law now being taught in fifth grade?

"Where did you hear that?"

"In the cookbook." She read: *"Take five pounds more or less of coarse fea-falt . . ."*

He took the book from her. It was a duplicate of a colonial cookbook. *"Sea salt.* They used to write *S's* like *F's.* He felt as if a comprehensive vision of life in Amworth had been revealed to him: children played with eighteenth-century cookbooks while half the world starved. Let them eat fea-falt. Had some factor in that dangerous equation triggered the countdown of Sterling Fairchild?"

"That's dumb," Joan said.

"I agree." He followed her to the kitchen. It was colonial, too, its oak beans festooned with dried herbs and roots. Metal surfaces had been camouflaged as wood. He took the pitcher of martinis from the walnut refrigerator and poured his second. "What's all this for?"

"Mommy said I could make hors d'oeuvres." Not only could she pronounce that, he noted with pride, but she could probably spell it. "For the party. To-morrow?"

"Oh, shit."

"If you're going to be vulgar, I shall have to ask you to leave the room."

"I'm sorry."

Joan had her mother's fine-boned, heart-shaped face and dark hair. She was going to be beautiful. She was beautiful. She could also be a prig. He pushed that unworthy thought aside. Children couldn't be fit into hard and fast patterns. They played roles. Now she was playing Miss Priss. But it was one of her favorites.

"Don't you want me to make hors d'oeuvres?"

"That isn't it. Go ahead."

He fled to the living room before she could press her interrogation. If he suggested that the party should be called off, she would tell Gwyneth, and Gwyneth would raise hell before he had a chance to advance the reasonable proposition that they shouldn't hold faculty parties while the corpses of students were still warm.

But he could no longer predict how Gwyneth would react to any situation. *Sweet* had fallen out of fashion as a word to describe a woman, but it had once seemed to sum her up. Pottering around with her ballads and her Jacobean playwrights, wondering whether she'd be laughed at if she wore a wimple to her lecture, seeming to spend most of her time in the seventeenth-century, but willing to abandon it completely in long, tender lovemaking, she had been sweetness personified. Now, to put it mildly, she didn't.

Maybe the unexpected appearance of the man who claimed to be her long-lost father had something to do with it. Philip Kemper had arrived in Amworth last year, and her symptoms had developed more recently, but they could have been caused by the strain of worrying that her friends and colleagues would connect her with the old man. Stuart remembered clearly the last time he had seen his father-in-law. Muttering to himself as always, he had been shuffling across the campus on a rainy day. He had been dressed for the weather in a green plastic garbage-bag, with holes cut in it for his head and arms, and with a rope for a belt. He had visited their home only once, to Stuart's knowledge, but the chance that he might come calling again was a constant threat.

Maybe her symptoms were his own fault. It was more likely that she'd found out about Malkin Gray, even though he didn't know how. It was a mistake, and he was trying to correct it, but he couldn't try to reassure Gwyneth by telling her that when he wasn't even sure that she knew. "I myself got no objection to eating a broad," he muttered aloud.

"Talking to yourself?"

"Damn!" His hand jerked, sloshing the drink into his lap. Had Gwyneth heard and understood? He couldn't tell from her expression. She dumped her heavy leather case in the hall without special emphasis—she didn't fling it at his head—so he supposed she hadn't.

"I've earned the right to talk to myself. It's been that kind of day."

"Mine, too." She sat beside him and kissed him, so he supposed that she hadn't understood. "The police questioned me about Sterling."

"Why?"

"The last normal thing he did, apparently, was to check my book out of the library. They found it with his clothing, opened to a suggestive passage."

"And so, inflamed to bestial passions by a treatise on folklore, he—"

"Something like that." The brusqueness of her interruption made him see that he could be as callous as the reporters who'd offended him.

"Some English psycho was inspired to vampirism by watching the Anglican mass, according to William O. Douglas. You can't say—"

"I don't." She laughed. "They thought his choice of book might shed some light on his mental state or his motive. They thought he might have been leaving a message by turning it to that particular page. Here, let me refresh your trousers."

He picked the wet polyester away from his thigh, debating whether to change his pants or let the martini evaporate, while she took his glass to the kitchen.

Everyone thought her book, an expansion of her doctoral dissertation, had been brilliant; brilliant, but unfashionable. One didn't get to be an English Lit star by writing about creaky old ballads that had long ago been abandoned to the anthropologists and psychologists, and even those trendy academies had since found sexier fish to fry than "The Great Silkie of Sule Skerry." Gwyneth was often referred to as a *folklorist,* and she sensed in that a touch of condescension. That was why she taught at a place like Amworth, and even Amworth made her keep up a front of respectability by teaching a course on seventeenth-century dramatists.

"And what was it?" he asked when she returned.

"What was what?"

"The message Sterling meant to leave."

"It was from 'Kemp Owyne':

'O was it warwolf in the wood,
    Or was it mermaid in the sea,
Or was it man, or vile woman,
    My true love, that misshapit thee?' "

Gwyneth didn't merely recite the eerie lines. She had shone in college theatricals, and her voice was a beautiful and various instrument. For a moment it had held the echo of a far-off Highland warpipe, and it sent banshees, or their Scots cousins, slithering their cold hands up Stuart's spine. He tossed off half his refilled glass.

"And what did the police make of that?"

"They wanted me to make something of it for them. The *vile* or *wily* woman—a witch, in this context—who had misshapen him could have meant one of his victims." She looked away. "Or me."

He slipped his arm around her shoulders. "You're kidding."

"No. They suggested—well, I suggested it, actually, I think it was true—that he had a crush on me. He was painfully shy. He blushed whenever I looked at him."

His first thought was that she was lucky the bastard hadn't happened upon her instead of his victims. His second was that her interview with the police had been a public relations disaster. What if the story got around that a deranged student had murdered two coeds because he believed his teacher had put a hex on him? Gwyneth, in one of her less sensible outfits, would have made the front page of the *National Enquirer.* He decided that neither thought did much credit, so he kept them to himself.

But she read his mind and said, "The police promised not to mention it to anyone." Then, with one of the sudden and grotesque changes of mood that had lately disturbed him, she laughed exuberantly and cried, "But just think what it would do for my book! They could retitle it *The Warwolf's Guide to Girls* . . . with a couple of naked tarts cringing in terror on the cover."

Anger drove him to blurt, "I've been thinking that we ought to cancel the party. At least until they've planted the tarts."

"Nonsense."

She spoke mildly, not reacting to his rebuke; and dismissing his objection to the party as offhandedly as if he were one of her students trying to weasel out of a test. Her attitude enraged him, and he left for the kitchen before he could say anything he might regret. Even at her most irksome, he still loved her.

People did change, after all. With the benefit of hindsight, he could see that her recent turn toward cynicism had been an almost predictable development in her character. The folklore she had studied abounded in grisly descriptions of cannibalism, incest, dismemberment, necrophilia, rape, murder, and torture. The dramatists she preferred wallowed in the same themes. Characters in the plays of Middleton or Webster would have thought Sterling Fairchild a frolicsome teddybear. Preoccupations like those hardly squared with sweetness. Deep down, she had probably always held a very dark view of life, and only now, in her mid-thirties, had some of the acid percolated to the surface.

Joan hovered over the oven while Arthur, her twelve-year-old brother, sat absorbed in a comic book at the kitchen table. Stuart had never seen her use the stove, and it made him nervous, even though a moment's reflection persuaded him that she was the Doyle least likely to cause an accident. He thought of reminding her to be careful, but that would have been ludicrous: a fatherly warning about knives from Jack the Ripper.

At his entrance, Arthur had sunk his nose even deeper into the comic book. He grabbed his son's ankles and pulled them out from under the table, upsetting his chair. He held him upside down, bobbing his head a few inches off the floor, and chanted:

" 'Fee, fie, faw, fum,
I smell the blood of an Englishman—' "

"For Christ's sake, Dad! Cut out the kid stuff!"

" 'Be he alive or be he dead—' "

"Don't mind Daddy, he's been hitting the bottle."

"I'll kill you!"

" '—I'll grind his bones to make my bread!' "

He bumped Arthur's head lightly on the floor and released him. "Say hello to your father."

"Hello to your father." In an undertone that Stuart chose to ignore as he assembled bottles and pitcher and ice, he added, "Son of a bitch."

Like himself, Arthur was fair. His pinched, fox's face—not an attractive face, but he had to admit that it was also like his own—was red with anger as he slammed his chair back into place and submerged once more into his comic book. Uncomically, a half-naked woman with fangs hissed menacingly from the cover.

Stuart was disconcerted by the sudden recollection of his own father flinging him around like a sack and quoting the same rhyme when he'd been old enough to feel that it compromised his dignity.

"Has either of you looked in on Grandma today?"

"I did," Joan said. "She's watching TV."

"Listening," Arthur quibbled.

"Watching," Stuart said. "You can't purge your vocabulary to . . ." He gave up. Arthur was trying to needle him into sounding pompous, and he'd succeeded. "Go and say hello to her, Arthur. See if she wants anything when—" but Arthur was already stamping and grumbling away on his martyr's path— "you get a chance."

"I didn't mean those poor girls," Gwyneth said. "Is that what you thought I meant? I was referring to lurid book covers, that's all."

"Of course." He wasn't entirely convinced. "But the party—"

"Do you think the caterer would refund the downpayment? Or that we could warn off a hundred people by tomorrow afternoon? And since this was Shaver's idea, he ought to be the one to cancel it, and he hasn't cancelled any classes or activities."

He winced. Only now did he realize that he should

have sent a memo to President Shaver suggesting such cancellations. Amworth's image, whose furbishment was his chief duty, might be tarnished. He had been too busy to think of it.

"On with the dance, let joy be unconfined." He stumbled against the edge of the coffee table as he went to sit beside her on the couch, but she pretended not to notice.

"Besides, the party was for Tom, and getting him to name a date was almost impossible."

He grudgingly admitted she might be right. He had only wanted an excuse to get out of the party. Edward Wheaton Shaver believed that organizing parties for visiting celebrities was one of Stuart's responsibilities. This time Shaver had even called upon him to provide a house for the festivities, since no place on campus would be available. ("Whoopee!" cried Prof. Robert "Barfing Bob" McWraith as, in Stuart's vivid premonition, he plummeted headfirst down the stairwell from the third floor.) At least the college provided the money, and Stuart would be sure to bill them punctiliously for broken glass, cigarette burns in the furniture, and personal trauma.

He wondered when she had started calling Dr. Tomlin Woodling—this year's writer-in-residence—*Tom*.

"I can't help thinking that it wouldn't have happened," she said, "if I'd seduced him."

"Who, Tom? What?"

White-faced, she stared at him for a moment. Then she laughed and said, "No, silly. Sterling."

Even before he had become an adulterer, Stuart had found that sort of talk embarrassing, and not only because he was a bit of a prude. Its fatuity embarrassed him. It typified the prattle of a generation that had misread Freud and believed it could screw its way out of all of life's little difficulties: out of disease, old age, death, and sin. He was surprised to hear her talk such nonsense; surprised, too, that it gave him a twinge of jealousy to think of her seducing a student.

"I don't think so." His tone was determinedly mild. "His problems run a little deeper than that. They've got him in the bughouse, you know, where he's convinced that he's a werewolf. Or a *war*wolf."

He wanted to say something more, but everything that came to mind would sound (Gwyneth reserved the word for their very worst arguments) sanctimonious. And she seemed too wrapped in her own thoughts to listen.

He trudged up the three grand flights of the central staircase—an elegant, mahogany wheel for human hamsters, his mother called it—and hesitated at the foot of the narrower staircase to the tower she had claimed as her domain. He noticed his father's toolbox under the stairs. Stuart had left it there to gather dust after fixing a loose step a couple of years ago. The sight of the toolbox evoked his father, jolly and generous, bubbling with bad jokes and ill-timed horseplay, and he was awed by the power of parenthood. Joseph Doyle had flickered briefly to life again when Stuart had picked his own son up by the ankles. Arthur wouldn't believe it now, but he might remember that moment affectionately some day and even unthinkingly inflict it on one of his children. Perhaps some ancestor who had been dust for centuries was recalled each time Stuart scratched his chin just so or walked the way he did.

The tower had the best view, Allison would say in her more sardonic moments, and that was true: its tall windows commanded the river, the college campus, and the hills beyond. He supposed she enjoyed the sunlight, even if she couldn't see it, and the privacy. She called it her penthouse.

"They were just talking about those two girls at the Mircalla Karnstein Residence." She switched off the TV. "Horrible."

"Are people getting nastier, do you suppose, Mom?"

"Ask Gwyneth to sing you one of her lullabies, if you've forgotten."

He had recently been thinking the same thing himself. He was forced to admit that the thought had originated with his mother, who had never respected

Gwyneth's field of expertise.

"Would you like me to read to you?" He picked up the third volume of *The Decline and Fall of the Roman Empire* and found his place. This was the third time around.

"No, thank you, James. There's almost no time until dinner, and after that, Arthur and I plan to watch *Kojak*."

"I've dropped 'James.' "

"I haven't."

She started when he snapped the book shut. "Call any Irish bar and ask for Jim Doyle," he had told her more than once, "and you'll not only get one, you'll get one pretty much like me." And she would remind him that he had been named for his remote ancestors, kings of England and Scotland; nonsense he had once believed. Until he was twelve or so, he had imagined that one day a Rolls would pull up to his house and a harassed nobleman with a crown under his arm would step out and say, "Your Majesty, we've had a bit of a cock-up on the other side, and . . ."

"I believe you've had too much to drink, James."

He stared at the black glasses masking her eyes and saw two James Stuart Doyles, both red-eyed and rumpled and pasty. She was right. But she couldn't know that no one on earth could hurt him so much with those words. He said only, "It's been that kind of day."

He went to lie on his bed for only a few minutes before dinner, but he woke up in cold moonlight. After soaking his head in the bathroom sink and flooding six aspirin down his desiccated throat, he lurched back to decipher the face of the bedside clock. It was past eleven. He peeled off his sodden jacket and twisted necktie and let them drop.

Gwyneth, her hair unbound, sat at the desk in her study. In horn-rimmed glasses and translucent nightgown, she looked like someone's fantasy of a seductive schoolmarm: his. Not everyone's, certainly, for she would have had to put on a few pounds to be a high-fashion model. She had suffered from anorexia in adolescence she still saw eating as no more than a tiresome necessity, whether the dish was beef Wellington or Spam. But she shared in the grace of the serpent, the fragility of the gazelle, and she was the standard by which he found most woman wanting.

He dropped into the leather easy chair and propped his head tenderly on a shaky hand. The tuneless humming that was her invariable accompaniment to concentration stopped. A moment later she asked, "How do you feel?" Seeing that the question was too much for him, she said, "Cassilda put your dinner in the fridge."

He parted his fingers to peer at her. Her long legs

were crossed, one of them bared to the hip. He wondered why hangovers made him feel sexy.

"You busy?"

After stacking her papers and closing them in a folder, she rose and stretched fetchingly, silhouetted against the green-shaded desk lamp. She shrugged out of her negligee. It was still floating in air when she snapped off the light, having given him only an inflaming glimpse.

"You know what we've never done?" Her voice swathed him like velvet in the darkness.

"Nothing."

"We've never made love in the playhouse."

"What a ghastly idea. Let's."

A carpetbagger named Marcus Aurelius Bloodstone had brought his loot home to Connecticut and built what was now the Doyles' home, "sparing," in the words of Allison Doyle, "neither money nor good taste." It had long lain vacant until Stuart's father bought it in 1960 for $30,000. He sank a fortune and his health into it, and died of a heart attack ten years later while carrying a load of slates to the roof. In his last words to Stuart, he had babbled with crazed intensity of the repairs still urgently needed on the *ravelin,* the *demilune,* and the *hornwork,* terms appropriate to the fortification of a castle.

According to Allison, the house had also cost him

his wife. She ran away with an artist who was only a
few years older than her son, she said, because her
husband had fallen in love with the place. Having
divorced her, he had left the house to Stuart. Taste
had changed, and it was now considered one of the
finest examples of Gothic Revival architecture in New
England. It had been featured in magazines and been
the star of an educational television documentary.
Stuart could have sold it for more than ten times what
his father had paid. He wouldn't have. Allison often
said he suffered from a compulsion to maintain his
father's tomb.

Stuart's father had never gotten around to restoring
one of the carpetbagger's queerer whimsies, the playhouse, an octagonal building large enough for a couple to have comfortably set up housekeeping. Bloodstone had built it for his only child, a daughter who
had died young and tragically. Joan would pester her
father to fix it up for her, "because I'll probably die
young and tragically, and if you don't fix it up now,
you'll never forgive yourself." He had promised
vaguely to do it, but then he got estimates for replac-
ing the four large French doors, now boarded up, and
repairing the pagoda roof, and he had shelved the
project with a shudder.

The interior walls had been painted with murals by
Sebastian Gowdie, an illustrator of Victorian children's books whose work was also again in vogue.

Selling the murals would have paid for the repairs to the playhouse many times over, but permitting their removal would have made Stuart feel like a vandal. He felt guilty enough as it was, since the paintings were decaying under the leaky roof.

Outside it was chilly and damp enough to discomfort Stuart in his shirt and trousers. Gwyneth, naked, didn't seem to mind. Clinging to his arm, she slowed his pace and breathed deeply of the dank mist that hugged the ground under a bloated moon.

"God, what a night! I feel like sucking your blood . . ." She darted up to nip his neck, then whispered in his ear: "Or something."

Cold and hung over but insistently tumid, he all but dragged her through the damp grass. Then he stopped. "There could be rats in there. Spiders, at least."

"Mmmm! If only we had a coffin to do it in. Would you like that?"

"No."

"You could pretend to be a naughty priest giving me last rites. And you could get carried away with passion and unwind my winding-sheet."

Now it was she who tugged him along. He wanted to tell her that he disapproved of mocking a sacrament. Instead he said, "You aren't supposed to give extreme unction to a corpse."

"You aren't supposed to fuck them, either, silly. That's the point."

She rubbed her hard nipples against his back and whispered further suggestions while he bent to unlock the door with an old, ornate key. The only remaining entrance to the playhouse, it was a child-sized door whose other side was painted into a mural to represent the door of the witch's gingerbread house in *Hansel and Gretel*. He pushed it open on shrieking hinges and crouched to step inside warily, fumbling for his lighter.

"I hope the rats—"

The door slammed behind him. Before he could react, he heard the key turn in the lock. For a moment he remained too surprised to speak. Then he called, "Hey. Hey, Gwyn?" He laughed. "Cut out the kid stuff."

He tugged at the knob. As he knew, the door was locked. He slapped his palm against it. "Come on, Gwyneth, open up! What the hell is this? What's the idea?"

He kicked the door and pounded it with his fists as he shouted pleas, then curses, then threats. He hurled himself against it. He had forgotten how small the door was; his shoulder hit the frame painfully and his jaw banged the wall above it. Dazed and gasping with pain, he sank to his knees on the cold floor.

At first he wasn't sure that he had heard her whisper at the keyhole. Then it was repeated:"Stuart?"

"What?"

"What would you do in case of fire?"

She had no matches. He tried to cling to that comforting fact. He tried hard not to think of her going back to the house to get some.

"Listen to me, Gwyneth. Fun is fun, you know, but this is . . . Sweetheart? Are you there?"

She giggled: "For the love of God, Montresor!" her giggle faded. He sensed that she was gone.

He panicked. Screaming, he threw whatever came to hand in the darkness against the door. If she was crazy enough to lock him in, his fear told him, she was crazy enough to start a fire. Crockery exploded against the unseen gingerbread house. Fragments ricocheted to sting his face.

He stopped, sucking hard for breath, when he heard her Jaguar's powerful engine ignite and roar down the driveway. He supposed she hadn't started a fire after all. His fear gave way to fury. He searched blindly until he found a heavy floorlamp. He used it as a battering ram, running it into the door as he shouted for help. The door didn't even rattle. It bounced him back solidly each time.

He dropped the lamp at last and fell beside it, his arms and shoulders aching. Did he really want help? Did he want a neighbor to come to the door so he could say, "My wife locked me in the playhouse and drove off for a night on the town"? If Gwyneth had taken the key with her, his rescuer would escalate the farce by calling the police or the fire department.

He began to hope that no one heard him. He was fifty yards from the street and nearly as far from the nearest neighbor's house. Since the playhouse was solidly built, his noise might have gone unheard. If the banging had disturbed someone, he would have cursed it and tried to go back to sleep. Stuart hoped so. In his own house, Arthur and Joan slept like the dead, or like the very young. Potent sleeping pills nightly obliterated his mother's consciousness; and Cassilda Oliphant was hard of hearing. ("Yes, officer, those are my husband's bones," a white-haired Gwyneth told the policeman. "I locked him in there forty years ago, but he was too timid to call for help.")

Struck by a new worry, he flicked on his disposable lighter and held it aloft. He had chipped some of Sebastian Gowdie's red paint off the door, that was all; he had done no damage to the details of the painting. In the flickering dimness, the mural unsettled him. Apple-cheeked and tow-headed, Hansel and Gretel sized him up with their steely blue eyes and found him wanting. Brown seepage from the roof had decomposed half the witch's face. And both of her eyes. Behind her, the oven door leaked flame. He let the lighter go out, but it was even less pleasant to think of them all staring at him in the darkness.

He made as thorough a circuit of the cluttered room as he could, snapping on his lighter only briefly. He seemed to have a talent for lighting it at the wrong moment. A cluster of dwarfs hatched plots under a toadstool. One of them stared piercingly over his shoulder at Stuart. A giant, his head a blur, advanced with an axe, his huge foot poised to squash him. He didn't know why Mistress Carpetbagger had died young and tragically (the phrase was a family joke that might have been spoiled by investigation), but perhaps this jolly hideaway had driven her to suicide. Its red jaws agape with fangs the size of railroad spikes, a black wolf prowled forward from the wall. He had never before really looked at these horrific paintings. Or perhaps he had made one forgotten tour when he was fifteen or so and it had fueled his nightmares for the rest of his life.

Whoever had boarded up the French doors between the murals, he found, had done his job with manic diligence. The thick planks had been mortised into the frames. Knocking them out with the bric-a-brac at hand would have been no easier than knocking out the walls.

He found a place on a battered sofa where the fewest springs extruded and sat down, trying not to think of the rats which might have made their nest in its mildewed horsehair. He examined a riddle he had been trying to forget: "For the love of God, Montresor." Those were Fortunato's last words when Montresor bricked him up in the cellar, in *The Cask of Amontillado*. Montresor had entombed him because Fortunato had made a cuckold of him. Gwyneth had been alluding snidely to his affair with Malkin Gray.

No. He was thinking of the movie version. Poe's story, he was almost sure, hadn't mentioned adultery. Gwyneth wouldn't get a literary allusion mixed up with a Vincent Price movie. So why had Montresor bricked up Fortunato? Again he felt like one of her students, unfairly used. This wasn't on our reading list, Professor Doyle.

Whatever the specific reason had been, it was a tale of revenge. She was getting even. And not just by locking him up. She'd gone tearing off in her XKE (Without putting her clothes on? She'd hardly had time to dress.) to get even with him the way wives traditionally got back at wayward husbands.

He didn't like the way she'd said *Tom*.

He wished she hadn't gone. He wished they'd been able to talk to each other. He wished he hadn't started fooling around with Malkin. He wished he had more than two cigarettes in the crumpled pack he now dredged from his pocket.

As he pulled it out, his fingers tangled in his rosary. He always carried it but never used it. He certainly had nothing better to do now. Wincing at cuts and bruises and strained muscles, he sagged from the couch to his knees and crossed himself. He heard the clitter of tiny claws among the springs behind him.

CHAPTER THREE

Gwyneth cut the engine at the corner and coasted to a stop in front of her house. She pounded the wheel, willing her car to roll the last few inches. Her knees were shaking so badly when she got out that she sagged against the car and clutched the door to keep from falling.

She stared at the satiny gleam of the hood in the early morning light. Not a mark on it, even though they had worked on the car for an hour with crowbars and an acetylene torch before they had been able to extricate her body from the wreckage.

Remembering how she must look, she pushed herself erect and stumbled up the long slope of the lawn. She clutched her raincoat about her more tightly. She knew it was unreasonable, but she couldn't help feeling that anyone who saw her, barefoot and bare-legged, would know at a glance that she was naked beneath it. Her hair hung tangled in her eyes, but she couldn't bring herself to release the coat and push the damp curls away. If any of the neighbors saw her and asked what the matter was, she would tell them the truth: she had been killed in an auto wreck last night. She had died on a marble slab, the severed halves of her spine rasping against each other as . . .

Bad as that was, real as that was, the true horror lay in her ignorance of what had happened. She remembered the wreck, she remembered what came later. But none of that was true. The car—she turned for one more reassuring look at it, sitting smug and shiny in the empty street—was in one piece. So was she. The pain of the stones that gouged her feet proved that she lived.

At the top of the lawn, she hobbled across the driveway until she had a clear view of the playhouse, as playful in its weathered dereliction as a pillbox left over from some irrelevant war. Maybe Stuart wasn't locked inside. She checked once again, hoping it wouldn't be true, that it had been part of her hallucination, but the heavy iron key weighed down her pocket.

She slipped into the main house and hurried up to their bedroom. He hadn't escaped, apparently, for the bed was empty, the spread disturbed only by some

Stuart-sized ripples from his afternoon nap. She hoped he hadn't died of a heart attack or, more likely from the way he'd been carrying on, of apoplexy. She'd never seen him so angry. It had started as a joke, and then he'd scared her—no, she told herself firmly, you can't worm your way out of it. You locked him in and meant for him to stay locked in.

She couldn't bring herself to examine exactly why she'd done it. She suspected it was because as a child, she'd once been locked in that loathesome place. One night wouldn't kill Stuart. It served him right for getting so drunk and acting so sanctimoniously.

She mussed up her side of the bed hastily and punched a depression in the pillow. She hesitated. Which would upset him more? That she'd left him to go tearing off into the night, or that she'd slept peacefully in their bed while he'd passed the night in a dank cell? "Neither of the above" was the only answer, but that option wasn't available. She decided to rearrange the bed as she'd originally found it.

In the shower-stall, she stood for a long moment with her hand poised at the taps. Joseph Doyle hadn't lived long enough to get around to the Victorian plumbing, and the pipes might bang. Worse, she might rouse the Haggworm, as she—to herself alone—called her mother-in-law.

For seven miles east and seven miles west,
   And seven miles north and south,

Nae blades of corn or grass will grow
For the venom of her mouth.

Screw her. She would curl up and die of self-disgust if she didn't scald and scrub herself this instant. She prayed (not to a God she didn't believe in, but to some vague Spirit of Plumbing whom she willed, of necessity, to exist) and her prayer was heard. The ancient pipes whispered considerately as the hot water stung her clenched face.

Last night she'd driven fast, so fast that the wind whipped the collar of her raincoat against her cheek hard enough to hurt. And that part was true: when she put her fingertips to her cheek, the spot was sore. In her hallucination, she took one hand from the wheel to adjust her collar. Her eyes left the road for an instant. She heard the bray of an air-horn. When she looked at the road, she could see nothing through the windshield but the big chrome grille of a truck.

She spun the wheel to the right. For a moment she thought, against all odds, that she was safe. Then something hit the left rear fender. The car became airborne. It struck hard and rolled over and over as it bounced down a wooded slope. Her back broke on the second bounce.

When she regained consciousness she could feel nothing at all. She could hear policemen and emergency workers discussing the best way to get her out. She wanted to tell them that she was conscious, but she couldn't speak. The crumpled roof in front of her eyes was illuminated at regular, rhythmic intervals by a splash of red light. Its pulsations irritated her, but she found that she couldn't close her eyes. That was when she tried to scream.

"Jesus, what a waste. Get a load of that body."

She couldn't scream. She couldn't tug her coat down to cover herself. *Get a doctor, you idiots!* Tearing metal shrieked in her ears. Blue-white light dazzled her, and sparks from its blinding core spilled over her. She smelled hair burning. It must have been hers. Then the work stopped.

"Can you get at her now, doc?"

"I think . . . maybe . . . yeah. She's gone. *Pow,* like that."

You incompetent asshole! I'm breathing! I'm thinking! I'm alive! Help me . . .

"She's got the engine in her lap, but there's not a mark on her. How do you figure that?"

"I don't. But people aren't meant to bend that way. Her spine's broken, obviously."

But I'm alive! Put a mirror to my mouth! Listen to my heart beat!

The renewed scream of metal drowned out her thoughts. The blue-white light engulfed her tiny world again. Sirens growled to life and wailed away, bullhorns squawked. Men cursed and gave each other conflicting advice. They talked about her as if she were a purely mechanical problem, a monkeywrench that had to be removed from the world's otherwise orderly works before they could go home to bed.

Don't move me! Don't move me! You'll kill me if . . .

But she didn't die, nor did she feel a thing. Her world expanded first to a mat of brown pine-needles, then, as they turned her over, to floodlit boughs and a black sky beyond. Then the world vanished as they pulled canvas over her face. It tightened suddenly as they buckled it down. It was too tight. She would suffocate. But maybe that would be best. Did she really want to live like this?

She screamed at herself in reply: *Yes, yes! Any way at all!*

A long time passed. She didn't suffocate. But she couldn't feel herself breathing against her shroud. Nor could she feel or hear the blood pumping through her body.

There was a logical explanation. Either her senses had been numbed completely or her heartbeat and respiration had slowed to the point where they were imperceptible, as in certain kinds of trance. But in such a state she would have been unconscious, wouldn't she? Obviously not. She was as alert as she'd ever been. They would soon discover at the hospital that she was alive.

She knew she was being carried from place to

place, a canvas-bound mummy on a stretcher. She heard footsteps on gravel, on concrete, on wood, on . . . carpeting, she supposed. They were bearing her into the hospital. The characteristic smell of a hospital was masked by a heavy perfume remarkably like fresh-cut carnations. It must be some new disinfectant. She didn't care for it. They carried her down a steep flight of stairs to a place where stronger, more reassuringly chemical smells prevailed. One of the men who carried her chattered incessantly and inanely about his brilliant daughter, Sandy, and her plans to become a lawyer. He seemed to be trying to convince the other one that there was nothing freakish in her ambition, although the other got no chance to express his views.

They unwrapped her in a blindingly bright, white room. After a while she realized that she was staring directly up at fluorescent tubes behind a glazed surface on the ceiling, but she couldn't shut her eyes or avert them. She was rolled this way and that as they removed her coat. Aunt Isabel's fondest fear had been groundless: on the day Gwyneth finally had her accident, she wasn't wearing soiled underthings. She wasn't sure whether she would have laughed or cried about this, but she was unable to do either.

A policeman drifted into the maddeningly narrow fan of her vision, a blue cliff rising behind her head. She told herself that he was the one with the smart daughter. He wouldn't let them file her away in a refrigerated drawer. He would imagine what it would be like if his Sandy were in this situation. He would want someone to search his daughter's eyes for a spark of sentience. He would look down. Perversely, he refused to do it. She willed him to. The struggle went on and on, but he never weakened.

" . . . called a priest," the policeman was saying. "We found a St. Christopher in her glove compartment."

Damn Stuart and his fetishes! She wasn't a Catholic, and Stuart himself hadn't been inside a church in fifteen years, but he kept planting his holy booby-traps. At last he'd caught her. Helpless, unable to protest, she would be forced to endure the consolations of the faith he'd abandoned.

Where was Stuart, anyway? The answer shot back like a bullet: locked in the playhouse. The police might pound on the door and ring the bell till morning, but neither the Haggworm, doped to the gills, nor the impossible Cassilda, with her hearing-aid on the bedside table, would respond. If the children heard, they might be too frightened to answer the door. Stuart might hear; but, out of embarrassment or sheer contrariness, he might not call attention to himself.

" . . . too late for a priest."

She focused all the force of will she could muster to

see who'd said that, but despite her soundless screams of fury and frustration, her eyes stayed fixed on the black pits of the policeman's nostrils. Too late? If she were in the hospital and the doctor had said it was too late . . . Would they perform an autopsy?

She heard the drone of an electrical appliance, and a gurgling, as of liquid being flushed away. The policeman's face paled. He turned aside and left her vision. She glimpsed a man in a white lab coat and heard voices at some distance. The sense of the words was lost in the echoes of the tiled room, in the relentless humming and gurgling.

A heavy door closed and one set of footsteps approached her. She sensed that the others had gone. A new face came to study her. It must be the priest—he wore a clerical collar—but she'd never seen, or even imagined, a priest like him. With his lank, oily hair hanging in his sallow rat's face, he looked like a walking advertisement for the Reformation. His clothes were dirty and his small, irregular teeth were bad. She wanted to look for the doctor, even though she suspected that she was alone with this man, but her eyes remained glued on the light directly above. And had he been a doctor? She tried hard not to believe that he had been an undertaker.

Unlike the policeman, the priest stared down at her for a long time; but never once at her face. His eyes traveled slowly up and down her naked body. The motions of his shoulders suggested that his hands were moving, too. His eyes glowed. He breathed more shallowly. He licked his lips.

For the first time it struck her that she might be dreaming. Except for the total absence of her sense of touch, every detail of this apparent reality was perfect. But no matter how perfect the details, the coincidence of living the very fantasy she'd told Stuart this evening was more than she could swallow. She must be dreaming.

It scared her when she tried to determine exactly when the dream had begun. Had she already crashed her car? If she willed herself to wake, would she wake to agony in the wreckage, to the certain knowledge that the last seconds of her life were pumping away? But suppose the crash hadn't happened and this interminable nightmare had lasted only a split-second. Suppose she had nodded over the wheel and was even now hurtling forward at a hundred-and-ten mies an hour.

The argument convinced her to will herself awake, but nothing changed. She continued to stare at the light until the priest interposed his face, only inches away from hers. His breath sickened her. He still didn't meet her eyes. He lay on top of her, but she felt nothing. Sweat beaded his lip. He grunted rhythmically.

She heard another rhythmic noise, a rasping and an

occasional click. She knew the sound was made by the ends of her broken bones scraping together. She raged at herself to wake, but instead she sank into oblivion.

She woke up in darkness.

"Stuart!"

She was eager to hold him and pour out the nauseous details of the nightmare that still made her flesh crawl, but when she reached for him she found that she was alone. Nor was she in her bed. She lay naked on a cold stone slab.

She sat up. She felt no pain or weakness, but no matter how hard she tried, she couldn't straighten her twisted back. When she reached to touch it, she felt the ragged protrusion of broken bones.

"This has gone far enough, God *damn* it! Wake up!" That she could speak gave her no comfort. The echo of her voice in the tiled void made her wish she had kept quiet.

She knew it was impossible that she should sit up, impossible that she should move her arms and legs, but she was doing it. Even more impossible was the absence of pain. On the contrary, she felt all a-tingle with a life and energy so real that it seemed as if it ought to be crackling visibly from her fingertips.

A friend who had taken mescaline had described one of her experiences in a similar way. She had felt, she said, like a human dynamo. Could everything she'd experienced tonight—the accident, the priest, and now her walking in some dark place with a shattered body—could it all have been induced by a drug? Had Stuart drugged her? Or his mother?

She dropped to the floor. She couldn't rise completely. Insanely, that didn't dampen her sense of well-being. Bent nearly double, half-supported by her hands, she nevertheless felt charged with a boundless dynamism. She could lurch along more vigorously than she normally walked.

Frustrated for a moment by the unfamiliar door, she was given a curious insight: the source of the enormous energy she felt was not within her. She could only absorb it at a distance and be drawn to it, as a flower is drawn to the sun. She had no life apart from it.

The insight was frightening because it implied such a violent reversal of her previous mode of existence. It was a change as drastic as if she had waked one morning to find that she could no longer breathe air and would have to live thenceforth under water. The center of her existence, the source of her health and happiness, was no longer within her, it was outside. She had no idea what it was. She knew only that she would find out, for now she was through the door and being dragged toward the source, growing stronger with each clumsy step.

She hobbled up a bare concrete stairway, through another door, and into a sumptuous and dimly lighted room. The center of its decor was a gleaming mahogany box surrounded with flowers. She knew that it should have alarmed her, this confirmation that she had waked in the workroom of a mortuary, but the fact seemed unimportant. The *Source* was everything, and it lay somewhere above her.

She passed two other rooms, one containing a coffin. She was in a home once nearly as elegant as her own that had been converted into a funeral parlor. She had been here before: the Bradbury Funeral Home. Aunt Isabel, who had raised her as her own child, had been laid out here. The place should have held sad associations. But she was different now: not just a different person, a different sort of being. She had undergone death and transfiguration, and the *Source* was greater than any memory of trivial, human grief.

Even when she caught a glimpse of herself in a pier glass in the central hallway, her reaction was only a mild, momentary curiosity. She knew that shock and loathing would have been more appropriate, but looking at the horror in the mirror was like witnessing a minor misfortune that had befallen a distant relative. She crawled up the carpeted stairway. She remembered clearly from her aunt's funeral that the carpet had been brown and threadbare. Now it was dark-blue and new. This difference had verisimilitude; this was no dream. She knew that the stairway led to the living quarters of the undertaker and his family.

At the top of the stairs she hesitated, overwhelmed by the naked strength of the *Source*. What she had compared to the sun was nothing less than a cluster of throbbing, radiant suns.

She didn't know where to turn first. She wanted to cry aloud with joy, but some unquestionable wisdom inside her stifled the impulse. Caution was essential. And crouching here, bathing in the *Source* near its heart, however wonderful an experience that might be . . . there was still something more to do that would transcend even this ecstasy.

She identified the brightest, clearest, and most life-giving of the four stars. It lay behind a door at the end of the hall, outshining the other three and nearly driving her back with its concentration of strength and nourishment when she approached. She had to move forward by slow degrees, acclimating herself to its richness.

She opened the door. In her former system of perceptions, she would have said that a beautiful boy lay asleep on a bed, dressed in blue pajamas decorated with white rabbits. She might have admired his rosy cheeks, his gold hair, she might have been touched by his innocence and helplessness, she might have fondly remembered Arthur when he'd been this age. Now she saw him as something infinitely more beautiful than that, something like a vision of a god. Love, sympathy, tenderness, innocence—those feeble concepts were only shadows cast by his brilliance. It wouldn't be a passing expression of affection when she clasped him to her breast; it would be Love itself, and it would last, because she would absorb it and make it part of herself.

She bent close to his tender neck and sank her teeth in deeply. She sucked hard as the hot radiance filled her mouth and pumped down her throat.

Standing beneath the shower, Gwyneth now felt all of the horror and loathing that had been absent from her hallucination. Her stomach rebelled, but she retched up only pale mucous. Thank God for that. There was nothing else to be ejected. It had been a dream.

The shower had turned cold. She got out and buffed her skin hard with a rough towel. She tried to remember what had happened—what had seemed to happen—next. A memory stirred that could be retrieved neither in words nor images. It was as elusive as the aftertaste of food or the afterglow of love, and like those it was a feeling of satisfaction, but unlike those satisfactions it was complete. It was analagous to a moment she remembered from her fifteenth year when she had sat watching a brick wall glow in late afternoon sunlight and had felt in such harmony with the bricks and the light that she had wished time would stop: but by recognizing the harmony and willing it to continue, by intruding her consciousness of herself and her will into the moment, she had lost it.

Last night a similar moment had seemed to last forever, because there had been no consciousness of self, no will, no possibility of disruptive intrusion between the utter peace within her and the inanimate world. But that ended, too, because a voice cried, "Gwyneth!" The vibration of that hateful voice buzzed in her bones as it destroyed the perfection of her mindless peace. "Gwyneth! *Come forth!*" Her long-stilled heartbeat returned, galloping, and pain returned with an intensity never even imagined before to each separate cell of her body as she struggled to breathe air that was thick as damp wool. Lashing and twisting in darkness, she found herself confined by unyielding walls of cold satin that were locked, she instinctively knew, in a six-foot embrace of dirt and rock.

That horror had ended in a blur of sick delirium. The next thing she knew she was driving, and it seemed as if she had been driving a long time. Only gradually, through a haze of guilt and shame and nausea, had it dawned on her that the car was undamaged; and that she was, too. Six hours had elapsed since she'd left home, but the gas tank was still nearly full.

Whatever she'd done last night, she hadn't slept.

The urge to crawl between the sheets and rest was almost irresistible, but she forced herself to put on a skirt and sweater. Fortunately, she had a couple of Saturday morning tutorials, and she had scheduled another interview with Tom. She would have an excuse to run away immediately after letting Stuart out. She would give him a full explanation only after her head had cleared and she'd had time to make one up. But she couldn't tell him the truth. He'd think she was crazy.

She tiptoed into the hall with her shoes in one hand, the key to the playhouse in the other. Maybe she was crazy. But she felt that her disbelief in her hallucination was important. A crazy person, she insisted to herself, would have believed it had all happened.

Only when she was turning the key in the lock of the playhouse door did she realize that the hallucination was the least of her worries. Whatever she had imagined that she'd done, the fact remained that she had really imprisoned her husband. That had been crazy.

She pushed the small door open at arm's length. She hadn't imagined locking him up: there he was. A wedge of light fell across him as he lay huddled on the dilapidated sofa. She couldn't bring herself to call him. She inched into the room, trying to distract herself with a survey of its contents. The Bloodstones had used it to store their junk, and the Doyles hadn't bothered to clear that out before depositing their own. There was a floor-lamp and a dining-room set, ugly and old-fashioned, from her Aunt Isabel's house. A shiny new microwave oven reproached her with its costliness: having read an article about radiation hazards, she'd been afraid to use it or even keep it in the house, where Joan might be tempted to experiment with it.

The light at last roused Stuart. He turned and stared at her coldly, his eyes red and puffy.

"I'm sorry. Really. Are you all right?"

He said nothing. He rolled slowly, painfully, to a sitting position and fumbled his feet into his shoes. She wanted to turn and run now, but spending the morning worrying about his reaction would have been unbearable. She had to know how he felt. She waited, her back pressed to the Hansel and Gretel mural.

He didn't look at her. His face was set in glum, weary lines. She wished desperately that she hadn't locked him in. Looking at him now, she felt as if he were a responsible, put-upon adult and she were a willful child. She had forced a wedge between them at a time when she needed him badly.

"Want to see something funny?" he asked conversationally. He stood up, grimacing and pressing his hands into the small of his back.

She watched him warily for some clue to his state of

mind. It was unthinkable that he should hit her; but her act had been unthinkable, too.

He limped to one of the Gowdie murals. It depicted *Jack and the Beanstalk*. The giant was emerging from his castle in a rage. With the goose under his arm, Jack hadn't yet made it to the stalk and safety. It was typical of the artist that you questioned whether he would. All the nightmares of fairy tales had been captured on these walls, but none of the happy endings. Perhaps Stuart was alluding to the subject of the painting and hinting that she should make a dash for her beanstalk, the Jaguar.

He passed his hand over a shuttered window of the giant's castle. To her surprise, it opened. It was the door of a cabinet. She inched closer for a better look.

"It occurred to me when I was looking desperately for a way to escape that *Hansel and Gretel* might not be the only trick painting. So I tried all the doors and windows. Take a look inside."

She came a little closer. The shallow recess was at the level of her eyes, perhaps only just accessible to a child on tiptoe. It seemed to contain a doll.

"Look," he urged. "I won't bite you."

She found it hard to believe that he wasn't in a vengeful rage, but apparently he wasn't. That he should be taking her prank so well made her feel even guiltier. She came up beside him as he reached in and removed the doll, piece by piece. It was tattered and mildewed, and it had apparently been deliberately dismembered. Its missing head had been replaced by a plastic jack-o'-lantern.

"The girl who died young and tragically—"

"That was the first thought that occurred to me. The doll looks old enough, and so does this." He pulled out a book on which the doll had rested. "But they didn't have plastic pumpkins in those days."

She examined the untitled book. It was leatherbound, the edges marbled with faded blue and orange, and it looked quite old. It was waterlogged and vile-smelling.

"I read what I could until my lighter ran out, but not much of it is legible. Most of the pages are stuck together, and I'll have to dry them before I try to open them."

She was reluctant to open the book. The smell and feel of it disturbed her obscurely. But Stuart waited, expecting her to show interest in his discovery. She lifted the cover and found that the contents had been written by hand in an old-fashioned, elegant copperplate. The first page, which might have given the name of the writer, was stuck to the cover. The text began:

Once upon a time in the land where Today follows Yesterday and Tomorrow follows Today like dutiful ducklings, a beautiful princess named Melody lived in a Castle on the edge of a horrid Abyss.

In the Abyss the days were more like naughty puppies who fought one another constantly with sharp little teeth and claws to determine which one should have precedence. A child who lived in the Abyss might wake with happy anticipation on Christmas morning and run downstairs to unwrap the toys that Santa had left her, only to find that Christmas had come and gone the previous week. It never happened that one would wake on an ordinary day to discover that it was Christmas, for the King of the Abyss was a very wicked king, and all of his surprises were unhappy ones.

The King enjoyed the power to change the faces of his subjects willy-nilly, so that the same little girl might think that she was safe in her mother's arms when she was in fact embracing a bad man whom she had been told never, ever to speak to.

The Abyss was a horrid place, and the King was a wicked King, and no one would ever have gone there if they could have helped it, but the fact was that Melody and the others who lived in the Castle could not see the Abyss. They were not even aware that they lived on its precipitous edge.

"Ugh!" Gwyneth snapped the book shut.

"Be careful." He took it from her before she could obey her instinct and fling it down.

"What a nasty story. But there you are. That was Young-and-Tragic's name, Melody."

"It still doesn't explain the pumpkin."

"Why are you looking at me like that? Do you imagine that I know anything at all about it? That I spend my time cutting up dolls and hiding them in strange places?"

"You have been acting peculiarly lately."

He said that with such long-suffering mildness, damn him, that she was goaded to reply: "So has your mother. I suggest—"

"By the way, where did you go last night?"

"I don't *know!*"

It slipped out, a wail of despair. She stared at him and wished she hadn't said it. He looked appalled: as if he believed her. She turned and blundered out the little door before he could question her; or worse, sympathize with her, for she knew that his sympathy would break down and draw out the insane story in its entirety.

"Gwyneth! Sweetheart, wait!"

She ran to her car and started it bucking on its way. While she drove she fumbled in the glove compartment until her hand touched—*bang,* you're saved!—

the St. Christopher medal he'd concealed there. She hadn't known about it. Not until the policeman had mentioned it.

In her hallucination.

CHAPTER FOUR

Allison Doyle had been hearing the little bells all afternoon, receding, approaching, but seldom out of earshot. The chime was fainter than the clatter of Cassilda Oliphant's bangles, and it was too musical for ice cubes. It must be someone's jewelry. She smiled at the picture of John Wayne moseying among the drab academics with bells on his spurs. Being blind could be an advantage at parties as dull as this one.

"What *is* that? 'Tinkle, tinkle, tinkle.' "

"Ice cubes." Bob McWraith rattled his glass, only proving that wasn't it; but when he stopped, she could no longer hear the bells. He said, "What were you saying?"

"That all this nonsense—witches, fairies,

werewolves—is nothing but metaphors that ignorant peasants created in order to give names to the areas of their ignorance."

"Just like psychiatry."

"Not at all. Psychiatry is a science—"

"Because they give *hydrotherapy* to *schizophrenics* instead of *dunking witches?* Because they prescribe Thorazine or Valium instead of vervain and hellebore? Giving new names to the victim and the treatment doesn't mean that you've made a significant advance in the understanding of either. Words, that's all, metaphors. I'll show you my succubus if you show me your libido."

"You're just arguing for the sake of it." He was also drunk, she thought. "Are you proposing that medical schools replace their departments of psychiatry with the Spanish Inquisition?"

"Not at all. I'm only suggesting that our metaphors for perceiving the world change and go out of fashion, and that those of a previous era are a perfectly fit subject for study."

" 'She rammed the silver bolt up the baby's nose,' " she said, quoting with a sneer one of the specimens she had culled from Gwyneth's garden of peasant doggerel, " 'Till the blood it came trinkling down the baby's fine clothes.' "

"I didn't say they were all worthy of Keats. Some of them are beautiful. 'The cock doth craw, the day doth daw, the channerin worm doth chide.' "

"Ugh. Worms. Death. Rot. It's all rot, if you ask me. 'He cut the paps from off her breast; Great pity it was to see.' No wonder that one of her students—"

"Sherry, wasn't it?" He took her glass and left before she could buttress her argument against the value of Gwyneth's specialty with Sterling Fairchild.

The tiny chiming passed quite close. She was about to call out—but what could she call out? While she was wondering just how to hail the phantom bell-ringer, her nostrils were assailed by a vivid ordor of dog. The sound of its claws on the uncarpeted floor of the drawing room suggested an enormous animal. Just then she heard young Arthur's voice, near the dog and the bell-ringer, and his words caught her attention: ". . . my grandmother."

The next voice was a young man's: "Fat, disgusting bitch. I'll kill all you scum. Especially Doyle. I've got this axe, and if he tries to take it away from me, I'll let him have it, ker-*chunk!,* and his head will go rolling and bumping away. . ."

"Arthur!'

"Is something wrong, Mrs. Um?"

"It's Dr. Shaver, isn't it? Is that you? Do you see my grandson, a blond boy, twelve years old?"

"No, it's crowded, Mrs. Um. I saw him just a moment ago. Are you all right?"

She bounced on the loveseat in frustration. Last

week the student newspaper had shocked her into some somber thoughts on the decline of common civility, never mind respect for authority, by referring to the college president as Edward Wheaton "Both-My-Hands-Are-Back-There-But-I'll-Be-Damned-If-I-Can-Find-My-Ass" Shaver, and it galled her to admit now that they had been dead on target. She couldn't have been stuck with a dimmer Argus in her hour of need.

"Who was with him? Did you see?"

"I believe he was alone. No, that's not true. I think he was with—it will come to me, I'm sure, the man in the green suit. With the bells?"

John Wayne was transformed to Danny Kaye in *The Court Jester*. "He's wearing a green suit with bells on it?"

"No, ha-ha-ha, whatever makes you say that, Mrs. Um? Oh, I see. I mean, may I get you a drink?"

"Where are the bells, Dr. Shaver? On the man in the green suit."

"Yes, exactly. You must excuse me for a moment."

"Doctor . . ."

"What's the matter, Allison?" It was Gwyneth.

"I'm perfectly all right. It's just that I heard Arthur . . ." She cut herself off. She had undoubtedly misunderstood. They must have been talking about some television program, or playing a game based on a horror movie. "He's apparently talking to someone in a green clown costume, or at least so President Shaver has told me. Is there such a person here?"

"Your sherry, Mrs. Doyle," McWraith said, taking her hand and placing the glass in it.

She was afraid that he would take advantage of his opportunity to leave her in Gwyneth's charge and disappear. She suspected that she had been holding him against his will. But she had remembered another choice morsel in his absence, and she couldn't resist ignoring Gwyneth for the moment to cite it: " 'Lambkin nipped the bonnie babe, While high the red blude springs.' "

"No."

"Mrs. Doyle has been quoting . . ."

Allison leaned forward to listen with her skin, as she would sometimes put it. Something was escaping her. McWraith hadn't heard Gwyneth's stricken murmur, but something (the look on Gwyneth's face?) had made him stop talking. She wondered if her daughter-in-law had seen something, and if it had anything to do with Arthur and the Green Man.

"It's nothing. That line gives me the creeps, that's all," Gwyneth said.

"I shouldn't wonder!" Allison cried in triumph. "You see, McWraith?"

"Why don't you sit down, Gwyneth?"

"A psychopathic killer named *Lambkin*." Allison was determined to enjoy the moment. "Not even

Mickey Spillane would impose on us so grossly."

"What's wrong with Mickey Spillane?" McWraith asked.

"You'll never guess who's outside, staring at your house. Gwyneth. Mrs. Doyle. Bob." Allison couldn't even guess who had hurried up to say this. Whoever she was, she continued, "The Old Man Who Wouldn't Say His Prayers."

Gwyneth had been sitting on the loveseat with Allison, who had sensed that she was wound up as tightly as she could be. Now she bolted. The woman who had brought the cryptic news squeaked in surprise and, after a moment, took Gwyneth's seat.

"I don't know why I call him that," she said, "but every time I see him, that just pops into my head—
'There I met an old man who wouldn't say his prayers;
So I took him by the left leg
And threw him down the stairs.'
He has these frighteningly intense, black eyes, in a face like white paper that someone with dirty hands has crumpled up every whichway and then tried to smooth out again, and I'll bet he never said a prayer in his life, not even, 'Now I lay me down to sleep,' when he was little, only he looks as if he never was. Little. But he looks like he's been thrown down the stairs more than once."

"Who is he?" Allison asked.

"I don't really know. He came here a year or so ago and set up housekeeping in an old shack in the woods. Nobody seems to know a thing about him, except that he looks so terribly *dedicated,* you know, only God knows to what. Probably he's working on a theory to prove that the CIA is controlling us through our electric toothbrushes. Or else he's just concentrating real hard on how awful he feels from drinking rubbing alcohol. I think he's the sort of person who's much more interesting if you don't know anything about him. I questioned the checkout clerk at the supermarket one day when I saw him there, and she said he spoke very nicely but he smelled bad. She assumed he was a professor at Amworth."

"That's us, all right," McWraith said.

"What is Gwyneth doing?"

"She went to—here she is now. Did you see him, Gwyneth?"

"Who is this man?" Allison demanded. Although she couldn't say why, or of what, Gwyneth's concern made her deeply suspicious. "Does he prowl around our home often?"

"No, of course not. I don't know who he is. Mattie keeps mentioning him, that's all, and I just wanted to get a look at him."

The newcomer, then, was Mattie Dreyfus, whom she had never actually met, the wife of an instructor in the anthropology department. She sensed that

Gwyneth was hiding something, but this didn't seem the time to dig it out, so she said lightly, "Perhaps he's Cassilda's secret admirer."

"Isn't that the perfect name for him, don't you think, The Old Man Who Wouldn't Say His Prayers?"

"Yes," Gwyneth said shortly. "You were asking me, Allison, about the man in green?"

"With bells on, yes. Don't forget the bells. You've given me this image—Dr. Shaver did, actually—or some elf in a bottle-green costume capering about the house."

"Not entirely inaccurate. The man is a dancing fool."

"Oh, do be quiet, Bob," Gwyneth said. "That's Tom Woodling, the guest of honor. Haven't you met him? That's terrible. It's not bottle green, it's a subdued, tweedy, heathery sort of green—"

"With an emerald necktie and handkerchief, don't forget those. I think he's a leprechaun."

"He can't be a leprechaun, he's English," Mattie said.

"Then," McWraith said gravely, "he must be a fairy."

"And the bells on his shoes—" Gwyneth tried to continue, but by this time all of them (especially Allison, who had nothing against which to gauge this surrealistic sketch) were screaming with laughter—"and the bells on his shoes—"

Allison heard the chimes approaching, but she couldn't speak. She signalled, trying to warn Gwyneth, but Gwyneth pressed on: "And the bells on his toes—his *shoes,* damn it—"

"This is certainly the liveliest corner of the party," said the man under discussion, throwing Allison into confusion: for although he was the man with the bells, his wasn't the voice that had spoken the bloody threat to Arthur. His voice was familiar, however, disturbingly so.

"You shall have music wherever you go," she said, and she was pleased to hear and feel this sally destroying the other's attempts at self-control.

"Oh, yes, quite, I see." He laughed along with them. "I'm surprised you were able to hear them at all, just idiotic little things on my shoelaces, I didn't know myself I had them until I'd got them home from the shop. Your hearing would be acute, of course, Mrs . . . ?"

"Doyle. Gwyneth 's mother-in-law. Arthur's grandmother. I overheard you—"

"Why didn't you take them right back to the store?" McWraith demanded. "Why do you wear them?"

"Really, Bob!" Gwyneth said. "You're wearing some loathesome cologne so you'll smell good, you're wearing your one and only necktie so you'll look good, why shouldn't a man try to sound good, as well?"

"I bet he even tastes good."

"Behave yourself! Bob's had too much to drink."

"There's no such thing."

"I overheard you talking to Arthur and some young man—a young man with a dog?—and I couldn't help wondering what on earth he was telling you. I must have misheard, but—"

"I was questioning him about his fantasies, that's all. It's for my research."

"Tom never stops working." To Allison's ear, Gwyneth's voice throbbed with admiration.

"Am I correct in understanding that someone at this party entertains the fantasy of chopping off my son's head with an axe?"

"Why, no." He laughed. "You did mishear."

"Not at all unusual, though, don't you agree, Mrs. Doyle, since you set such store by psychiatry?" McWraith said. "Like every red-blooded American boy, Arthur wants to chop off his father's head—and Freud would find that method of execution significant—and sleep with his mother. The—"

"It wasn't Arthur," Allison insisted.

"—last part makes a lot of sense, of course," McWraith had continued in an undertone intended only for Gwyneth.

"However, Arthur didn't say it," Woodling said. She wondered if he and McWraith were conspiring to be deliberately obtuse about the homicidal young man. "What's your dearest fantasy, Mrs. Doyle?"

"To be an artist, of course. Or perhaps a ballerina."

It annoyed her that only McWraith laughed. She had tried to make a joke, and everyone but the drunken fool had chosen to interpret her remark as the embarrassing bile of a bitter old woman. She laughed to show she had been kidding.

But Woodling said, "I assume you were being quite honest. One's potential has nothing whatever to do with one's fantasies. Quite the contrary, most often. A celebrated wit like Professor McWraith, for example, doesn't fantasize himself as a brilliant conversationalist, but perhaps as a great lover. You—"

"I say, old boy, that's a bit thick." McWraith's mockery of Woodling's accent didn't conceal that he had been stung.

"—were blinded as an adult, were you not?"

Allison stiffened. "Yes."

"But in your dreams you can still see, of course."

"I even dance." She thawed slightly. "Bizarre as that may seem."

"And, of course, in your fantasies you have sight, too. There's no reason why you shouldn't daydream of painting pictures."

Mattie asked Woodling why she fantasized of being

interviewed by Mike Wallace, and Allison drifted inward to examine the picture of this house that she had lately been painting. She had never liked the house. She had once believed that she loved it, but the fact was that Joseph had swept her away with his eloquence, as he so often could. Living in this ruin of the Gilded Age, to hear him tell it, would be a continuous adventure in which little crises would arise that they could always cope with in clever ways, that they could laugh about later together. But the constant battles with plumbing and termites and weak floorboards and broken sashes hadn't been fun, she hadn't coped very well, and there hadn't been much laughter.

Much as she disliked the house, she nevertheless found in it now a complex challenge for her memory and her imagination. Remembering all the intricate details of the scrolls and gargoyles and grillwork, the placement of the many windows, the shapes of certain stains on the brick foundations, the patterns of colored light and shadow falling into the central hall through the stained and etched glass surrounding the baronial front entrance, light whose quality changed with the season, the day, the hour: when she got it all just right, she would feel the elation of a god whose universe has inconveniently imploded, but who has recreated it all as good as new from memory. Unlike a proper god, she would usually forget some silly little thing like the weathercock on top of her tower.

Lately she had experimented with painting people at the windows: Jamie at twelve years old, wearing the bemused and hurt expression of one who persists in playing a different game from the rest of the world; Gwyneth as she'd last seen her in one of her flamboyant outfits. Sometimes she painted Joseph in his overalls, red-faced and obsessed, Captain Ahab going down for the last time under his crushing white whale of a house. More often she painted Alan Braden, her own artist, who would have made a cutting remark about her daydream of being a painter.

She slid past the side of the house and found herself in the overgrown orchard beyond the playhouse. It was twilight, and it must have been spring, because the orchard was in flower. Fireflies glimmered in the green gloom; the pinkish-white blossoms seemed to glow with their own inner light. It was a piercingly beautiful scene, but she knew that something profoundly unpleasant lurked at the end of the orchard. And she was being drawn to it.

She saw an unnaturally lean shadow. Its long arms and legs had a spidery quality, its movements were too quick and furtive to be human. *Beware of Long Lambkin that lies in the moss.* As she got closer, its more grotesque qualities faded into the semblance of a man. She could have been mistaken about his deformities, fooled by distance and dubious light, but it was almost as if the disappearance of those inhuman proportions and mannerisms had been activated automatically by her approach: like the disappearance of a swarm of vermin at the approach of a human being.

Man or not, he still radiated menace. His face was an immobile wax mask, and through it burned eyes with catlike slits for irises. His hair was silver, although the mask was youthfully smooth. She was extremely glad to be invisible, as she often was in her dreams. He watched her house the way a cat watches a mouse-hole. And then he turned his eyes on her.

He saw her.

She woke with a violent start. Her terror dissipated into the shame of having dozed off. Woodling was speaking: ". . . blame myself. I should have known that his sadistic compulsions were something more than fantasies, and that talking about them would give no release. I may have lent them a certain respectability by listening so uncritically."

"A rare admission," McWraith murmured. "Haven't you just dismissed the basis of psychoanalysis?"

"I'm only an experimental psychologist," Woodling said mildly, and his bells tinkled as he got up. "Would you care to dance, Gwyneth?"

"So was Dr. Mengele," McWraith said under his breath, but Allison heard him.

For all Allison knew, she might have been snoring

among them for the past ten minutes, but she resolved to brazen it out: "My mind wandered for a moment. Was he talking about Sterling Fairchild?"

"Apparently he lent a sympathetic ear to the lad's dreams before he went out to make them come true. It's what he does. A sort of highbrow Nancy Friday," McWraith said. "At least, I'm told he's a highbrow. And the police have been questioning him, now that his protégé has flown the coop."

"Do you mean to say that horrible boy has escaped?"

"He didn't even have to chew his way out. Some computer overlooked him as he was being handed from one set of bureaucrats to another, and now he's free to fold, bend, spindle and mutilate the populace. Excuse me."

Finding herself suddenly alone, Allison listened to the music from the next room and wondered how one would dance to it; or why one would want to; but her feet moved nevertheless, and she stilled them sternly. She heard more talking than dancing, a continuous volley of voices competing to be heard above one another and the music. Out of the wave of noise she distinguished James's voice approaching. He was speaking angrily but too softly for her to make out his words, and he lowered his voice further when he entered the drawing room.

"Shaver . . . humiliation . . . gone too damned far

this time . . ."

"The caterer is being paid by the college. Why not me?" That voice, clear and shrill, was Cassilda's.

"Because you're not doing anything, are you?" His voice rose, too. "And because I agreed to pay you fifty bucks for whatever extra cleaning up you'll have to do, which is absurd, but which leaves you with no excuse for trying to extort a hundred from Dr. Shaver—"

Amused, Allison held still, hoping they wouldn't notice her and take their quarrel elsewhere. Knowing Cassilda, she could see her approaching the president in her chummy, flirty way, abundant bosom all but bared by her cocktail dress, to all appearances another guest at the party. She had fun picturing Shaver's attempt to puzzle out the solicitation.

Joseph had collected strays, and he'd moved Cassilda Oliphant in when her husband had gotten fed up with her scatterbrained ways and left her. James later hired her to take care of the children while Gwyneth studied for her doctorate. He kept her on, she supposed, because he was fond of her and therefore imagined that everyone else was, too. She worked hard at keeping her status ambiguous. Although she was paid as cook and housekeeper, she promoted the fiction that she was the old friend of a family that shamelessly imposed on her good nature.

Beneath a show of affection, she and Allison despised each other. Cassilda never entered Allison's room without switching a few articles from their clearly established places: her hairbrush from the right to the left of her dressing table, for instance, or the toilet paper from its holder to the top of the bathroom hamper, causing her minutes (sometimes hours, if Cassilda was inspired) of anger and frustration. To call her back and ask what she'd done with her chocolates or her slippers, or where she'd hidden the lunch tray today, would be to admit defeat, which Allison never admitted to anyone under any circumstances whatever. To lose her temper and make a scathing remark would reduce Cassilda to tears, a sweetly reasonable woman who had merely been trying to make things nice or cosy or more convenient for her unfortunate old friend. Allison believed that her old friend would have liked to put a nice, cosy chair in some convenient place like the head of the stairs, where she would trip over it and break her neck, but that she lacked the courage; besides, it would bring her game to an end. Their game, she grudgingly amended, for she enjoyed it when she could beat Cassilda.

Allison had a more compelling reason not just for tolerating this cruel eccentric but for desiring her company. As the only person she knew who remembered Alan Braden at his best, Cassilda was the custodian of her past. She was like an irreplaceable phonograph record with a deep scratch in it, one that she couldn't bear to play but couldn't bear to throw out.

". . . has thrown up all over my bathroom," Cassilda was saying. *"My* personal bathroom."

"Oh, shit."

"No, Stuart, if that had been the case, I presume he would have been sitting on his intended target and able to hit it. I'm talking about *vomit:* a spray, a cataract, a deluge of malodorous, alcoholic *vomit.*"

"God damn it, I'll make him clean it up." James's voice receded. "Or *I* will."

"I knew there was a reason why he had a black aura." The angry rattle of advancing ornaments told Allison she had been spotted and was being addressed. "I never before saw a human being with a black aura." The loveseat sagged beside her under a gin-scented weight. "It's disappointing, if it only signified that he was going to puke."

She had been telling Cassilda that her occult enthusiasms were hogwash for—good Lord, for all of forty years now: she'd met her, appropriately enough, at a Halloween party when she was fifteen. Cassilda—then Cassie Castaldo—a couple of years younger, had been reading palms. She'd told Joseph Doyle that he would soon make a long ocean voyage because of something terrible that was going to happen at Pearl Harbor, even though none of them, in October of 1941, could recall having heard of a place with that name. Everyone in those days had known in their hearts that "something terrible" was going to happen, and the name *Pearl Harbor* could have slid unnoticed into her subconscious from any number of sources, but Cassilda (and Joseph, too) had taken the Japanese attack five weeks later as proof of her clairvoyance. While her contemporaries collected scrap metal and knitted khaki sweaters, Cassilda had spent the war writing voluminous letters about her dream to President Roosevelt.

Allison didn't say "hogwash" now, because she wanted a favor, but she didn't have the patience to listen to a lecture about auras, either, so she came to the point: "Would you mind taking a walk out to the end of the orchard for me, Cassie? The fresh air might do you—"

"Are you accusing me of being drunk? You people are going to regret all the abuse you've heaped upon me when I'm gone. Which won't be very long." She was even drunker than Allison had suspected. "A black aura. God!"

"No, no, not at all. I was told there's a strange man prowling around the house, or there was. And I have a feeling that he might be out there, at the end of the orchard."

"A feeling?" Cassilda didn't just brighten; she incandesced. "A premonition?"

"A vision," Allison asserted. "I saw a man—not

the old man they described, really, but a thoroughly undesirable sort of individual—at the end of the orchard, watching the house. It isn't dark yet, is it?"

"Almost."

"Don't go all the way. Just go out and take a look. Would you? As a very great favor?"

"Very well." Rising in a jingle of ankhs and amulets and zodiacal gewgaws, she sounded like an army of elves girding their loins for battle. "But it doesn't mean I've forgotten all those things Stuart said to me. Or that I'm going to tolerate people with black auras, even if they don't throw up in my bathroom."

Mattie Dreyfus returned with a plate from the buffet and explained its arrangement with the eagerness of a child playing a new game. When they were eating, she said, "Do you mind talking about your handicap?"

"Affliction," Allison said. "Handicap suggests a racehorse, and the image of a blind racehorse is altogether grotesque. It also suggests the universal cure for disabled horses, and I'm not quite ready for that. I don't mind talking about it."

"It's just that when I was a kid, I used to get into a silly discussion with my friends about which we'd rather be, blind or deaf, and I always was laughed at for saying blind. I wanted your opinion of my choice."

"What's your own opinion?"

"It seemed to me—it still does, I guess—that the things you really need to see, like your plate, can be described by others, or figured out by touch. The things you need to hear would create problems—like, 'Stop!' or, 'Duck!' And so far as the things I want to see or hear are concerned, I've never seen anything that could compare with hearing Bach. I wouldn't want to give up music, or the sound of voices I love."

Allison was moved. No one had given her a choice, but hers would have been the same. Voices would have been hard to give up. James's, for instance. He had an extraordinary voice. With proper training he might have sounded as good as Raymond Massey or Richard Burton, actors whose voices gave her gooseflesh. If James was in the right mood, his reading could send shivers down her spine. If he had stuck with his youthful ambition, he would have made a spellbinding priest, the kind whose sermons raised blisters when he spoke of hellfire. But he had never stuck with anything he'd started. She'd pitied her husband for taking the game of renovating the house with such deadly earnestness; she pitied her son for taking the real world as a game.

But his voice, even when he was talking nonsense, was a pleasure to hear. She doubted that she would have been pleased, if her sight could be miraculously restored, to see the changes in his face through the years of heavy drinking and petty disappointments; or pleased to see her own. It was bad enough to feel her sagging jowl and shapeless body.

Alan's voice—and thinking of it, she knew instantly whom Woodling had reminded her of. Woodling's English accent had distracted her from the similarity. Also, he spoke in coherent sentences, while Alan had tended to speak in elliptical grunts. She hoped to hear Woodling's voice again before the evening was over.

"It allows me to concentrate on music and voices more intently, too," she said. "And on words, when books are read to me." Afraid that she might be in danger of compromising her reputation as a curmudgeon, she added., "Considering the benefits, I'm only surprised that everyone doesn't pluck his eyes out."

"Would you like me to come and read to you some time? I'd really enjoy it."

Mattie's voice was tentative and wispy, though pleasant enough. It wasn't in James's league; or even in Gwyneth's, who'd been a pretty good actress, by all accounts. But then Gwyneth had never volunteered to read for her. Arthur was very dutiful, but he tended to stumble over the longer words, and he couldn't conceal his lack of enthusiasm for her favorite authors. She had never asked Cassilda, whose voice suggested a saw cutting metal.

"If you're free some afternoon, I'd be grateful. I

hope you don't mind Edward Gibbon?"

"Not at all." She added shyly, "I wrote my master's thesis on him."

Twenty minutes had passed since Allison had sent Cassilda on her errand, and she asked Mattie to see if she had returned to the house without reporting or, what was more likely, had never left the house. ("A plump woman, not as fat as I—no one is, of course— with a bleached blonde fright-wig of frizzy hair, and probably wearing an immodestly low-cut dress and too much junk jewelry.") When Mattie couldn't find her, she shrugged off the girl's offers of assistance and went upstairs for a sweater. She wanted to keep Mattie at arm's length until she decided how she felt about sharing her pleasure with someone who probably knew more about Gibbon than she did.

Descending from her tower with the sweater, she suffered an attack of vertigo. That was how she explained it, although it failed to describe the symptoms exactly. The staircase leading down to the third floor seemed to have developed a twist to the left, so that she couldn't descend three steps without bumping into the wall to her right. She had sipped only three glasses of sherry in two hours, and she knew she wasn't drunk.

She stopped for a moment to pin down firmly in her mental diagram of the enclosed staircase to the tower. After the seventh step there was a narrow landing, where the stairs did make a sharp left turn. But both flights were perfectly straight. She must have reached the landing without noticing and blundered her way around it.

However plausible that explanation might be, it didn't jibe with her best recollection. She could have sworn that she'd descended only six steps, and that she'd bumped into the wall after each set of three. She now took what she believed to be the seventh step. She would normally have turned confidently on the landing at this point, but she was compelled to jab the space ahead with her cane: and she discovered another step. And another. And still a third, where she struck the right-hand wall with her shoulder for the third time.

The tip of her cane gave neither the right touch nor the right sound as it tapped the stairs. She scraped it on the next step. It sounded and felt as if it were scraping stone, but the stones to her tower were uncarpeted wood.

She must have taken the wrong door and descended the wrong staircase, but she knew the house perfectly, and there was no wrong door, no wrong staircase to take. Only one set of steps led down from her tower, and it was made of wood. The house simply did not hold a spiral staircase made of stone.

Counting the steps as she continued, she was conscious of a deep, muffled vibration occurring at irregular intervals of a few seconds. It might have been made by someone beating a padded hammer against a cellar wall, but only if the house were infinitely larger than it should have been, the cellar infinitely deeper, and the hammer the size of a wrecker's ball.

She strained her ears for the sounds of the party, but she heard only the sigh of a spectral breeze in vast spaces and, very far off, the sound of one man singing. She could determine neither the words nor the melody.

Having counted fifteen steps, she came upon a level space that should have been the third-floor hallway; but wasn't. She cleared her throat loudly, and the sound was wrong. The hall was far too big, and, like the stairs, its floor was made of stone.

She had no intention of shouting for help. Everyone would rush to her assistance, making her feel weak and cowardly. Worse, they would all tell her exactly where she was and how she had gotten here, and she would feel like a fool for not having known it all along.

She proceeded on the assumption that she was exactly where she should have been, in the third-floor hallway of her own home, but she proceeded with extreme caution. Searching for reasonable explanations, she theorized that the thudding in the depths of the cellar was actually the beating of her heart—but that was wrong: her heart was beating very fast indeed.

She heard an indistinct cry to her left. She turned toward it and crossed the hall, noting the time-worn concavity of the floor. The tip of her cane ruffled a very heavy drape. She clutched at the thick brocaded material and felt it tear easily, as if it were disintegrating with age. It was damp and smelled musty. She sensed that someone in the room beyond this hanging was watching her.

The acoustics of the hall abruptly changed. The sense of vast distance, the chill of obscure drafts, no longer prevailed. The man who had been singing very far away was not singing just beneath her, noisily and drunkenly, over the general din of the ongoing party. The quality of these sounds suggested that she was on the second floor of her home, not the third. She was relieved to find an explanation for the inordinate number of steps she had descended, and she clung to it as if it explained everything; even though she knew that it didn't.

Without realizing it, she had apparently opened the door to James's and Gwyneth's bedroom. She shut it and hurried down to the entrance hall, and she was out the front door before anyone could detain her. She breathed deeply of the smokeless air to clear her head of what she now dismissed as vertigo. The air had a crisp bite to it, but she refused to run the gauntlet again by going back for something more substantial than her sweater. She strode confidently past the side of the house, whipping the air with her cane.

When the noise of the party had faded behind the playhouse, she called out sharply: "Cassie!"

Cassilda might not be here, but she had to assure herself that there was no monster in a human mask, either. If she once gave way to things that weren't there, if she began to take seriously the terrors of her imagination, her dark world would become uninhabitable. She had to assert her courage by going to the very place where Long Lambkin lay in the moss and daring him to do his worst.

"Mom!"

That was James, far behind her, but she didn't answer him as she pressed forward—too hastily, for she tangled with something hanging from an apple-bough. She beat it off with her cane, disgusted by the feel of it. Whatever it was, it was long and limp, the diameter and texture of sausage, and it was coated with slime.

Damn Cassilda Oliphant! Her previous pranks had never been so bizarre, but perhaps Allison's ill-considered suggestion of a supernatural experience had inspired her to outdo herself. It seemed a lot of trouble to go to, hanging a rubber snake over a limb on the slim likelihood that she would look for her if she didn't return and stumble into it. But perhaps Cassilda could predict her actions better than she was willing to admit.

Turning to find the ropy loops again with her cane, she stumbled on some rubbery thing and fell against the stone fence. This was the approximate place where the lean creature had crouched, and it wasn't here. Not even her annoyance at Cassilda's trick could prevent her from feeling elated by her little victory.

The light breeze died, and she noticed for the first time the vile odor of her surroundings. As she began to retreat, the soft objects she trod on—there were many of them—took on an unpleasant significance. She poked at them with her cane. But they weren't excrement. They maintained a resilient integrity when she jabbed at them.

"God damn you, Cassilda Oliphant." She spoke in a firm, carrying voice. "I was with you at that Halloween party forty years ago, and I remember it as well as you so obviously do, and I'm not going to be upset by the same trick that scared me when I was fifteen years old."

The game had been Joseph Doyle's, and she hadn't forgiven him for it until two years later, when she'd seen him on the eve of his departure for the war and fallen in love with him. "This is the old witch's liver," he'd whispered portentously in the dark room; "This is the old witch's heart," as he'd passed around his grisly props, some borrowed from his mother's icebox, others made up from things like Jello and rubber gloves. Cassilda had done him one better by somehow providing an odor for the illusion.

"Mom, what are you doing out here?"

He was much closer, but she didn't believe he'd seen her yet. She went forward hastily, not wanting him to see what Cassilda had done, for it was a skirmish in a private war that he didn't understand. As it often was, her exasperation with her old antagonist was mingled with their shared nostalgia. In her haste, she stumbled and fell over a larger, round object.

She groped for the thing that had tripped her. It proved to be a pumpkin carved with a grinning face. To her, it seemed the signature on Cassilda's work; or, more properly, the switching on of the lights to prove that it had been just a Halloween party game.

She couldn't understand at first why James, when he came upon her, cried out in horror and revulsion.

CHAPTER FIVE

"Elephants' Graveyard, I said!" Arthur was trying hard to look the picture of outraged innocence. "I was telling Joan how I was reading about this place where the elephants all go to die. Jeez!"

Stuart said, "She used to change your diapers when you were a baby, Arthur."

He shouted further denials, but Stuart turned his full attention to Joan as she asked, "Who killed her, Daddy?"

"The police think it was the same boy who murdered the coeds."

"Arthur thinks it was Grandma."

"Shut up, you stupid little bitch!"

Stuart held Arthur's arms to keep him from attacking his sister while he addressed the question as if it were reasonable: "It couldn't have been. Mrs. Drey-fus told me when Grandma went outside. I followed her within five minutes. More like three minutes."

"Just like Agatha Christie," Joan said. "Will the police make everyone at the party give everyone else an alibi?"

"No. As I said, they think they know who did it."

"What a shame. Arthur doesn't have an alibi."

She knew that he wouldn't hold her brother in his chair all day, so she sprang to her feet and dashed out of the house. Stuart said, "You know she only needles you because you've got a rotten temper. If you didn't rise to the bait so predictably every time, she'd get tired of doing it."

"Yeah, okay, can I go now?"

"If you promise to leave Joan alone."

"Joan alone," he mocked. "Yeah, sure. I want to go see Grandma."

"That's a good idea. She'll be lonely now, without . . ."

"Come on," he groaned, shambling toward the stairs. "They hated each other's guts."

Stuart dropped into the chair his son had vacated and stared at the mosaic of lights and shadows in the front hall, where Gwyneth would presently appear, if she planned to appear. "Where have you been?" he would demand, stubble-faced and red-eyed. He should have a shotgun over his knees to complete the picture, and a can of beer in his hand. He could do something about the beer, at least. He got up and went to the kitchen.

Beer in hand, he entered the pantry and took down the book from the playhouse where he'd . . . no, not where he'd left it to dry: where he'd hidden it, with that sickening doll. He tried to pry open the hidden pages, but they disintegrated soggily. He looked at the oven. He hadn't dared to touch a stove in fifteen years. It was ridiculous: this tasteful walnut cabinet didn't even look like a stove, and it operated by electricity. But nevertheless, his hand began to shake when he thought of using it to dry the book. He hurried back to the parlor with his can of beer.

"Oh!" He hadn't heard her come in, but Gwyneth was now sitting in his chair.

"Didn't you go to work?" she asked disarmingly. Instead of looking guilty, she looked concerned for him.

"I called in. Considering the murder and all . . . What do you care?"

"Why, what's wrong?"

He sat opposite her and searched her face. She was much better at feigning innocence than her son.

"I woke up at three o'clock this morning to find you gone."

"I may have gotten up. I . . ."

He couldn't understand it, but she seemed unprepared for his questions. She averted her eyes, and her hands began to move restlessly about her skirt and the arms of her chair as if busy on their own aimless errands.

"Your car was gone, too."

She folded her hands together firmly and looked him in the eye. "I couldn't sleep. So I went for a drive."

"And have only just now returned."

She smiled, although she didn't seem amused. "So it would seem."

"You don't really remember, do you. Leaving the house. Or where you went."

"What nonsense!" She laughed convincingly, having warmed to the story she'd just made up, he was sure. "I couldn't sleep, so I went for a drive. That seemed a foolish waste of time, so I decided to make the most of my insomnia by going to my office to grade papers. I napped there on the couch for a while and then went to my class."

"Sterling will get you, if you don't watch out."

"I can't let Sterling rule my life. Besides, I don't think he'd hurt me."

"Tell me next time, will you? Wake me up."

"You don't like being waked—"

"I like even less, waking to find you gone! With a maniac loose, with people being murdered in our own backyard, I don't like it at all, God damn it! While we're on the subject of what I don't like, I don't like being locked in the playhouse while you . . ."

His anger faded into a dull ache. Shouting at her would solve nothing, nor would it elicit responsive answers. He stared at his side of the rug, she at hers.

At length he asked, "Do you suppose he made a habit of hanging around our house?"

"I saw him a couple of times. In the orchard. I mean, in retrospect, I think now it could have been Sterling I saw."

"You should have told me."

"I thought nothing of it. This was before he ran amok, before anyone suspected he was capable of it. I thought it was just kids, or. . ."

"Or your father."

He was disappointed in himself. Unwilling to press his interrogation about last night, perhaps because he was afraid she might tell him where she'd been, he tried to provoke her by picking at an open sore. Talking about her father—if that's who he was—upset her.

Gwyneth's Aunt Isabel Underhill, a dotty old maid who had been principal of the local grammar school since three years before the discovery of chalk, had told her as a child that her immediate family had "gone away on a long trip." When Gwyneth was older, Aunt Isabel confessed that they were dead. As dottiness became senility, the cause of their deaths had varied from cholera to shipwreck to a house fire.

Even at her most lucid, Aunt Isabel had never given Gwyneth a consistent picture of her parents, her brothers or sisters, and Gwyneth had come to suspect that there had been something unsavory, even shameful, about the family and the manner of their deaths. She hadn't dug any deeper when her aunt died without telling her more.

Just last year, Stuart had come home to find Gwyneth talking to a morose tramp who called himself Philip Kemper and claimed to be her father. If the man were telling the truth, one explanation for his absense immediately suggested itself: that he had murdered the rest of his family and been confined for the crime all these years. Like no one Stuart had ever seen, he looked the part: furtive, guilty, socially inept as from long imprisonment, but with a certain exasperating arrogance that hinted he knew more than the common herd could ever hope to experience or understand. Gwyneth's own childhood suspicions and the fact that her aunt had seen fit to change her name to her own reinforced Stuart's theory, but he hadn't confined it to Gwyneth; and she declined to say what she believed, or what Kemper had told her.

The old man had presumably come to Amworth to be near his surviving daughter, but he had seen her only that once, to Stuart's knowledge. Since then Stuart had seen him lurking near the house once or twice, but he had turned and scurried away from friendly advances.

So he felt it was unfair to mention her father now, but while he was thinking of a way to word his apology, she astounded him by saying, "I wish . . . I think maybe you should talk to him."

"Me? Why?"

"It was just a thought. He doesn't want to talk to me, obviously. I thought . . . Never mind, it's hardly important."

He believed she was trying to tell him that her father might be able to shed some light on her behavior, which even she didn't understand; but that she was afraid to find out for herself. He saw it as an appeal for help, and it moved him, but he doubted that Kemper could tell him anything worth knowing. She might believe that she had inherited a strain of mental instability, and her father might believe it, too, but that wouldn't make it so. Her problem was her own. And his.

"Have you thought of seeing a doctor?"

She laughed at him. Maybe he had read too much into her words. Or not enough, and she had convinced herself that the Curse of the Kempers was immune to medicine. He saw that this wasn't the time to bring up the subject of psychiatry, so he said: "I asked whether Sterling had been hanging around because it occurred to me that the things in the playhouse might have been his. A book of gibberish, and a doll to practice on."

"Why didn't you mention it to the police?"

It was a good question; too good. He said, "You didn't, either."

"Allison couldn't have murdered Cassilda, Stuart, really—"

"Good God!" He found himself standing up. He watched his beer can foaming into the rug for a moment before he regained the presence of mind to pick it up. "Whatever gave you an idea like that? Do you think I suspected her for a moment? Have you been making such suggestions to Arthur?"

"Of course not. Why didn't you tell the police about the doll?"

He started for the kitchen, then changed his mind. "I think I'll shave. And dress. And go out."

The book was old enough to have belonged to Miss Young-and-Tragic. But the doll, he admitted to himself as he shaved, could have been his mother's. Or his father's. If it had been secreted in the hidden cabinet years ago, as its condition would seem to indicate, the likeliest candidate for ownership would have been Alan Braden.

Braden had turned up on their doorstep one day and introduced himself to Joseph Doyle as an artist who would restore the Gowdie murals. He was a very skinny, very nervous young man with thick spectacles who blurted his words in random clusters ("I've always wanted to see the Gowdie. Playhouse and since. I happened to be in the area I didn't want to pass. Up the opportunity.") The knapsack on his back held everything he owned.

"I'm not dumb enough to pay money to that pipsqueak for fooling around with valuable artwork," Joseph Doyle said, but he allowed Braden to examine the murals. This examination proved to be a long and involved process, and the artist had soon moved into a spare bedroom. The arrangement wasn't unusual. Joseph acquired freeloaders, whom he called "pensioners and protégés," like barnacles as he sailed majestically through life. Braden did spend a lot of time sketching the murals, and he would grunt about them thoughtfully if asked, but before long he had moved the junk from the playhouse onto the lawn and converted it into his studio, where he worked on his own paintings. Since he had no money at all, he touched Joseph for several hundred dollars to buy art supplies.

Sometimes he would try to lend a hand with the ongoing renovation of the house, but Joseph refused his help unless he was desperate. He claimed that Braden had a wild talent for destroying any mechanical device he touched. "Don't let Michelangelo get his mitts on your watch, whatever you do," Joseph warned

Stuart when he came home from his second year at seminary to find the artist in residence. He thought his father was exaggerating, so when Braden asked him for a light one day, he handed over his indestructible Zippo without a second thought. It wouldn't work for Braden; it never worked again.

The artist would flatter his patron by painting unflattering portraits of him and giving them to him. He always managed to make Stuart's father, a bluff, easy-going, uncomplicated man, look more autocratic and less stable than Nero. But his favorite model was Allison, and they spent a lot of time with each other. Since she was a poised thirty-nine and he was a scruffy, neurotic, inarticulate, undernourished boy (he would have been twenty-two-or-three, but he seemed much younger), Joseph didn't give this a thought.

To Stuart's eye, the eye of a nineteen-year-old virgin preoccupied with the Meaning of Life, Alan Braden seemed implausible in the role of Young Lochinvar. He had skin the color of library paste, a beard that grew in patches, and the kind of mouth that had not yet been fully authenticated by Mick Jagger. He alternated his compulsive blurting with spells of surly withdrawal, and he could have given lessons in thin-skinned irascibility to a samurai.

If the artist planned to sweep anyone off her feet, Cassilda Oliphant, another of Joseph's protégés, seemed a much likelier target. She wasn't at all bad-looking then, and she had the blowsy, comfortable, undemanding appeal of an unmade bed. Even on Stuart, who was deeply unnerved by it, she exerted a guilty attraction. But beyond peeking down the careless decolletage of her bathrobe and writing some very bad verses about what he glimpsed there, he did nothing about it.

Cassilda would rise at eleven, but she "wasn't herself" until three, by which time she would have made two pots of coffee and spilled most of it over the dream books and horoscopes littering the kitchen table, where she would hunch, muttering over and scribbling on scraps of paper, a disorganized Druidess. If you believed her, she dreamed dreams rivaling *Finnegan's Wake* in length and complexity every night of her life, and anyone who wandered into the kitchen between eleven and three would get a fully annotated account of last night's phantasmagoria and be invited to assist in its interpretation.

Her dreams were often preceded and ended with lists of credits, like movies; not, as one might expect, "Produced, Written and Directed by Cassilda Oliphant, Additional Dialogue by Cassilda Oliphant, etc.," but a citation of names and functions that she seldom remembered, but that seldom made sense when she did. For years she kept stuck in the corner of her bedroom mirror a tattered and greasy list derived from one particularly vivid dream she'd had on May Eve, 1960. Stuart remembered this marvel clearly, because she would frequently consult it and solicit comment on it:

Head Gourd	Will o' the Wisp
Anachronist	Sebastian Gowdie
Trepan	Sylvestris Tenebrion
Resurrectionist	?
Act Three	Axcabala
Third Murderer	Jamie Stewart
Lampreys, Leeches, Raptors	
summoned by	The Eldritch King
The Pestilence That Walketh	
in Darkness	Leesome Bairn
Scavenger's Daughter . . .	Old Scratchy Claw

Almost everyone avoided the kitchen during those hours when it became Cassilda's salon. Stuart sidled in at least once a day for a cup of coffee and a look down her bathrobe, but he regarded the bilge he had to listen to as penance for a venal pleasure.

But Braden soon took to planting himself in the kitchen for the full four-hour seminar. He would sit and grunt, occupying himself by rolling her daily supply of sixty Bugler cigarettes, a task he performed so well that they looked as if they had been made by one of the machines he could have demolished with a glance. Before he took on this job, Cassilda would wander about with disintegrating packages of burning tobacco dangling from her lip that would periodically unravel completely, often in someone else's food or lap. Stuart thought Braden did this to scrounge tobacco, which he did, or to catch glimpses of Cassilda's loosely guarded charms, which he also did, but it became obvious that he was genuinely interested in what she had to say and that they shared a passion for the fantastic. But whereas she would become a convert to whatever theory was put forward in the latest issue of *Fate,* Braden was single-minded in his silliness.

He didn't talk to her about his obsession, at least not while Stuart was present, but he once told Stuart a story that made Cassilda Oliphant at her craziest seem as sane as Margaret Mead. Alan Braden was firmly convinced that he was Sebastian Gowdie: not the artist's spiritual heir or his reincarnation, but the very man himself.

Stuart had mostly ignored Braden since coming home, but one rainy night when he had no one else to drink with, it struck him that the artist was the best of good fellows, and he set a circuitous course for the playhouse with a quart of gin to seal their friendship. Braden was pleased to receive him, and the playhouse, lit like an execution-chamber by a bare, 200-

watt bulb on an extension cord from the house, seemed to Stuart like the most delightful place on earth, with its heady atmosphere of turpentine, mildew, and bohemianism.

Braden had shrouded the murals with an assortment of dirty tarpaulins and army blankets to protect them from flying paint, he said, and to keep them from distracting him. Preternaturally bright flowers and bloated fungi showed beneath the drab hangings, and a baleful eye observed them through a moth-hole. Stuart's gaze kept fixing on what looked like a coarse, humanoid foot, tensed beside the hairy hoof of some other creature in the picture as if about to catapult its owner forward into the room.

More intriguing was the painting Braden had been working on, a nude study of Cassilda that captured the untidy earthiness that Stuart saw as her essential appeal. The painting had a shaggy texture that Stuart couldn't account for until he examined it closely and saw that the oils had been mixed with thousands of shreds of tobacco. Braden—who also rolled paint from his fingers into his cigarettes all evening—called this a lucky accident that he had capitalized upon.

After they'd both had a few pulls from the bottle, Braden twisted his bony body into the irregularities of the couch and began to blurt the facts of Gowdie's life. He was born to a prominent old family in Carcosa, New York, in 1870. His early indications of artistic talent were encouraged by his parents, who sent him to study in Europe. Although he was considered a master of technique, his works lacked vitality, and he never lived up to the promise of his childhood.

In the 1890's, he turned his hand to illustrating children's books and rapidly achieved enormous success. By 1895, the year he painted the playhouse, his popularity had already begun to decline. He alienated his public with bizarre experiments, and his publishers and patrons with his heavy drinking and ferocious incivility. In 1900 he abandoned painting completely— "The eyes are a hindrance to sight," he reputedly said—and devoted all his time to occult research. He died on June 23, 1917, in London. He might have died of starvation if a bomb from a German zeppelin hadn't gotten him first.

According to Braden, the bomb completely destroyed the house where Gowdie lived in a cramped closet under the eaves. The bodies of the twelve other residents were pieced together after a fashion, but not a fragment that could be identified as Gowdie's nor a stitch of the only clothes he ever wore were found.

Those were the facts stated in reference books, Braden said, but his independent research had disclosed that no other bombs were dropped on the night of June 23; no one reported hearing the usually noisy engines of a zeppelin over London; and the pertinent records of the Imperial German Navy, which he claimed to have examined, indicated that no airship had been in action over all of England that night.

Braden said that he himself was found wandering naked in a field near Gowdie's birthplace in 1958. His apparent age was fourteen, and he had no memory whatever of a previous life. His speech was unusually courteous and formal, except for odd lapses into out-dated slang. He objected to the "cheek" of someone who had "given him the go-by" when he asked for help, he called safety matches "lucifers;" he amused everyone by saying that he felt "knocked-up" when he meant he was tired, and baffled them by saying that he was "hippish," meaning that he felt unwell. He displayed quirkish pronunciations, too, such as "deef" for "deaf." His amazement and delight with such apparent novelties as modern automobiles and neon signs seemed spontaneous, and his custodians were beginning to suspect they had a genuine time-traveler on their hands until he was taken through a door activated by an electric eye at the police station and he enthusiastically cried that it was "Out of sight!" The phrase was only just coming into fashion, and it carried allusions of "beatniks and hopheads" to the Carcosa police.

No one claimed him, and his description couldn't be matched with that of any reported missing person in the region. A psychiatrist ruled that his selective amnesia was genuine, either traumatic or drug-

induced, but that his archaisms and his professed ignorance of the modern world were a smoke-screen
thrown up by a bookish and badly-frightened boy.
(Braden claimed that he was trying hard by then to
modernize his vocabulary and adapt to his surroundings. He said he succeeded so well that he soon forgot
his old-fashioned speech and manner and lost the
sense of wonder he had felt on first entering the
nineteen-fifties.)

. The boy was put in an orphanage, where he was
adopted a year later by a doctor named Braden who
had become interested in his case. The doctor discovered that Alan, as he named him, had an astounding
facility for painting in oils, watercolors and casein.
His favorite subjects were storybook scenes. Dr. Braden thought he had a genius on his hands, and he ar-
ranged to have the paintings exhibited locally. Some
of them were brought by the doctor's friends. When
Alan's work was given wider circulation, it was revealed that he had been copying Gowdie's paintings
exactly. He could have seen the originals easily
enough in old children's books.

Some of the paintings could not be matched with
Gowdie's known works, in particular a series of oils
that Alan had painted to illustrate classical mythol-
ogy. They were every bit as good as Gowdie's paintings, and perhaps even better, but they abounded with
nudes so sensual as to have been considered indecent

in Victorian times, and which caused a furor even in the Carcosa of 1960.

Two years later, Professor William Gregg of Haverford, a Gowdie expert, bullied his way past Dr. Braden—who had been humiliated by his role in Alan's artistic debut and wanted no more fuss about it—to look at the paintings and talk to Alan. Gregg was astonished when he saw the mythological series. In 1894, he said, Sebastian Gowdie had been commissioned to illustrate an expensive gift edition of Ovid's *Metamorphoses*. He slaved over the commission, doing what he considered his finest work, but the financing fell through and he never collected a penny. The paintings were misplaced in the general disorganization and wreckage of his life, and it was thought that they had been destroyed. No reproductions of them had ever been made.

The previous year, however, Gregg had tracked down Gowdie's long-lost sketchbooks. He and a few others had been the only persons to set eyes on them since the artist's mistress had packed them in a trunk and stowed it in her attic in Malneant, New Jersey, sixty years before. Nevertheless, all of Alan's paintings had been prefigured in Gowdie's sketches, with just the sort of changes that Gowdie might have made between sketch and finished work.

Neither Dr. Braden nor Professor Gregg seriously considered the possibility of a supernatural explanation. The professor theorized that Gowdie's originals must exist somewhere, and that Alan had seen them. The house where these paintings were hung, where Gowdie's other works were also available, and where Alan's efforts to copy them must have been encouraged, would be his original home.

At Haverford, Gregg had a file containing several thousand names: students and collectors of Gowdie, his heirs and their descendants, the descendants of his friends and most of the people who had ever crossed his path. Alan was scheduled to enter Harvard that year, but Gregg implored him to change his plans and come to Pennsylvania with him. Together they would work their way through the file by name, until they hit a jackpot that would contain an identity for Alan and a treasure-trove of lost Gowdies for the world. Gregg even promised to get him academic credit for the work. Dr. Braden, who felt that his good name might be redeemed by their success, and whose curiosity had been thoroughly aroused, promised to underwrite the expense of the project.

Alan refused. He was sick of being considered a freak, he was sick of the mystery surrounding his origins, he was sick of Gowdie, and he was sick of painting Gowdie's pictures; he wanted only to get on with his own life and work. Although he didn't say so then, he thought Gregg's theory was foolish, and he suspected that the truth would be insupportable. He and Dr. Braden quarreled bitterly, and their quarrel still rankled when he left for Harvard.

Braden's notoriety as an art-forger had preceded him to Cambridge, but it carried no stigma there. He was seen as a raffish celebrity, and he was persuaded to put on a show of his work that was praised in the *Crimson,* given a wry paragraph in *Time,* and earned him five-thousand dollars.

Through the show he made the acquaintance of an associate professor of Medieval metaphysics named Charles Montgomery, who told him that a very curious manuscript of Gowdie's called *The House Across the Way* was kept in Widener Library. Braden wasn't interested at first, but Montgomery kept teasing him with hints of its bizarre contents, and he finally accepted the professor's offer to provide him with access to it; the manuscript was kept under lock and key and was not usually available to undergraduates.

The manuscript had been written in 1900, the year Gowdie gave up painting. It began with an account of a commission he had received from Marcus Bloodstone to decorate a playhouse for his daughter in Amworth, Connecticut, in 1895. Gowdie wrote that he had always been sensitive to psychic influences, and that the invisible forces he sensed to be at work in the Bloodstone house were the most powerful and inimical he had ever encountered. He wanted to leave immediately, but Bloodstone offered to double and then to triple his promised commission. Nor would his patron permit him to return to his studio, then in Malneant, to do the work. His daughter Melody was one of the artist's most enthusiastic admirers, and she wanted to watch Gowdie at work on her very own paintings.

The banal title of Gowdie's manuscript was a pun: by "Way," he meant a path to another world, and he asserted that the Bloodstone house lay across it. One night as he lay awake in his bed, troubled by visions more fearsome then those of fever, laudanum, or delirium tremens (all of which he knew about firsthand), and wishing that he hadn't succumbed to greed and accepted the commission, he was alarmed by the distant clang of iron falling to a stone floor.

Getting up to investigate, he found that he wasn't in a Victorian mansion, but in a medieval castle. He assumed that he was dreaming, but every detail of the dream was clear. Clearest of all was a pervasive atmosphere of ancient and insatiable hatred: hatred not just for him, not just for all human beings or all living creatures, but hatred for the very principle of life itself. This castle was the seat of the enemy, where entropy reigned over souls not only damned but destroyed beyond redemption by Divine grace or mortal tears.

Gowdie crept out into the shadows of a gallery that

overlooked the great central hall, where Bloodstone sat with the twelve members of his family at a long banquet table. They were dressed in medieval costumes and attended by similarly dressed servants who reminded the artist of those dead whom the sea will give up on Judgment Day. An animal that prowled at the limits of the torchlight may have been a gigantic hound, but something about its erratic gait and the quality of the sounds it made deterred Gowdie from spying on it too closely. Around the table strolled a huge man in green, wearing a crown. He was playing a lute and singing ballads that Gowdie, who was neither a prude nor a churchman, described as obscene and blasphemous.

In spite of the grisly atmosphere, the Bloodstones appeared to be having the time of their lives. Normally aloof and reserved to the point of hostility with one another and the world in general, they gorged and swilled and thumped the table while shouting lewd pleasantries over one another's clamor—all, that is, except Melody, who sat stiff and pale and silent with a crown of flowers on her hair. She looked like a human sacrifice stoically awaiting her fate among savages.

Although Gowdie was scared nearly out of his wits by the castle and everything in it, he was gripped by an overwhelming urge toward self-destructive heroism. He adored little girls (and his frankness on this subject may have been the reason why the library kept his manuscript out of unauthorized hands). He was on the verge of dashing down to rescue Melody from this vision of hell when she chanced to look up; and he cried aloud. The others were just rowdy, the servants just sickly, the hound and the minstrel petulant and the castle itself gloomy compared to that which illuminated her pale green eyes as they burned into his cringing soul and knew it for what it was. She was no frightened lamb, she was mistress and instigator of these Satanic revels, a puppeteer to graveyard disgorgement. He dashed upstairs and hid under his covers until dawn, when he at last dared to peek and found that the castle was gone and the house was as it should be.

More than ever he wanted to flee Amworth, but even more compelling was the need to stay and paint the subjects he had found in the tapestries hung about the great hall in his vision. Normally a methodical craftsman who considered every step in a sketchbook before he touched a brush, Gowdie attacked the walls immediately, while his vision would still be fresh, and completed the job in six days.

Melody came to watch him work. He ordinarily would have welcomed such an audience and stretched the job out to enjoy her company as long as possible, but he found her presence intolerable and barely spoke a word to her. He saw nothing in her eyes of what he had seen in his dream, but he lived in constant fear that he would. When he was finished, he fled without saying goodbye or collecting his fee; and it was never paid.

Gowdie had always been fascinated by occult phenomena. He would go a hundred miles out of his way to examine an allegedly haunted house or consult a publicized crystal-gazer. But he had never seen anything like his vision in the Bloodstone house, and it converted him wholly to a belief in the supernatural.

He believed that the Otherworld, even more than this one, is entirely what you make of it. That he had looked beyond the veil and seen horror wasn't proof that horror lay beyond the veil, but that it lay within him; and that it lay within the Bloodstone house, built by rapacity and packed with repression. He resolved to purify himself by austere self-denial, to fortify himself with knowledge, and to look for a Way to the Otherworld in more tranquil surroundings.

That was where the manuscript ended, and Braden said that it changed his own life profoundly; not just because, as he had seen at once, it had been written in his own hand, but because he remembered having written it and remembered the events it described.

He left college to view the scenes of Gowdie's life, to search out and read the letters and journals he had written, to see all the pictures he had painted. Memory came flooding back with each step, and his obsession intensified; he was arrested twice for breaking into homes where Gowdie had lived or visited. Not wanting to share what he knew with Professor Gregg, he broke into his college offices and stole his card-files. Dr. Braden threw up his hands at these developments and disowned him. When the money from his Cambridge show ran out, he found to his annoyance that the fad for bogus Gowdies had died; but he pursued his quest up and down the eastern seaboard and to Europe by begging, stealing, and stowing away.

Now, Braden said, he remembered every detail of his—meaning Sebastian Gowdie's—life up to the point of his disappearance on June 23, 1917. At that time he was trying to correlate some curious aspects of medieval diabolism with other equally curious aspects of non-Euclidian calculus in an effort to open a Way to the Otherworld. Braden only hinted at the details of this process, which involved drawing certain symbols, speaking certain words, and making a certain sacrifice. He succeeded: he was assumed into the Otherworld, with the incidental destruction of his earthly surroundings.

"That other amnesia. Was nothing, that was easy. Remembering," he blurted, reaching for the paint-smeared bottle that sat on the floor between them. "But I can't. For the life of me remember what happened in the Otherworld. Forty-one years, blotto. A blank. And that's forty-one of our years, *positive* years. Equalling thirty-three *negative* years on the other side. Which is why I was fourteen when I returned to this world. Does that ring a bell there, Father Doyle? Thirty-three years? Maybe I spent my time being the Messiah of the Otherworld. Got booted back here when I was crucified by fairy Romans and elfin Jews. Maybe my present sojourn in the Untied Snakes of America is my descent into Hell. What do you think, Father? What would be the church's position?"

Stuart realized that the story was at last over and some kind of comment was required. He said, "I am drunk beyond redemption by Divine grace or mortal tears." Instead of taking offense, Braden laughed. Stuart said, "When the cops found you, why did you say 'out of sight' if you weren't just a stoned hippie?"

"Oh, shit, that's easy. Out of sight. Popular expression at the turn of the century. Just happened to be enjoying a comeback. Like me. Look at this."

He went to rummage in his knapsack and produced a sepia-toned photograph, crazed and faded, in a gilt frame. It might have been Gowdie, *circa* 1895; it might have been Braden, gotten up in a high collar and flowing bowtie; it might have been, since it was so overexposed and poorly focused, any man with whiskers and spectacles. But Stuart agreed that it was astonishing proof of Braden's identity.

He discovered that he could no longer see, from his perch on a trunk, the manlike foot and cloven hoof he had seen before under one of the makeshift hangings. He concluded that he must have changed his position, but now he couldn't find it anywhere. Cassilda Oliphant, in tobacco and oils, looked so desirable that he wanted to go wake her up and tell her so, but he knew he wouldn't.

"So what are you doing back here at Bloodstone Manor if it's such a horrible place?"

"Best for last. Or worst. Wanted to make sure I remembered everything. Was strong enough to take it. But." He shrugged.

"But what?"

"Nothing. Zip. Like a broken radio. Not receiving. Cassie. More to her than meets the eye, only not much. Her list is worth reading. Have you exorcised this goddamn place? Sprinkled holy water around?"

"No. You think I should?"

"Christ, no! That would really piss them off. Nasty sense of humor, that's their trademark. Sleep," he said, and he dropped as if he'd been shot. He immediately began to snore.

For the life of me remember what happened in the Otherworld. Forty-one years, blotto. A blank. And that's forty-one of our years, *positive* years. Equalling thirty-three *negative* years on the other side. Which is why I was fourteen when I returned to this world. Does that ring a bell there, Father Doyle? Thirty-three years? Maybe I spent my time being the

Messiah of the Otherworld. Got booted back here
when I was cricified by fairy Romans and elfin Jews.
Maybe my present sojounr in the Untied Snakes of
America is my descent into Hell. What do you think,
Father? What would be the church's position?"

Stuart relized that the story was at last over and
some kind of comment was required. He said, "I am
drunk beyond redemption by Divine grace or mortal
tears." Instead of taking offense, Braden laughed.
Stuart said, "When the cops found you, why did you
say 'out of sight' if you weren't just a stoned hippie?"

"Oh, shit, that's easy. Out of sight. Popular expression at the turn of the century. Just happened to be
enjoying a comeback. Like me. Look at this."

He went to rumage in his knapsack and produced a
sepia-toned photograph, crazed and faded, in a gilt
frame. It might have been Gowdie, *circa* 1895; it
might have been Braden, gotten up in a high collar
and flowing bowtie; it might have been, since it was
so overexposed and poorly focused, any man with
whiskers and spectacles. But Stuart agreed that it was
astonishing proof of Braden's identity.

He discovered that he could no longer see, from his
perch on a trunk, the manlike foot and cloven hoof he
had seen before under one of the makeshift hangings.
He concluded that he must have changed his position,
but now he couldn't find it anywhere. Cassilda
Oliphant, in tobacco and oils, looked so desirable

that he wanted to go wake her up and tell her so, but he knew he wouldn't.

"So what are you doing back here at Bloodstone Manor if it's such a horrible place?"

"Best for last. Or worst. Wanted to make sure I remembered everything. Was strong enough to take it. But." He shrugged.

"But what?"

"Nothing. Zip. Like a broken radio. Not receiving. Cassie. More to her than meets the eye, only not much. Her list is worth reading. Have you exorcised this goddamn place? Sprinkled holy water around?"

"No. You think I should?"

"Christ, no! That would really piss them off. Nasty sense of humor, that's their trademark. Sleep," he said, and he dropped as if he'd been shot. He immediately began to snore.

Their paths didn't cross again for a few days. When they did, Stuart asked for clarification of some detail, and Braden laughed in his face. He had made up the story, he said, to go with an old photograph of an unknown man who bore a slight resemblance to him. He had told it to "Father Doyle" because he assumed that a person who believed in God would believe anything. As a matter of fact, Stuart hadn't believed the story, but he was convinced that Braden did; but he dropped the subject.

He often wondered what Allison had made of Braden's delusion. The subject hadn't come up when Stuart had visited them two years later as a couple, and he couldn't bring himself to discuss Alan Braden with his mother now.

He had considered his mother something of an eccentric when he was growing up. She had always been committed to the rational and practical; she could abide no music and very little literature produced after 1800. Although she'd never come out and said so, she had thought Stuart's religious vocation absurd. She had seen it as the essence of rational practicality to do exactly what she pleased, and public opinion— or Stuart's and Joseph's perception of public opinion—be damned: she used to work out with weights, and for a while she ran a judo salon in their home. It seemed sadly ironic now, but she had been the one who wired the house for electricity when it became obvious that this held the lowest priority on Joseph's renovation plans.

Stuart came to realize that what he had seen as eccentric in his mother was really conformity to an old Yankee prototype of the strong, competent individualist. No one, it seemed, could have had less patience with Braden and his fantasies. Nor did he know what Braden saw in her. He had always thought that Allison, viewed with whatever objectivity a son could bring to such a question, had not been particularly attractive. She hadn't been at all fat then, but her appearance had seemed plain and her style rather severe. But when they ran off together, the artist left behind a nude painting of Allison that had shocked Stuart's eyes open. He had made her look like a goddess; and seeing it, Stuart had known that she did. He burned the painting, an act deplored by his father: "Who knows? It might be worth something some day."

So Braden, who had spent more time in the playhouse than anyone, and who had been crazy enough to do such a thing, could have left the doll and the plastic pumpkin-head. But he couldn't have come back to murder Cassilda on Saturday night. Stuart had killed him a long time ago.

Concurrent with that thought, he nicked his chin with his razor. He stuck a scrap of toilet paper on the cut and continued, paying closer attention to what he was doing.

It could have been Gwyneth's doll. And although he'd looked for her sometime before and after the discovery of Cassilda's body, he hadn't been able to find her. The last he'd seen of her she'd been giving her light fantastic toes a workout to The Incredible String Band, of all things, with Woodling. He'd turned his attention to the caterer for a few minutes, and when he'd looked again, she was gone. So was *Tom*.

But Gwyneth hadn't killed her, nor Woodling, either. He looked far too neat and self-contained to be

capable of murder, or—so he tried hard to believe—
of any passion. When Stuart saw him again, not one
of his hairs had been out of place. The only one with
blood on her had been Allison. It would be a long
time before he would stop seeing her as she'd looked
stumbling out of the orchard, extending the grinning
jack-o'-lantern in her bloody hands.

Sterling Fairchild had killed Cassilda, and therefore he had hidden the doll. Telling the police about it
would have complicated the issue and drawn unwelcome attention to Stuart's home and family. That
sounded, at last, like a plausible answer to Gwyneth's
question.

Gwyneth jabbed a poker at the fire on the hearth.
"Are you cold?"

Then he saw what she was burning. He tried to take
the poker away from her, but she pushed him back
and returned to her work of burning the doll and the
book. A black bug scuttled out of the plastic pumpkin
as it began to sizzle and melt.

"That might have been evidence." He looked for a
chance to seize the poker, but it was obvious that she
wouldn't give it up without a fight. "A clue."

"It was evil, I knew it when I saw it." She shot him a
nervous glance and tried to soften the melodramatic
word: "Disgusting. Creepy."

He started to leave, then turned back. "The funeral

is tomorrow at eleven." Exasperated by her uncomprehending, startled look, he said, "Cassilda's. Remember her?"

"At Bradbury's? I don't think—"

"No, he's had a death in the family. The other place, Whozis. Wakefield."

"A death?" she called after him. "Who?"

"His little boy."

She hadn't liked Cassilda much, and he didn't expect her to feign grief, but the incongruity of her response annoyed him: she had taken Cassilda's death unemotionally, but now she burst into tears at the death of an unknown child.

He drove to the campus and parked his car in the lot of the Erich Zann Conservatory. Taking his time to see who might be observing him, he crossed the street to one of a row of dowdy stucco houses that faced the campus and went cautiously up the outside stairs to the second floor. He tapped lightly, willing her to hurry and rescue him from standing on this scaffold for all the world to see.

Malkin: it means a scarecrow, a mop, a swab for a cannon; a name for a woman of the lower classes; a demon, a specter, a cat, a slut; an effeminate man; a rabbit. Or, as she had also told him, a nickname for her own name, which she disliked: Matilda. But he could never think of her, or see her, without dragging up one or the other of those connotations, and somewhere in the ragbag of old allusions that was his mind, each connected firmly with an aspect of her mutable personality.

Gray was her maiden name, but she didn't use it. He used it in his thoughts of her as a way of obliterating her superfluous husband, Dreyfus. Thoughts of her husband naturally led to thoughts of his own wife, so he called her Malkin Gray and tried to pretend at some level that they were both unattached. And of course the Shakespearean echo amused him. Once, at a crucial moment, he had cried out, like Macbeth's witch: *I come, Gray-Malkin!* His erudition had earned him a left hook to the ribs.

He reminded himself that he wasn't here to rhapsodize about her name, nor to daydream about former intimacies. That raised the question of why he was here at all. He had wanted to break this off. She hadn't come to the door yet. Instead of knocking again he took a step backward, hoping she wasn't home. But she was. She opened the door.

"I was taking a nap."

When he stepped inside she sagged against him, totally relaxed. Gwyneth never quite did that. In their closest embraces she always held a little back. Malkin was a dead weight in his arms, trusting and childlike. She had been napping in the nude. Seeing him through the curtain, she hadn't covered herself to answer the dor. She purred against his chest, eyes closed, while he caressed the outward swell of her haunch, the sleek chunks of her buttocks.

"Have you ever noticed that it's difficult to sympathize with a really crazy person?" He paused to blow a smoke-ring at the water-stained ceiling. "There's something about them, something physically different from a sane person, that makes them repulsive."

"I wouldn't say that as if it were a universal law." Her gray eyes, peering up over his chest, were wide awake now. The pupils had fascinating, coal-black flecks of brightness in them. "Some people find any kind of sick person repulsive. Others don't."

"Have you ever known anyone who was genuinely crazy? I mean, not just your typical Amworth neurotic, but—"

"The Old Man Who Wouldn't Say His Prayers."

She must have felt him stiffen, but she couldn't have known why. He had been thinking of Philip Kemper when he'd asked his question, and of Alan Braden. Nobody knew who Kemper was, he hoped.

"You don't actually know him."

"No, but I'm always making up stories about him. This week I think he's Howard Hughes, who didn't die at all."

She snuggled closer, her breasts against his ribs, one thigh across his legs. She said, "I had a pet chicken once when I was a kid. She got a rash or something that made her lose some of her feathers. So all the other chickens ganged up on her and pecked her to death."

"When did you start speaking in parables?"

"When you started complaining to me about your wife."

"I didn't . . ." He found that he couldn't work up the appropriate degree of indignation. He hadn't been willing to admit it, but Gwyneth's current antics had produced in him a kind of repulsion. Maybe that was why he was here. "So I'm a birdbrain for being put off by her . . ."

"If you say so. I only meant that such a reaction to illness is probably instinctive. A kid's natural reaction to the Old Man, *et cetera,* would be to throw rocks." She shivered. "Except that one of his piercing, black looks can soil your underwear at fifty yards."

"And we should rise above our natures."

"You could try," she whispered, fondling him intimately.

While she prowled around the room later in just a sweater, looking for cigarettes, he said, "I guess I wanted some advice. I don't know how to cope with her."

"She seemed perfectly okay at the party Saturday night. She wasn't flapping her lower lip."

He shouldn't have expected sympathy. Making love to her, then expressing concern for his wife: he probably looked as if he were missing some feathers. He could not guess what she would think if she knew that sometimes, in their closest moments, he shut his eyes and pretended she was Gwyneth. He was here only through habit, and it was a habit he should break.

"I'm sorry."

"What for? You did just fine, kid." She dodged his lunge. She pinned back her thick red hair, unconcerned that her lower half was naked. Gwyneth would have posed; she was just being herself.

"My husband is coming over for dinner."

"Oh." He sat up and untangled his trousers.

"You don't have to go on his account. He's very understanding about this separation."

"You haven't told him about us, have you? I wouldn't want—"

"You wouldn't want it to get back to Gwyneth. Not because she'd be mad at you, or jealous, but because you're afraid of further upsetting her mental balance. And for the same reason, you can't leave her now that you realize she needs your help."

"I didn't say that!" Having surprised himself by shouting, he lowered his voice. "I said nothing like that."

She winked at him exasperatingly as she stepped into her jeans. "I haven't told anybody. Did your mother tell you I was going to read for her?"

"What?"

"Most of my afternoons are free. We got along great at your party."

"That's—" he almost said, "out of the question," but he changed his mind; he knew he couldn't stop her—"very nice of you. With Mrs. Oliphant gone—"

"Hey! Why don't you hire me to replace her?"

"Knock it off." He hurried into his clothes.

"Wouldn't it be decadent? The lord of the manor humping the housekeeper. We could poison Gwyneth for her money."

"She doesn't have any."

"Gwyneth and I will poison you, then. That would make even better sense. Just like the wife and the mistress in *Diabolique*. This is great! I'm going to ask Allison to hire me. I'm getting damned sick of the daycare center."

"Malkin—"

She fell back across the bed, flinging her arms and legs wide. "I go all soft and helpless when you call me that. Ask me anything."

"Quit screwing around, will you?"

"Anything but that, Jim."

CHAPTER SIX

It seemed as if Stuart would never get going. His car crawled down the driveway, then stopped as he examined the overgrown hedge to his right. Looking for her father, Gwyneth supposed.

She wished she hadn't politely put aside her mistrust of Philip Kemper and introduced him as her father to Stuart. Beyond his word, and a dim but uncomfortable feeling of familiarity, she had no proof. She wished she could have said, "This wretch claims to be my father, Stuart. Please beat the truth out of him." But she could never say such a thing, nor would he do it. He only hit people who were twice as big as he, and he hadn't done that in years. But sometimes her husband's affable, foxy face recast itself in rigid lines that looked disturbingly medieval. In another age, she could see him sadly but resolutely applying the boot or the thumbscrew.

She had been able to get nothing from Kemper. He had extracted the truncated story of her life while evading all her questions. They hadn't been very determined questions, for she'd been half afraid he might answer them. But if he had a story to tell, and if Stuart could get it out of him, he might ration the truth to her in digestible bits.

She ran back into the living room to poke the smoldering book aflame, but her task was complicated by her unwillingness to look at it. She had set the fire on a sudden, irresistible impulse. It would have been intolerable to have the filthy things in the house a minute longer. She had felt their moldy contagion spreading as it seeped from the closed pantry.

Only now did she stand back and look at herself, scuffing at the pages with the tip of the poker. She had grown up with an almost superstitious reverence for the written word. In her community, book-burning—it made no difference what book—was an act of vandalism, if not fascism. To put it charitably, she was behaving oddly.

She was tempted to retrieve what was left of the book and redeem her own opinion of herself; and in the moment of temptation she was struck with redoubled force by a sense of the book's utter loathesomeness. The feeling resisted all attempts at examination.

Venting her anger at herself as much as her distaste for the book, she scraped at the pages more vigorously and heard them puff into flame.

She ran back to the front door and hovered at the colored panes that flanked it. Stuart's car was still at the bottom of the drive. She willed him to go, pushing tensely at the air. At last he drove away, his car alternately condensing and elongating as it melted through phases of red, yellow and green.

It occurred to her that her gown would be unsuitable for her errand. She couldn't waste time changing. She snatched down Allison's black shawl from the coat rack and flung it around her shoulders. The fog of lilac cologne evoked the Haggworm in all her nastiness, but she had no choice. She took one last look to assure herself that the book was burning brightly and fled to her car.

And where will it take me this time? Her hand held back, unwilling to obey her command to grip the door-handle. She forced it. She forced herself not to imagine things. The things she imagined lately had a way of coming true.

And even things she had never imagined. She would have assumed the events of last night were a dream and forgotten them if Stuart hadn't told her that she'd left the house. This morning she'd found herself driving to work with no recollection of getting up, getting dressed or leaving home; with only the fading and disjointed memory of an unpleasant dream. Since she was on her usual route to the campus, she had supposed that she had done all things that habitually led up to it in an automatic way. It was unusual that she should have done so many things and spent so much time in a state of automatism, but it was certainly true she'd had a lot on her mind lately. She hadn't been seriously worried until Stuart had revealed that she'd left home in darkness and that the episode must have consumed five or six hours.

Only then, while trying to fend off his exasperating questions, had she made an effort to recall her dream. She had been waked by a formless but urgent fear for the safety of the children. Her fear couldn't have been greater if she'd smelled smoke in their drafty old firetrap.

She hurried out of the bedroom without disturbing Stuart or turning on a light. The hall seemed darker than it should have been. She extended a hand to touch the wall and make sure of her way, and that was when the strangeness began, for what she felt under her fingertips was not the wallpaper of the corridor outside her bedroom, but damp stone. She turned hastily back to the bedroom door, but she couldn't find it. It wasn't there. Nor did she see the glow of the night sky through the window at the end of the hall. Although the darkness was complete, she sensed that the hall went on for a very long way, far longer than any hall in her home.

"I'm dreaming," she said aloud, "and now that I know it, I can wake up."

The charm didn't work. She became aware of a sound that was more like a feeling in her bones, an irregular thud of enormous power that originated deep in the bowels of the . . . Castle? It was the sound of the sea assaulting eroded walls and vibrating the whole massive structure like a lute-string wrested to the breaking-point. As she crept along the corridor she found that the stones of the floor sloped to a trough at the center, worn down by the passage of innumerable feet through centuries.

" 'The Abyss was a horrid place,' " she found herself reciting from the book in the playhouse, " 'and the King was a wicked King, and no one would ever have gone there if they could have helped it, but the fact was that Melody and the others who lived in the Castle could not see the Abyss . . .' "

Her recollection began to fragment at this point. There had been a man, lean and lupine, whom she had never seen in waking life, but whom she had known well in the dream. She had been ill, but her illness was oddly literary. It was centered in no part of her body, it produced no pain. Lassitude and lack of will were its sole symptoms; and a certain knowledge that she was being consumed in the fire of time. At one point she saw her reflection in a glass. Her teeth and eyes had seemed enormous in a face whose colorless skin was stretched tight over the skull.

But her gloomy, Byronic companion had thought her beautiful. He hadn't been able to take his eyes off her. He had gazed not at her so much as at her component parts: especially at her teeth. And she had read to him:

"By a route obscure and lonely,
Haunted by ill angels only. . ."

That was Poe, of course, just as his fascination with her teeth came from Poe's "Berenice." The "wasting illness," the sinister hero, the crumbling Castle—the setting of the dream had been the cluttered attic of Gothic melodrama, furnished with odds and ends by every practitioner from Horace Walpole to Roger Corman. The mental landscape was so remote from her own that she felt as if she were merely a supporting player in someone else's dream.

Over a lifetime, it seemed, the conditions of the dream changed. The power and importance of her companion drained away as the Castle asserted itself; it was as if the Castle had digested his essense, leaving him an empty husk who lurked in the shadowy fringes. He no longer seemed handsome or even entirely human. When he walked, she heard the clicking of claws.

She couldn't remember all of it. The fragments of remembered dreaming dissolved into the reality of driving to work this morning, dressed in the same outfit she had worn in the Castle. It was more elaborate than most of her gowns and immodestly, in Stuart's opinion, low-cut. Maybe he had been paying her a sly compliment; she knew that most men would consider the opportunity to ogle her breasts not worth taking.

Sterling Fairchild had been an exception, she remembered only now. She had worn the gown once this year, on the first day of classes, and she had thrown him into red-faced confusion every time she looked his way to discover his molish gaze glued to her neckline. As a supporting player in his dream, she would have worn this dress.

She had reached her destination: the Bradbury Funeral Home. She sat and studied it through the fuzz of a light drizzle. It looked coldly official, not at all like anyone's home. The basement held a tiled, fluorescent room . . .

The chill of the afternoon drove her from the car and up the walk, cluttered with a fresh fall of slimy leaves. They muffled her footfalls and made them unlike the sounds the policemen's shoes had made. She remembered to lift the hem of her gown with one hand, to arrange Allison's shawl more decorously with the other.

The door was locked, and no one came to answer the bell. They would be in the basement, of course, working the gurgling pump that drained their clients. She wrenched her mind from that image. A man came at last to answer her persistent ringing, shrugging into his suit-jacket as he opened the door.

"I'm sorry," he began, "but the—"

"I heard there was a death in the family. The little boy."

"Oh, I see. Are you a friend?"

"Yes, may I—" She tried to enter, but he didn't step aside.

"You don't understand. The funeral is being held from Wakefield's." When she continued to stand dumbly, he said, "There's no one here but me. Mr. and Mrs. Bradbury are at Wakefield's."

She didn't know him from her dream. He was a young man, probably an assistant or apprentice. He would have just come from working in the tiled room. She thought she detected the odor of familiar chemicals through the lilac wall of Allison's cologne.

As much as she wanted to see the dead child, she wanted to see the inside of the building. She wanted to mark the location of the door to the basement, of the pier-glass in the hallway; she wanted to check the color—but it would be dark blue—of the carpet on the main stairway. She could think of no good reason for asking to be let inside. She could only stare at the young man as he grew steadily more impatient and suspicious.

"Like doctors," she said.

"I beg your pardon?"

"Not treating their own relatives." She knew she sounded like an idiot, knew it from the look in his eyes. "That's why they. . . at Wakefield's, I mean."

"Yes." The door began to press against her.

"The little boy—what did he die of?"

"The family can tell you." When she stepped back, he shut the door.

She couldn't see through the white curtain. She didn't try very hard, sensing that he still stood just beyond it. Now that the door was closed, she thought of ways she could have gotten in: asked for a glass of water, the use of the telephone, the bathroom. I suffer from a wasting illness, and I must languish on your couch awhile. She turned and walked back to her car.

She didn't want to go to the other funeral parlor. Cassilda was laid out there. She would have to accept the condolences of unctuous coffin-salesmen for the loss of a woman she'd disliked. She would have to play the mourner in a green gown and vile-smelling shawl. She had a vague recollection of relatives who were even more affected, malicious and stupid than Cassilda herself. They would resent her for having exploited and abused their lost lamb. They would sneer at her clothing and mock her way of speaking when they trooped home to eat their tuna casserole and watch TV. Worst of all, their brutish cunning would enable them to see behind her eyes and to know that at the very moment when their loved one was being hacked to pieces, she had been opening her body and wrapping her legs around the naked flanks of a man who was not her husband.

But she drove on grimly, determined to see little Bradbury in his satin box.

She didn't know why she had been unfaithful to Stuart. It was the first time in twelve years of marriage. She had thought of her fidelity as intellectual rather than emotional or reflexive, and for that reason she had thought it would remain invulnerable.

Some people found her husband stuffy, but it was one of the reasons why she loved him. He was safe and predictable and solid, like a somewhat dim but well-founded lighthouse in a very treacherous sea; a sea whose black depths and irresistible tides he, from his limited perspective above the waves, couldn't even imagine. He had his rulebook, the technical manual that came with the job of lighthouse-keeper. It held all he needed to know about good and evil. She saw nothing wrong, in any absolute sense, with making love to someone who struck her fancy, but Stuart would have. And when she'd married him, she had resolved to play the game by his rules.

But her attachment to her husband transcended

cold reason. The symmetry of his certainty gave him a purity, a goodness. Like everybody else, he fell far short of his ideals, but at least he did have an ideal of goodness that he tried to live up to. Stuart was a nice guy; so people said who had never tried to be nice guys themselves, who had never thought that compliment had much value, and who were a little surprised and apologetic to find themselves using the cliche about someone and knowing it had meaning. At about the time Cassilda was being murdered, at about the time his wife was making love to another man in his bed, Stuart had been cleaning up McWraith's vomit in Cassilda's bathroom: because it said in his rulebook that McWraith was his guest, therefore his responsibility and because he was a nice guy.

She'd started by being intrigued with Stuart—or Jamie as he'd been called then—before she'd actually met him: a dutiful, pencil-thin seminarian with a death-row haircut; an odd product for a pair of breezy, larger-than-life parents whose eruptions into bouts of shouting and dish-smashing had been the talk of Amworth.

Joseph Doyle in his fleshy craftiness had reminded her of Broderick Crawford in *All the King's Men,* a back-slapping glad-hander who would walk over you with a joke and a smile to embrace his next new friend of the moment. It had taken her awhile to see through his jovial facade. His apparent tolerance for human foibles was no virtue, it was a total lack of involvement in others' emotions; he saw other people, even his own family, as cleverly animated toys. Stuart had adored his father. Because Joseph would sometimes praise the Catholic clergy and lament that he'd never had a vocation (to annoy Allison, she suspected), Stuart had dreamed up a vocation for himself. When it proved to be an illusion, he'd felt beaten and worthless, mostly because he imagined that he'd let his father down.

Joseph earned a reputation for soft-heartedness by giving free room and board to all sorts of eccentrics and misfits, but he was neither charitable nor gullible. In his hospitality he resembled some decadent aristocrat diverting himself with a private zoo. By being so uncritical and understanding, he would encourage his creatures to become even more maladjusted, and he would manipulate them into grotesque involvements and confrontations with one another. Whenever one of his inmates turned on him, Joseph would get all the sympathy: a saddened but forgiving zoo-keeper, one who kept his cattle-prod well hidden. Everyone had blamed Allison when she left him.

Gwyneth didn't like to admit it now, but Allison had been her early ideal of wit and sophistication and even glamor: the kind of glamor surrounding a woman who knows she is too beautiful for makeup and styled hair and fashionable clothes, and who upstages everyone by scorning such adornment. She had the exotic distinction of being a judo expert. This became the subject of many local jokes when she undertook to teach the skill in her home, the jokes hinging on her quarrels with her husband or the need for defending herself from his imperfectly housebroken guests. Surprisingly, some of the leaders of Amworth society joined her classes. Learning from Allison Doyle how to unman mashers became the thing to do for a couple of years.

Gwyneth had no desire to chop wood with her bare hands, but she was dragged along to some of the classes as an observer by an enthusiastic friend. Allison seemed to like her, and she once jokingly said to her, "You have to meet my son. I bet a girl like you could knock all that God-nonsense out of his head."

That would have been the summer of 1964, the year before she went away to the state university. One thing and another kept her from meeting Stuart until the following June, when Allison invited her to a party for her son. She hadn't enjoyed it, and Stuart had been only barely civil. She had sensed the unpleasant interaction of complex alliances and enmities among the guests that she hadn't understood until much later, when she'd understood Joseph's hobby.

That September, Stuart came to the University of Connecticut in the class ahead of her, having left the seminary. He lurked around the fringes of the drama department—he wanted to be a playwright then, and she hoped to be an actress—but he was moody and self-involved, and their acquaintance never went much beyond an exchange of comments on the smallness of the world. About that time Allison Doyle surprised everyone by running off to live on a houseboat in New Jersey with a hippie. Gwyneth thought of saying something consoling to Stuart, but she couldn't think what, and he receded further from her sphere as she grew more interested in the study of obscure playwrights than she had been in acting.

The summer after he graduated, Stuart went to visit Allison on her houseboat and clumsily triggered a soap-opera disaster that blinded her and killed her boyfriend. He may not have been to blame, but he never doubted that it was his fault. In darker moods, he believed that he had engineered the accident with the subconscious—or even drunkenly conscious—intention of accomplishing exactly what was accomplished.

Joseph had overcome his Catholic scruples and promptly divorced Allison after she left, wanting to make sure, he said, that she never got her hooks into the house, which had already appreciated greatly in value. When Stuart returned from New Jersey he tried to persuade his father to take Allison back as a pensioner. Joseph laughed so hard at this suggestion that he actually rolled on the floor, pounding his fists with mirth, then got up on his knees and loudly thanked God for having punished her.

Stuart got a part-time job on a newspaper and settled into the tower of his father's house to work on the play he'd been trying to finish since college, *The King in Yellow*. Alan Braden (she learned much later) had introduced Stuart to the book on which this play was based, and he may have seen his work as some kind of expiation for Braden's death; but he never finished it.

After the argument about Allison, Stuart and his father communicated with each other solely by letters, carried between them by such hangers-on as Cassilda, while father and son furtively went their separate ways.

Dear James:

 If you persist in pounding your typewriter until five in the morning, I must earnestly request that you obtain a pad for the machine and a rug for your floor to moderate the din.

Cordially, your Father,
Joseph A. Doyle

Dear Father:

 As my car is being repaired and I must go to Hartford this evening on business, I would greatly appreciate the loan of yours. I will of course reimburse you for gasoline.

                    Respectfully, your Son
                         J. Stuart Doyle

But Gwyneth knew nothing of the Doyles' lives at this time. She had heard conflicting accounts of the events in New Jersey. The most popular rumor had it that Joseph sent Stuart with a bomb. She knew Stuart only as a failed priest, once mildly interesting, now something of a reclusive oddball. She was therefore surprised one winter morning to find that Stuart had slipped a fat envelope under the door of her dormitory room during the night. It told his life story in forty pages of single-spaced typing: his struggles with God, the houseboat incident, his current lunatic domestic arrangements, his ambition to be a playwright. He wrote well. He even wrote amusingly, but the pain came through. He baffled her by claiming that she had been the only person in college who had understood him or spoken kindly to him. He protested that he wasn't in love with her, that he had no wish for any romantic involvement, but she dismissed that as nonsense. You don't sneak a forty-page letter under a girl's door in the dead of night to tell her that you don't love her unless you are obsessed with her to the point of insanity.

Though moved by his suffering, amused by his eccentricity no less than by his wit, and flattered by his choice for a Grand Passion, she was nevertheless annoyed. He had popped up from nowhere to dump a responsibility on her, to muddy the clear channel of her life. It was an obvious plea for help, a plea for the understanding and kindness she'd somehow unwittingly shown him. It might even be a suicide note.

Like the Ancient Mariner, he said, he wanted only to tell his story. He didn't expect her to call or write back. But she was sure he would get in touch with her. He still hadn't dropped the other shoe by the time she was home for the Christmas holidays, so she went and cornered him. He must have spent an hour apologizing for having written so stupid a letter.

Implicit in the letter had been the fact that he had gone through college and reached the age of twenty-one while somehow managing to preserve his virginity. He believed that his plays would be better if he sublimated his sexual urges into his work. At this time Gwyneth believed that she had invented sex, and that it was not only what he needed, but what he was asking for. She steered him onto his cot (another sacrifice for Art, or a way of spiting Joseph; the house held plenty of unused beds) while creating the impression that he was doing the steering. It was like popping the cork on an ill-used champagne bottle. He ejaculated on her belly before he could come into her, and it took awhile to talk him out of his agony of shame. He got it right on the second try, and he even pleased her on the third.

Hindsight told her that she should have known what she was letting herself in for, but it shocked her when he changed from her Ancient Mariner to her albatross. ("Who was that?" Aunt Isabel would ask when she put down the phone. "Albert Ross," Gwyneth would sigh. "What a nice boy," Aunt Isabel would say.) Even while she was home for the holidays, two blocks from his home, she would get booklength letters every day. He still found time to call her on the phone, turn up wherever she went, and throw pebbles at her bedroom window in the small hours. He followed her back to college with the same routine, and it diverted her until he started picking fights with every man he caught her talking to. She would have hated him for it if he hadn't lost almost all of the fights.

When she finally convinced him that she wanted to work and persuaded him to go home and court her in a more sensible way, even persuaded him to stop writing letters she didn't have time to read, she found that she missed him. She looked forward all week to seeing him on weekends.

She didn't know if she loved him. She liked him a lot. She was used to attracting male attention, and it usually didn't mean much to her. But it was exhilarating to have a man who was, in the truest sense of the word, crazy about her. But by that time she knew what she wanted with her life, and her plans didn't include a husband or even a fiance.

Or a baby. But shortly after her graduation she discovered that she was pregnant. She made the mistake of telling Stuart, who began planning their wedding. It took days to penetrate his euphoric visions with the information that she wouldn't marry him and that she planned to have an abortion.

The Stuart she had known before was a fickle drone compared to the single-minded demon of energy now uncaged. The voluminous letters came twice a day, but she never was able to finish them because of all his visits and phone calls. The letters were now illustrated with ghastly photographs of aborted fetuses that he had probably kept from priest-school. He alternated these shock tactics with onslaughts of Jesuitical nitpicking and rhapsodies about the potentially idyllic childhood of the rosy-cheeked little Einstein or Mozart she was plotting to squelch.

He convinced her that it would be wrong. She knew that she would probably carry her crushing burden of guilt to the grave. But screw him and Einstein both. She hadn't driven herself to the edge of a nervous breakdown working successfully for a Columbia fellowship in order to throw it away now and become an incubator, diaper-changer, and milk machine. She thought of those unkempt maniacs, him and his father, prowling around in their dismal zoo and itching to get a woman who would "tidy it up," and her stomach rebelled.

But he had won the battle. She dawdled. Time passed. She began to think of having the baby and giving it up for adoption. She foolishly let that idea slip to Stuart, and it encouraged him to shove his campaign into high gear. He shocked her by getting a full-time job with a handsome salary. He promised to hire a woman to take care of the baby and even produced her: Cassilda Oliphant. It must have been the most bizarre way of proposing ever devised, trotting out the frizzy-haired, balloon-breasted Mrs. Oliphant for a job-interview with the prospective bride. But the convincing argument was his promise to support her in New York, visiting her only at her invitation, until she had gotten her doctorate.

Young Mozart (Arthur, as it transpired) beat the pill. Next thing she knew, Joan had outwitted a diaphragm. She was in her turn deposited at the nursery about the time of Joseph's death. Stuart had made up with him, they had stopped communicating by letter and had even become close, but he bitterly regretted all the chances he'd now lost forever to tell his father he loved him.

Joseph had left them fairly well off. He had sold something called ferrites, which neither she nor Stuart wanted to know anything about, but which were apparently indispensible to the existence of mod-

ern industrial civilization. The house had been only
the most conspicuous of his good investments. She
took a couple of months off to bury the ferret-
salesman—as Stuart used to call him—and help her
husband pull himself together. Actually, she did most
of the pulling. Left to his own devices, Stuart would
have atoned for his sins by giving the inheritance he
considered undeserved to the starving orphans of
Franz Josef Land, or to his mother, and turning the
house into a leprosarium.

Allison's return to Amworth was then imminent,
but Gwyneth, concerned then with evicting Joseph's
lingering strays, didn't contest that; nor did she notice
the horizon turning black. She remembered Allison
fondly and looked forward to seeing her again. She
was shocked by what she saw and by what she felt for
this grotesque, embittered creature, but she reasoned
away her feelings as flaws in her own character that
ought to be overcome. By the time Gwyneth had
come home for good with her doctorate, the Haggworm was ineradicably rooted in the tower where she
and Stuart had first made love.

Things would never have gone so far with Tom
Woodling if she hadn't believed at first that he was
homosexual. His alert, glittering eyes, his fussy manner, the prematurely silver (possibly even bleached)
hair that he kept so neatly in place, all suggested it.

Even more suspicious was the graceful way he consciously used his whip-lean body when he moved. He kept fresh flowers in his office, which was always neat as a pin: and despite his disclaimers at the party, he had a taste for such pert fripperies as those bells on his shoes.

So when Tom wormed a promise out of her to participate in his project, she cooperated without reservation, talking to him about her fantasies as if he were one of the girls. But her total frankness might have had an even deeper source. He reminded her of someone from her forgotten childhood. She had no idea where the point of similarity lay, and she had a vague impression that the memory was an unhappy one, but she hoped that she might jog it loose by being near him and talking to him.

Telling her dreams to him was like telling them to a marble statue: which he resembled. In his pale, immobile face with its colorless hair and eyebrows, only his eyes had life or color, almost like the eyes of another person—a strange, catlike person—peering through a wax mask. He never interrupted, seldom commented, only nudged her on with incisive questions when nudging was required.

She had told him the darker fantasies that she'd never hinted at to anyone: the vampire, for instance. When she was younger than she should have been, her Aunt Isabel had let her go to see Bela Lugosi in

Dracula. It was too old-fashioned and melodramatic
to be really scary, or so she'd thought, but it gave her
dreams that were. The image of Dracula's brides had
fascinated her in the film, she'd regretted that they
had such small parts, and it was this image upon
which her nightmares revolved. She was one of them,
and her victim was most often a small boy. As she
grew older, she cultivated the fantasy with sexual variants. She often imagined making love in a coffin, as
she'd told Stuart. But she'd told Tom first, and that
was why she'd at last been able to overcome her long
reticence about that fantasy with her husband.

Tom seldom required more than one interview with
a subject, and she'd had three, by which time he'd
pretty thoroughly exhausted her fantasy-life. They
had spent most of the third session in an exchange of
Amworth gossip. There had seemed no reasonable
excuse for a fourth, although she'd wanted one, until
she began fantasizing about Tom himself. Sometimes
she would pretend, when Stuart made love to her, that
he was Tom.

She wondered if she ought to tell Tom. He might
think she was making fun of him. But she convinced
herself—deluded herself, she now admitted—that
these daydreams were significant, that they would
give him an interesting perspective on his work and its
effect on his subjects.

Her fourth interview came on the Saturday morning following her vivid hallucination of death, necrophilia, and vampirism. She hadn't slept, she was a nervous wreck, and the fantasies she told Tom weren't the uppermost things on her mind. She hardly knew what she told him. Whatever it was, he wasn't fooled about her reason for telling him. He grabbed her and kissed her. She responded. She began trying to fight him off when he slipped his hand under her sweater to fondle her bare breasts. He pulled her to the floor and tried to undress her completely.

When the utter nastiness of the situation struck her, that she was actually about to be raped on the rug of an Amworth office by one of her colleagues, she screamed. He desisted immediately. His face showed some color for the first time, but it was expressionless as ever as he stood up and rearranged his clothing.

"Forgive me. I forgot that this sort of thing was your national pastime," he said icily. "See you at the party."

She had sensed a promise or a threat in his words, but she hadn't been able to worry about them. She went home and collapsed, and Stuart had trouble waking her when it came time to prepare for the party.

Tom was his usual, epicene self at the party in his honor, seeming to flirt with McWraith rather than her. Maybe his act was a well-considered cover for a seducer of other men's wives. Maybe he was bisexual.

Maybe he simply didn't realize how his style played to an audience of provincial Americans. Whatever he was, she knew that he liked girls.

He completed the seduction by dancing with her. Dancing hadn't been on the agenda for the stuffy reception envisioned by Stuart and President Shaver, nor music of any kind, but some oaf who thought Vivaldi was appropriate background music for noisy chatter had put a record on the turntable. Tom replaced it with one of Cassilda's rock 'n' roll records and started dancing with the housekeeper. Others began dancing, and Gwyneth soon found herself dancing with Tom.

They seldom touched, but a bond of energy vibrated between them and united their bodies into one new creature whose existence was defined by rhythmic sound. She seemed to be directing his body as much as her own, willing his movements as he willed hers. Their steps were words, their words were music. She couldn't say what the music was. She couldn't recognize it because it was inside her, because she was the music.

It seemed impossible that one of Cassilda's stupid records could have produced something that came close to descriptions she'd read of religious ecstasy, or that dancing could have done it; she'd never been a particularly good dancer. It could have been liquor or an unexpected onset of desire for Tom, but she had begun to suspect a more sinister interpretation.

She couldn't listen to the music she was part of, but she had the impression that it had slipped unnoticed into something weird and unearthly, that it originated even more in the bells on his shoes than from the phonograph. She could see nothing in his eyes, and yet she had the strong feeling that the room and the people had vanished and they were dancing on thick grass in a green gloom. She began to feel much as she had in the previous night's hallucination, that she had no control over events or her own actions.

She didn't even think to note who might be observing them when Tom led her up to her bedroom. Not a word passed between them. She undressed quickly and gave herself to him. Only when it was happening did she come back completely to herself. She wasn't dancing with the Eldritch King to the music of the Otherworld. She was lying on her own very real bed, hers and Stuart's, with a man she didn't know very well.

"This is insane," she said.

"Hush, love," he said, kissing her.

Light fell on them as the door drifted open. A vast black blot stood there, capped by a massive, pulpous face with round black lenses for eyes. Gwyneth congratulated herself on not crying out. She dug her nails into Tom's back and clutched him tight with her thighs, wanting to caution him that the intruder could detect the slightest sound of motion. But he moved. Smiling at the blind woman who stood there for an eternity, he continued to move. Gwyneth clenched her eyes and bit her lip as she felt herself dissolving.

"Is someone in there? Who's there!"

" . . . ah . . . ah . . . ah," said the rebellious breath in Gwyneth's throat.

But as she faintly vocalized her ecstasy, a drunken male voice boomed out from below:

"O Allison Gross that lives in yon tower,
    The ugliest witch in the north country. . ."

She must have imagined it. None of their guests would have been so ill-mannered as to sing such a thing at the top of his voice. But it might have been McWraith's voice, and he was capable of any social atrocity. And she hadn't imagined it, for after an eternal pause, the goggle of the Haggworm swiveled toward the noise. The door slammed, darkness returned, and Gwyneth sobbed and whimpered into the man's bare shoulder.

At Wakefield's, the haggard man in black gazed at her closely as he rose from his metal folding-chair. He searched her face.

"I know you . . . don't I?"

"It was years ago, Mr. Bradbury." But it had been only Friday night. He had stood at the foot of her slab in a white smock. "Gwyneth Underhill—Doyle, now. My Aunt Isabel?"

"Yes." But he obviously didn't remember.

"My housekeeper—" she struggled to think of a euphemism for "died" that an undertaker would recognize, but her mind was blank; she concluded—"is here. And I heard that your son . . ."

"Passed away, yes."

"I'm sorry. What did he—" he startled her by avoiding her intended touch of compassion—"what did he pass away of?"

She moved toward the glowing mahogany coffin, all but buried in flowers. The bright satin lining of the raised lid—she dragged her mind away from unseemly thoughts. But she was still unsettled by the memory of Tom. She should have waited until she had composed herself. But she had to know.

"Loss of blood."

Bright spots swam in front of her eyes. She forced herself to breathe evenly. "Loss . . . ?"

She looked down at the still, unreal face against the white satin and gasped with relief. It was a much older boy, almost a man. Bradbury took her arm as if afraid she might faint.

"A hemorrhage in the night. A congenital condition."

"I'm terribly sorry."

"We were prepared for it. Thank you for coming."

"I'm sorry," she said to the shape she took to be the mother. "I'm sorry," she repeated to the others, all of whom she tried hard not to see in her embarrassment as she blundered out of the room, "I'm sorry."

"This way, Mrs. Doyle," said a man who took her firmly by the arm and propelled her into another room.

"I'm a mother, too," she said, realizing only as the words escaped her that she had spoken them too late. Her guide pretended not to have heard.

She found herself staring at the broad back of the Haggworm, installed on two of the chairs, with Joan and Arthur on either side of her. Before them lay a gray metal box, shut tight, with not nearly so many flowers.

"Oh," Gwyneth said, knowing only now what she had fallen into.

"Gwyneth?" The black lenses glittered at her. "I must say, you're the last person I expected to see."

"You vicious old bitch!" Gwyneth muttered, and this time her guide couldn't maintain his pretense. He gaped at her, but she left him quickly to take the seat beside Arthur. She held his hand. "I'm sorry. She was more of a mother to you than I was, at one time."

The expression he showed her was suitably solemn, but then he leaned to whisper in her ear: "Since they couldn't find her real head, do you think they'll bury her with the pumpkin?"

CHAPTER SEVEN

Viewed from the town, the hills north of Amworth looked as if they must always have been thickly wooded; but walking up through the woods, one found them honeycombed with stone fences that had formerly separated neat little farms. The stones were sinking back into the spongy earth from which they had been wrenched by generations of men and mules, but the fences were surprisingly intact beneath their garlands of briars. The farmers and their houses were gone, but the stones that they had fitted one on top of another without mortar had stayed just as they had put them. Stuart reflected that his life's work, the speeches that he put together for President Edward Wheaton Shaver, tended to fall to pieces even as they were spoken.

He looked back the way he had come. Fallen leaves carpeted the forest with gold. Bright lances shot from the lingering drops of yesterday's rain as the sun struck them. He could only just make out the "road" he had followed. "The old carriage-road," the yokel down below had called it. A gap in the trees, that's all it was, a little longer and straighter than the other gaps. He could see nothing of Amworth. A hundred-and-forty years ago, before the farmers had gone off to find richer land in the west or graves at Gettysburg, the spot where he stood would have given him a dollhouse-maker's view of the town and the college. Standing here then, he might have been seen from Main Street, a tiny figure in the midst of brown and green quilting-squares. "The Union forever!" he shouted, waving at women in bonnets and bustles, men steering buggies through muddy streets. He turned and trudged upward sheepishly, remembering that the yokel could probably hear him and would think he was crazy.

He was reminded of *The Jungle Book,* which he had read again and again as a child, especially of a story called "Letting in the Jungle," about a village completely digested by the forest. It had surprised him to learn later that Kipling had written the book in Vermont, with snow piled high at his door. It might have surprised Kipling to learn that, given a little more time, even the cold earth of New England could reclaim its own.

His memory flashed a card he hadn't known it held. It was a Saturday afternoon. He was fourteen. They had just moved into the house, a leaky, barely habitable shell, and his father was knocking down a superfluous wall with one of his cronies, Albert Barnhill. His father asked him where he was going, and Jamie told him that he was going to see the film of *The Jungle Book,* which was being revived at the local movie-house. Barnhill volunteered that his son, Jamie's age, was going to the high-school football game, and he volunteered it with just enough smugness to suggest what he thought of boys who chose to watch childish movies instead of manly games.

He hadn't been able to enjoy the movie because he felt that he'd let down his father. The next year he tried out for the football team and made it. Barnhill's son, who also tried, didn't.

He wondered how he would have felt toward his father if he had farmed him out to a dotty old aunt, without explanation, when he was twelve; and if that father had only recently returned to wander around town dressed in a plastic bag. He really couldn't fault Gwyneth for being ashamed of hers, even—so it seemed—frightened of him. He was more inclined to fault himself for not having taken firm charge of the situation when Kemper had first shown up. He should have offered help. Perhaps he should have gone so far as to get help for the old man, whether he'd wanted it or not. But Gwyneth's feelings had been muddled, she'd given conflicting signals, and he'd been too wrapped up in his own concerns to sort things out. Now he was belatedly doing so.

He hadn't imagined that hills could have swamps on them, but the path took a downward dip and he found himself slogging through one. He stopped to make sure of the so-called road, even though standing still caused him to sink, slightly but most unnervingly. He felt water trickling into the eighty-dollar oxfords he had worn to Cassilda's funeral that morning.

To his left, a sheer cliff rose beyond a clump of thicker woods. It shut out the sunlight and lowered the temperature perceptibly. To the right and ahead of him lay the swamp, dank and misty in the local twilight. He thrashed to the left, holding his toes awkwardly curled to keep his shoes from being pulled off.

"God damn it all to bloody hell!" he shouted as he stumbled to his knees in muck.

"If you are trying to walk on water, those are probably not the right words."

Philip Kemper stood a little above him on dry ground, leaning on a staff. If another man had held it, Stuart might have called it a stick or a pole, but *staff* was the word that came to mind when he saw his father-in-law. If the mat of his yellow-white hair had

been cleaned up and his scruffy beard allowed more
than its apparent three-day growth, he might have
looked Biblical. The polished anthracite of his eyes
hinted at the unworldly preoccupations of a prophet.

"Give me a hand, won't you?"

He held out the staff, and Stuart gripped it. The old
man looked frail, but he was surprisingly strong and
agile. Stuart was soon standing on solid earth and
flapping his wet trouser legs ineffectively.

"You're trespassing, you know."

Stuart straightened up and extended his hand. "I'm
your son-in-law. Stuart Doyle."

"I know that." Kemper ignored the hand.

Though outraged by this discourtesy, he put his fel-
ings firmly aside. "I know you didn't invite me, and
I'm sorry to intrude on your privacy, but I think we
have to talk." He looked for a hint of response in the
other's face and found none. "I am your daughter's
husband, after all."

Kemper turned his back and walked away. After a
moment of indecision, Stuart followed him. Soon
they came upon the old man's shack, lying hard by the
cliff among tangled undergrowth. Its tarpaper siding
and tin roof showed the hand of an indifferent work-
man, but its site had been picked by a skillful dissem-
bler. Stuart knew he could have spent a week looking
for the place and not finding it if the old man hadn't
chosen to show himself.

Kemper made his first, grudging acknowledgement that he had been followed by standing aside when he opened the door. He waited without comment as his guest removed his shoes, encased in shapeless blobs of mud. Stuart felt foolish when he entered and the chil of a bare dirt floor penetrated his stocking feet. Light stingily afforded by one window revealed inner walls packed solidly with books and papers. The minimal furniture had a scavenged look, and all of it was weighted down with more books and papers. A new kerosene stove and a few boxes, haphazardly stowed with canned foods, completed the appointments.

"How can you live like this?"

He regretted blurting out the question, but he had meant it literally: he wondered how the old man had survived the last winter. But his father-in-law chose to interpret it as a cry of protest against a disregard of banal aspirations.

"What do I lack, a television set? A sauna?" The scorn in his voice escalated: "A princess telephone?"

"A floor, for openers," Stuart shot back. His feet were so cold now that they hurt, but Kemper had closed the door on his muddy shoes. Retreating to get them would have made him seem even more ridiculous. Without pausing to examine his impulse, he said, "Why don't you come and stay with us? There's plenty of room and all the privacy you could want. My father and I lived there for two years once without seeing each other for weeks at a time."

"Would you like some tea?"

"Thanks." There was a little room on the cot, so Stuart sat there, drawing his feet up with him. The iron frame creaked but it held him.

Kemper lit the stove and a lamp, immediately filling the small room with an unpleasant, oily odor. He filled a kettle from a five-gallon jerry-can. He said nothing more, so Stuart examined the books crowding him on the bed. They were very old and mostly in Latin, the works of forgotten quacks, crackpots, and pseudo-scientists. Some of them would have been valuable for their bindings or their bizarre engravings, and it seemed a shame that they should end their long lives rotting in this damp hutch. But the same thing could have been said of the old man, and he told himself it was discreditable to waste his pity on books.

Kemper wasn't wearing his garbage-bag today. Stuart looked for it but didn't see it anywhere, so he assumed it had been a spur-of-the-moment improvisation. He saw no clothing at all except what his host wore: a blue jacket and brown pants from different suits, both too large and both extensively stained and crudely mended, and a holey gray sweatshirt lettered "AMWORTH" in faded red. His dirty feet showed through the broken seams of his canvas shoes.

He made what Stuart supposed was a hospitable

gesture: he gave him the dirty mug and kept the dirty jar for himself. The mug was scalding, and there was no saucer, so he balanced it on the mattress as close to his feet as he could tolerate it.

"You have rather a notable ancestry, on the maternal side," Kemper said when he had shifted the books from the chair to the perilous pile on the table and sat down. "When Gwyneth mentioned it, I looked it up."

Stuart only just managed to keep a straight face. Having decided after a long, internal debate to extend his hospitality, Kemper had apparently racked his brains for an appropriate subject of conversation with a son-in-law and had hit upon one suited to an old-fashioned parent in an elegant farce. Considering the man and his surroundings, it was grotesque. But Stuart was encouraged by the unexpected thaw, and he said, "My mother believes that we're distantly related to the royal Stuarts."

"Oh, my, no. No, indeed. The name indicates that your family and theirs may have had the same occupation in remote antiquity—stig-ward, or sty-warden, keeper of the pig-sties—but that's the only connection."

He had put no faith in Allison's airy castle for a long time, but he was nevertheless ruffled to have them dragged so abruptly and thoroughly to earth. "And what might the name Kemper derive from?"

"It means a champion, but that's beside the point,"

he said, and he ignored Stuart's impolite laugh to concentrate on the delicate task of putting on his jury-rigged eyeglasses without destroying them altogether. The wings were fixed to the lens-frame with bits of wire that stuck out from his temples at odd angles, like the antennae of a battered insect. As he searched for something on the table, he hummed tunelessly, and Stuart felt a weird little chill; for Gwyneth had the same habit. He came up with a piece of paper which he unfolded and consulted before he resumed: "You are, however, apparently descended from James Stewart—" he spelled out the variant—"who was an infamous Bailie of Glenwearie in the early 1600's."

"Infamous?"

"He was more than ordinarily zealous in his persecution of witches, so much that he was remembered for three-hundred years after his death by the local peasants as a kind of bogeyman, under the name of 'Auld Catchy-Claw.' The name may have derived from his frequent and enthusiastic use of the caschielawis."

"You've lost me there."

"Quite a few others were lost there. It was a device for compressing a suspect into the smallest possible space, in which condition he would be left for hours or weeks. But another tradition has it that he got his nickname from his withered hand. According to the story, your ancestor was so skillful and relentless that

he succeeded in hunting down the Eldritch King himself. As James was pursuing the King through
Foulbogschiel, he reached out and grabbed him with
his right hand, which was instantly twisted into a claw
that he could never straighten."

Stuart felt a shiver of recognition. He had first
heard of the Eldritch King through Gwyneth's ballads
as a most unwelcome tourist from the Otherworld.
Not just through an effort to please her, but because
anything that she touched at that time became
dragged into the vortex of his obsession with her, he
had incorporated the legend into his unfinished play.

But his shiver owed more to his recollection of the
list of dream-credits Cassilda had once made. The
King had been mentioned, and so had "Old Scratchy
Claw." He reasoned away his disquietude: she and
Kemper had both come across the same book of
Scottish folklore in the Whateley Memorial Library,
that was all.

Kemper was saying: " . . . great-grandson, Alexan-
der, took part in the Jacobite rising of 1745, at which
time he claimed a kinship to Prince Charlie and took
to spelling his name as you do. When the rebellion
failed, he fled to Canada. Which is why you're here."

"Instead of minding the pigs in Scotland," Stuart
said, laughing, and Kemper smiled for the first time.
His smile was no less odd than anything else about
him. Engaging all the muscles of his face and throw-

ing well-worn ruts into kindly alignment, it suggested a man of great goodwill and capacity for enjoyment; but he averted his face slightly when he smiled, and his eyes held their habitual look of wary calculation. His smile was that of a man permitting himself a convivial moment while awaiting a phone call from his doctor. The image seemed so apt that Stuart wondered if Kemper were not seriously ill; if he had not come here in order to die near his family, but not so near as to cause them inconvenience.

Stuart's darkest suspicions now seemed groundless. Although the old man took a certain grisly delight in talking about torture implements and witch-hunts (and he would find a kindred spirit in his grandson, Arthur), he seemed nothing more than a harmless, scholarly oddball. Taking his first sip of strong, bitter tea, Stuart resolved to trust his instinct and press his impulsive invitation. "I'm quite serious about your coming to stay with us. Living like this—maybe it doesn't concern you, that you might freeze to death or die of pneumonia or malnutrition, but how do you think your daughter is going to feel when you do?"

"It's better that I stay away from her." Stuart felt as if an iron gate slammed in his face.

"Well, look, since you've already come this far, since you're virtually in our backyard—where have you been for the past twenty-odd years, anyway?" He added lamely, "If you don't mind my asking."

Stuart could see the iron gate cracking. Whatever he may have resolved, it was obvious that Kemper desperately wanted to talk. He said at last, "I've been detained against my will. I'm not the sort of person you would want to have around your wife and children."

"I don't see why not. There are all sorts of reasons for putting people away, and some of them may not be very good ones." He decided to push a little harder: "You don't seem particularly crazy to me. Are you?"

"If any man has a right to be . . . No. But I know that I'm bad luck. A Jonah. Leave it at that. Human attachments are dangerous, and I've chosen to eliminate such dangers from my life."

"Dangerous! Do you know what's dangerous? It's living by yourself like this without any human attachments." Searching for an appropriately horrifying example, Stuart stumbled on one that horrified himself as he spoke it: "Suppose your stove blew up, and nobody was here to help you?"

"I know you're trying to be kind . . . but I need no more proof. I'm dangerous to those I love."

Stuart had to settle the matter. He asked, "Did you kill your family? Gwyneth's mother? Is that why they put you away?"

Kemper seemed to shrivel himself under Stuart's gaze until his pained eyes looked enormous in his tissue-frail face. "I didn't kill anyone," he almost whispered, "but in a way—no, in every way, I was to blame for certain events which deprived Gwyneth of her loved ones."

Stuart saw that he had pushed a little too hard, but he believed he might win the old man's confidence if he took no false steps. Again acting on impulse, he said, "Let me tell you a story. I loved my mother very much. But when she left my father for a . . . a . . . I have no word for him. If the human race had gone on strike, and God hired scabs to take over for them, one of them would have been Alan Braden, my mother's boyfriend. It took me two years to separate my love for her from my distaste for what she'd done, and for my detestation of this Braden. After I graduated from college, I went to New Jersey to make my peace with her. They were living on this rotting houseboat in a pestilential bay, near a town called Malneant. If you'd known my mother, how orderly and rational and—well, that's beside the point. I had hoped to come to accept her arrangement, but I hadn't known myself well enough. I wasn't big enough to accept it.

"About the time I left the seminary—I suppose Gwyneth told you about that—I made the unfortunate discovery that thorny social situations can be smoothed with alcohol. I knew this reunion would be difficult, so I started drinking on the bus. I arrived with an edge on, I soon acquired a glow, and I got progressively more drunk for two weeks. My mother would have been glad to see me on any terms, but it was obvious my drinking distressed her. Her distress made me feel guilty, so I drank more to overcome my guilt.

"Braden simply dismissed me as someone beneath his notice, drunk or sober. Most of the time he seemed to treat my mother that way, too. I think I qualify as a male chauvinist pig, but I believe that women are human beings. Braden didn't. Sometimes he would spin out his theories about how they are an inferior species—with my mother listening docilely—God, if you'd known her! It was as if he'd drugged her, or had her under an enchantment, that she should listen to this bullshit without speaking up, without walking out, without slugging him.

"I got into a couple of arguments with him that would have become fist-fights if she hadn't intervened. She would always jump in on Braden's side, even though the subject of the argument was invariably his rotten treatment of her. And even though he would sneer at her while she was scolding me.

"Before two weeks were up, I had begun avoiding both of them as much as possible. I would leave the houseboat early in the day to mope around the beach—the bay was on one side of Malneant, they had a pretty nice ocean beach on the other side—or to hang out at a bar, staring covertly at girls and wondering how to pick them up. But afraid to try, in case I might succeed. Nothing was settled, I hadn't made peace with my mother, I knew I ought to go home, but I couldn't bring myself to admit defeat.

"Finally she took me aside and told me bluntly to go home. I wasn't doing any good, I was merely 'upsetting Alan.' I would have liked to upset him. She insisted I leave that day, she virtually threw me out. But I went to a bar instead, and I spent the day there. In the afternoon, I managed to walk back to the houseboat. I wanted to get something to eat, and I couldn't believe, in my condition, that my mother had meant what she'd said. I tried to heat up a frozen chicken pot-pie, but I couldn't get the oven lighted. I went back to the bar for a hamburger and then, sometime after dark, fell asleep on the beach.

"I don't think the explosion woke me up. It was the sirens. It sounded like the Chicago Fire, every volunteer department in three counties converging on this one little town. I crossed from the beach to the bay and blundered in among the firemen and ambulance workers to gawk at—well, at nothing. At some burned odds and ends floating in the bay. I stood there like all the other rubbernecks until it leaked into my brain that I was looking at the ruins of my mother's houseboat.

"Braden had opened the door first, said, 'Do you smell—?', and flicked on the light-switch by the door. Those were his last words.

"The oven could have been defective. It was Braden's oven, after all, and he had a genius for screwing up mechanical devices. There could have been gasoline in the bilges, and a short-circuit in the electrical wiring could have touched it off. I may have turned off the gas when I was unable to light the oven. The destruction was so thorough that nobody was able to figure out exactly what had happened. And I couldn't remember exactly what I'd done before leaving the house. Whatever the reason, Braden was dead and my mother was blind."

Now that he'd told the story in its entirety, Stuart felt only embarrassed. He couldn't bring himself to say any more. Kemper sat for a long time as if deep in thought. At long last he said, "I don't suppose they found Braden's body."

"How—?" But the answer was obvious: Gwyneth must have told him the story. "They looked hard, but they assumed the tide was just right, that it had swept him out to sea."

Kemper's shoulders spasmed so violently that Stuart went to him, upsetting his tea from the cot. He thought that the old man might be having some kind of seizure, but it appalled him to see that he was laughing.

"I really don't think it's all that funny."

Kemper found these words hilarious. He nearly fell off his chair. Stuart winced in sudden terror as a ball

of fire shot across the floor towards him, vanishing
before it reached his feet. Another whipped past him
on the stacks of books. He felt ashamed of himself,
but intensely relieved, when he had determined that
these darting, fiery imps were nothing but the light of
the kerosene lamp refracted through Kemper's spectacles as they danced on the string about his neck.

"You have no idea how funny it is." He stopped
laughing abruptly and wiped the tears from his eyes
on his moldering sleeve. "I'm not laughing at you.
What you did was praiseworthy. If you did it on purpose, it was even heroic. But it was useless."

Stuart was surprised to see that it had grown dark
outside the little window. He no longer had any desire
to stay, but he returned to the cot to keep his feet off
the floor.

In a tone that was again deceptively lucid, Kemper
said, "I suppose you think I left those curious items
for you to find in the playhouse."

"The thought had crossed my mind, yes." Annoyed to see that Gwyneth must be reporting to him
regularly, he added belligerently, "Who else?"

Kemper turned and apparently addressed his next
remarks to a picture above his table: "Sometimes I
think it must be an enormous game, where men land
on the moon to culminate a combination of plays that
began when your toothbrush happened to be missing
one morning, or where the Civil War is effectively

countered by my tripping over a mislaid rollerskate."

Stuart believed he had heard similar nonsense emanating from the Amworth philosophy department, and he said with some assurance, "You mean that cause and effect are illusions."

"Oh, no, not at all!" Kemper started laughing again, so Stuart got up to leave. "There's a reason for everything. It's all part of a game, and we're the pawns. Considering your illustrious heritage, you might even be a bishop."

Stuart now saw that the picture on the wall was an extremely professional sketch of Gwyneth as a little girl. The artist had intended it as a historical exercise; both her costume and the sentimental style of the picture evoked the flavor of the preceding century. He would have liked a closer look, but he was anxious to regain his shoes. Outside the door he began banging them together to dislodge the mud.

Kemper had followed him, and he continued: "The game holds some very curious pieces, ones more durable than us. And far less forgiving. You might read Paracelsus on the subject of Umbratils and Sylvans."

The woods around them were quite dark, but the sky was a clear, bright blue, bisected at an enormous height by a glowing orange contrail. The appearance of this technical marvel jolted Stuart into a realization that modern reality began only a mile away; the contrast of its simple geometry made the woods, and

Kemper himself, seem less baleful than blighted—oversights in the march of progress that would soon be tidied out of the way.

"I have to go now." Having witnessed his father-in-law's performance, he regretted his invitation. But nothing had been solved. Kemper was still loose to cause them embarrassment, or to do himself harm. "Why don't you come to dinner tomorrow? We can talk about . . . something better for you." But Stuart had been touched by Kemper's devotion to Gwyneth's childhood picture, and the spineless sound of his own words angered him. He added: "I mean, about coming to stay with us."

"You think I'm mad, don't you," he said without rancor. "I couldn't stay with you. That would be making it too easy for them. But tell Gwyneth to come here, that's important. I can tell her how to defend herself against them."

Stuart sometimes felt empty without the passionate faith that had filled him in youth, but he had never been tempted to replace it with Cassilda-esque absurdities, and such talk could sometimes exhaust his patience; as it did now.

"She isn't a fool," he said sharply. "If psychiatry didn't cure *them* for you, you might try prayer."

"I pray all the time," Kemper said, his voice quavering with fury, "but not to your dead Jew. I often wish I could have lived then and helped them drive the nails. And kept a proper watch on his tomb."

Stuart stared at the abruptly-closed door in baffled rage for a moment, then turned and went on his way.

CHAPTER EIGHT

The woods were dimmer than Stuart had expected, but he was confident of finding his way. Nor was he the least disturbed by Kemper's babble. He assumed his father-in-law had meant, by Sylvans, the demons once associated with forests; his Latin suggested that Umbratils would be the demons who lurked in shadows—or by contrast with the Sylvans, the fiends to be found indoors.

Hogwash. It still irked him that he had flinched at the fire-imps. Maybe Kemper had noted that reaction, taken him for an utter fool, and been encouraged to perform his Old Wizard of the Woods routine. Maybe he wasn't so much crazy as he was cursed by a whimsical sense of humor. His very first words, mocking Stuart's attempt to walk on water, suggested that.

Mulling over the unsatisfactory interview, he sprawled headlong over a stone fence. His cuts and bruises were unimportant compared with the proof this gave him that he had lost the path. The sky teased him with fading light, almost none of which seeped down to the wooded hillside. At his level, all he could see clearly were the paler stones of the fence that had tripped him.

He told himself not to worry. He was no woodsman, but it seemed axiomatic that continuing downhill would lead him to one familiar road or another. Although the fence cut across the slope, he followed that for a while, hoping it would connect with one of the fences flanking the old carriage road.

As he followed the wall with his hand, he felt the need to assure himself that snakes wouldn't be up and about this late in the year; but his hand didn't believe that, and it jerked back to his side. It occurred to him that abandoned farms implied abandoned wells and cellar-holes. He slowed his steps until he was inching forward, scuffing up the moldy leaves in his path: where the snakes hibernated. Who needed forest-demons?

"Jamie!"

The call was quite clear, but he thought at first that he must have imagined it. Some acoustical quirk made it seem to come from nowhere, or from everywhere. Most probably it had originated in his own mind. Although no one but his mother would ever call him "Jamie" nowadays, the voice had been a man's.

But it seemed foolish to assume that the call had been an illusion without testing it, and he yelled, "Hey! Here I am," at just the moment he fetched up hard against the angle of the fence. He cried out, fell, and thrashed for a moment, cursing, in a tangle of briars. When he held still and listened, he heard nothing; but the answer might have come while he'd been floundering noisily.

"Yo!" he called, but he got no answer.

He ventured a few steps beyond the intersecting fence and saw nothing that resembled the overgrown road. The woods seemed to have thickened. The dim sky was now freckled with stars. He tried to be clever and identify the Pole Star by following the handle of the Big Dipper, as his father had taught him, but he couldn't find the Big Dipper. He began to go cautiously downhill.

A tiny ball of fire shot past him. Another streaked by. He cried out in fear. These couldn't be explained by Kemper's glasses and the kerosene lamp. Will-o'-the-wisps? He had only read about such things. Lights now danced through the forest on all sides. Something was burning in the woods ahead of him; but unlike any fire he had ever seen, it expanded as tongues of spontaneous flame sprang up all around him and converged on the blaze. It looked like the ruin of a small house that was burning. As the fire brightened, it reflected on a still area of water around it.

"Jamie Doyle!"

Years ago in Malneant, one of the firemen had called him by that name, shocking him into the realization that he was gawking at the burning houseboat where his mother had been living. "Is anybody here named Jamie Doyle?" he had called.

And now the huge figure advancing from the fire on the water began to shout: "Is anybody—"

"No!" Stuart screamed, running toward the fire just as he had that other time, and falling once more.

He fell very hard. His head hurt when he looked up, and the present moment didn't quite connect with the preceding one. He saw no fire. He smelled no smoke, only the mold and decay of the wet woods. Bob McWraith stood over him with a flashlight.

"Where's the fire?" Stuart asked.

"That's my line, surely. You were the one sprinting through the woods."

He got shakily to his feet and tried to describe what he had seen. McWraith explained it as the effect of his flashlight, flickering through trees, reflected by rocks streaked with mica, by moisture on spiderwebs. He flashed his light around, giving a demonstration that satisfied himself alone.

"Why were you looking for me? And calling me by that name?"

"Forgive me," said McWraith, who always seemed a little drunk and very jolly. It was said among his students that he looked like the illegitimate son of Santa Claus, with his cheeks like apples and his nose like a cherry, who would come down the chimney to molest children. His thick mustache bristled upward toward his shoe-button eyes, and his red beard merged with the hairy tangle rising from his chest. "I tried several variants—" here he roared them, making the forest ring, until Stuart begged him to stop—" but that one seemed to have the most carrying power. Your daughter is not with you?"

"No, of course not. Why?"

"Gwyneth thought she might be. She asked me to look. Now, don't worry, I'm sure Joan's turned up by now. Gwyneth hadn't even checked all the places she might be before I left your house. I have my car down below, I'll shoot you straight home."

Stuart almost said, "Mrs. Oliphant must know," but he remembered that they had buried Cassilda that morning. Keeping track of the ever-footloose Joan had been one of her principal duties. A couple of years ago she had tried to hitchhike to New York City to see some rock star, but she hadn't gotten beyond Cornwall Bridge. He told himself that Gwyneth had gotten out of the habit of coping with her, that was all, and had panicked over nothing, but he chafed at the way McWraith dawdled down the hill.

They came to a slapdash wooden bridge that Stuart recognized from his upward journey. He found it hard to believe, but he must have been following the carriage road ever since he'd fallen over the last stone fence. As they reached the bridge, McWraith snapped off his light and seized his arm. "Listen!" he ordered sharply.

It made him extremely uneasy, straining his ears in darkness—for what, he had no idea—beside the shadowy bulk of the other man. All he heard was the splash and gurgle of water beneath them, and at last he said so.

"No, the nymphs won't speak to us tonight. You must be harboring impure thoughts, Stuart." McWraith released him and trod confidently across the bridge, making it creak and sway. "One night I camped in a ravine like this one and was absolutely convinced, after darkness fell, that two young women were whispering to each other across the stream. After a time I went looking for them, yoo-hooing among the rocks like Tarzan at extreme risk to life and limb, and all to no purpose. It was obviously the sound of water and its echoes, operating on a mind susceptible through isolation and weariness to auto-suggestion, but you couldn't have told me that then.

Often they would giggle, seeming to mock me. I was certain that I would be able to understand what they were saying if only I listened hard enough, and they kept me awake half the night, tired though I was.

"After that," he continued when Stuart said nothing, "I could understand perfectly why our ancestors believed in sprites and naiads and nymphs and whatnot. I'm not entirely unconvinced of their existence myself. Some day I'll go back to that spot and find the White Rock Girl leaning out of her diaphanous nightie."

They had reached the road and McWraith's car. Only when Stuart was settled inside it did he realize how tired and sore he was. "Something like that just happened to me. I mean, something that an old pagan would have accepted as quite normal. Until we started walking, the road I'd been looking for simply wasn't there. Growing up as I did in towns, I never realized that being lost could be so—" he looked for a better word but could find none, and he laughed weakly—"disorienting."

"Puccahs are responsible for that," McWraith said firmly, slamming the car into gear and accelerating in typically reckless style, "of whom *Harvey* is the paradigm. They lose your way for you, and they make you trip over things that aren't there. All of these little marvels and nuisances of daily life wouldn't disturb us half so much if we simply admitted the inadequacy

of our bankrupt rationality and accepted the obvious.
Then would the scales fall from my eyes, then would I
perceive the secret entrance into the Hollow Hill and
dwell in the house of the White Rock Girl forever."
He remembered to turn on his lights. "Amen.

"Do you want to hear my theory on the current
vogue of supernatural horror in trashy books and
movies? Of course you don't, but it's the price of the
ride, as I tell my students while they sit and excavate
their nostrils and fondle their genitalia, waiting for
my hour to crawl by. It's because the generation now
in its early thirties was the first one to grow up without proper fairy tales. When the poor wee bairns tod-
dled to their mothers' knees to beg for ghoulies and
ghaisties and long-leggedy beasties, tales to scare the
bejesus out of the little buggers and send them to bed
without daring to whimper, what did they get but stories printed out by computers in the hire of the National Educational Association, designed and pre-
tested to assure them that everything out there in the
vast, horrid dark beyond the feeble fire of the home
cave was just ginger-peachy. The nasty, Pecksniffian
mouth-breathers who had been itching for years to
snip the balls off the Boogieman finally, for that unhappy generation, succeeded, and the onanistically
beslimed fingers of Pure Reason filched *The Wizard
of Oz* and *Alice in Wonderland* from the cribside table. The young louts couldn't even sneak home a

good, gory comic-book, Dr. Wertheim saw to that.

"They were marooned without metaphors for externalizing and conquering the horrors they had to suffer, the very real fears that they would lose their way home, that their mothers would die, or that some big giant like daddy would catch them and eat them. Without the mythic exorcism they should have gotten from the Brothers Grimm, they all grew up to be a little bit nuts. So now, when they flock to movies about mothers who have devils for babies, about neighbors who are vegetables from outer space, they're really trying to clear up the unfinished business of childhood, which they'll never, ever be able to do. Which is why—" he pounded the wheel exuberantly, making the car swerve— "that neurotic generation has given us women's liberation, marijuana, Bette Midler, down jackets, the effeminist movement, frisbees, Stephen King, the designated hitter, UNICEF collections on Halloween, the English mass, a world owned by Wogs, a Post Office run by baboons, Ernest Angley, the Manson Family, and Debby Boone."

"You're getting old, that's all," Stuart said, because he felt old himself; but since he was thirty-four and McWraith was—he only guessed—ten years older, it struck him that it might have been a tactless observation.

But McWraith dismissed it. "I'm a mere sprat," he scoffed, "and were I so young as to reckon my years in negative numbers, I would still gag at words like *Zip Code, laid back, senior citizen,* and *spokesperson.*"

"Consider the state of the world when Gwyneth's ballads were big hits. Everyone should have been happy as a lark, if your theory is correct, but they burned old women for giving them bad dreams, or—" he showed off his newly acquired erudition—"stuck them in the caschielawis."

"Don't forget the scavenger's daughter and the pilliwinks. But—" he gestured grandly at the highway they now traveled, an endless oblong box of mercury-vapor light glutted with neon signs, filling stations, fast-food stands, utility wires, and tinny autos; whose light excluded the old humps of the hills, so that they could just as easily have been driving in an identical box in Illinois or Texas—

" 'For all the plagues that are in hell
Light on the fruits of this countrie.'

I rest my case."

Stuart assumed that his friend was just talking to hear himself talk. Tomorrow he might maintain with equal fervor that earth's Golden Age had just begun anew. But as he often did, he had touched on many of Stuart's own unspoken and formless discontents. He had given shape to the feeling that everyone around him, whatever his generation, was coming unglued. Malkin Gray wanted to read for his mother, Gwyneth vanished in the night (to tryst with Woodling?), Kemper peered under his ratty cot to look for Umbratils, and McWraith lusted for naiads; Sterling Fairchild's dream differed only in its militancy.

"Who's Woodling?" Stuart asked.

"A prancing English god, God slit their gizzards."

"I mean, who is he, really? What's he doing here?"

"Stuart, Stuart, you wrote such a masterly press release about him when he came here. You ought to read it."

"His name is an English version of 'Sylvan.' "

"I thought it meant 'termite.' We could write a modern, upbeat fairy tale, *Woody the Termite,* about a lovable little fellow in a green suit. With bells on all six of his shoes."

While McWraith expanded on this, devising adventures for Woody at a college like Amworth, Stuart brooded on his own former literary ambitions. Through family connections, he had gotten the job as public relations director solely to impress Gwyneth that he was serious about providing for her and the unborn Arthur. He had needed the salary while she was going through graduate school, but with his father's legacy and her tenured position, his job had become superfluous. He did it now because he felt he ought to do something, but that was a poor reason to stick with drudgery. Why didn't he quit and try again to become a playwright? The notion that he was free to do it hit him like a revelation. Instead of hiring someone to replace Cassilda, he could do the housework and see to his mother's needs. . . . His eager planning petered out as the answer to his question struck him with equal force: because he was afraid of discovering he couldn't do it, that's why.

McWraith had ended his tale by having Woody bore a hole in President Shaver's head. Before he could launch a second installment, Stuart asked, "Did you ever hear of Robert W. Chambers?"

"The Shooting of Dan McGrew?"

"No. I'm surprised at you. He more or less invented the modern horror story with a book called *The King in Yellow.* The book took its title from an imaginary play of the same name. No one could read the second act, according to Chambers's account of it, without going mad."

"A popular idea with decadent Victorians, to be ruined by a book."

"Anyway, I tried to write the play, as it was hinted at in the book." He added glumly, "I never got beyond the first act."

"How could you? You'd never be able to live up to your advance publicity."

"I was thinking of digging it out and reading it after

all these years. If I think it's worth continuing, I'd like your opinion—"

"What's this?"

It was a police car, and it sat in front of Stuart's house. He had hardly given Joan's absence a second thought, and guilt as much as fear impelled him to jump out of the car before McWraith had stopped it. The presence of the police put an ominously official stamp on what had seemed only a bit of Gwyneth's chronic absentmindedness.

He burst into the living room and stared hard at each person in turn, and he sensed that the worst hadn't happened. Gwyneth looked tense, and his mother was unruffled. The policeman had been writing calmly in his notebook. His revolver, handcuffs, nightstick and black leather jacket seemed incongruous with his gray hair and glasses; he looked like a storekeeper at a costume party.

"Joan went out to the playhouse after school, James, saying that she planned to start work on its renovation, since you hadn't stirred yourself to do so," Allison said. "We haven't seen her since."

"What connection with the family do you have, James?" the policeman asked suspiciously.

"I'm her father, for Christ's sake." The policeman consulted his notes, so he added, "James Stuart Doyle."

It was six-thirty by the clock on the mantel. Joan

would have gone to the playhouse only three hours ago, at most. She hadn't been missing long. But neither had Cassilda.

"Have you looked—"

"We've searched the grounds thoroughly," Allison said.

"I told the officer how independent she is, how. . . . But with Sterling . . . and everything. . . ." Gwyneth's lips barely moved as she continued to stare at the policeman with unremitting, wide-eyed intensity.

"You did right to call us," he said, and he seemed about to go when McWraith entered and had to explain himself. It developed that he had arrived around four to return a book to Gwyneth and had spoken to Joan and Arthur outside before ringing the doorbell. The policeman seemed disappointed that McWraith had still been here, half an hour later, when Arthur had come inside looking for Joan and started the panic.

Stuart got the impression, from the way the policeman had pounced on him and now on McWraith, that he was more interested in degenerate friends of the family than in Sterling. But he needed more reassurance, and he asked, "Have you caught Sterling Fairchild yet?"

"We've checked everywhere he might be hiding, so we think now he's probably left the area. I'm sure your daughter will turn up safe, don't worry about things like that."

He was about to leave again. But at the door to the hall he turned to Gwyneth, who still stared at him, and said, with an unofficial, sheepish smile, "You know, it's a real pleasure to meet a lady professor, if you don't mind my saying so. Sandy, that's my daughter, she's smart as a whip, and she's got her heart set on being a lawyer. I'm behind her a thousand percent in that, but her mother thinks—"

Gwyneth bolted from the room.

"Hey, I'm sorry. I didn't mean to. . . . Gee."

"It's not your fault. I shouldn't have mentioned Sterling Fairchild. But since he was apparently in our orchard only on Saturday—"

"He likes big girls," the policeman said as he left. "And he's sure as hell not in any of his local hangouts."

"Perhaps I shouldn't intrude now," said McWraith, who had drifted to the front door with them, "but I've never seen the inside of this famous playhouse."

"I was going to take a look myself."

The key was missing from its hook in the kitchen. The door to the playhouse was open, however, and a light shone inside. Stuart saw that someone had rigged a long extension cord from the house, just as Alan Braden once had. Trunks and useless furniture were piled on the lawn, again reminding him of Braden's tenure.

A huge shadow moved in the fan of light from the door. Stuart dashed the last few yards. He didn't exactly expect to see Braden, but that face rose vividly in his imagination. It was only Arthur, however, who told them he had been helping Joan clear the place out.

"That's why she took off, she was going to pay me a dollar an hour," he said. "She thinks I'll forget about it. She'll come home and everybody will make a big fuss over her. What I ought to do, I ought to move all this crap back inside."

"Well, what happened to her?" Having all but shouted, Stuart struggled to keep his voice in check. "You were here all the time."

"She was here, then she wasn't. You think everybody hasn't asked me that ten times, for chrissakes?" He shot McWraith a malicious look. "They told her not to take candy from strange men, but would she listen?"

McWraith pried a cellophane bag out of his pocket and extended it to Arthur. "Would you like some now?"

"It rots your teeth. Now she's not only lost, but she's got rotten teeth."

Stuart supposed that everyone had been quizzing Arthur relentlessly. Beneath his normally bristling facade, he was probably as worried as anyone, so he didn't press the questions he wanted to ask. He had thought for a long time that the best way of breaking through Arthur's tough shell was by not trying, but it hadn't seemed to work. He tried to touch his son's shoulder in a comradely way, but Arthur twisted free and scrambled like a monkey to the top of a pile of trunks and packing-crates.

"Interesting!" McWraith boomed. "Gowdie was quite mad, wasn't he."

"From what you were saying before, you ought to like these."

"Oh, I do indeed. But he saw these fairy tales as a child does, and he's communicated his terror and impotence probably more forcefully than he intended."

"The girl they were painted for died young and tragically, so I've always been told."

"Oh, yes. Don't you know the story? When she was twelve or so, her father refused to take her to a production of Gilbert and Sullivan's *Ruddigore* in Boston, or to let her go by herself. She poisoned her family and the servants with strychnine, left them to lie where they'd fallen, writhing in agony, and went to Boston to see the show from a first-class box. I suppose she'd given no thought whatever to the consequences, for she returned in splendid high spirits and was quite put out to find the police waiting to arrest her. An angry mob gathered to see her on her way to jail, and she was killed by a thrown brick."

McWraith surprised Stuart by going straight to the window of the giant's castle and opening it. Looking in, he said, "Aha."

Stuart hesitated, suspecting the niche might contain some new horror, but it was empty. "How did you know that door would be there?"

"It was ajar. Why? Does it have some significance?"

"No. The entrance to the playhouse, too, is painted into—" He started to turn and found that he didn't want to look at the oven belching flames, at the witch with eroded eyes, and he merely gestured behind him; but it was no more pleasant to face the stalking wolf or the oncoming giant with his axe.

"Oh, my. You should do something to avert such disasters, Stuart." McWraith seized his arm and forced him to face the blind witch and her oven. "It's downright criminal."

"Mind your own goddam business!"

"Oh, I do apol—"

"No, no, no, I'm sorry, Bob, really." It took great determination to ignore Arthur, snickering from his high perch. "My nerves are shot. You're absolutely right, of course. It's just that I had promised Joan to fix up this place. . . ." *Because I'll probably die young and tragically,* Joan had said, *and if you don't fix it up now, you'll never forgive yourself.*

McWraith gripped his shoulders with a massive arm. He was alarmed to discover how close he was to tears, and he brought himself under control only with an effort.

"What do you say we look for her?" McWraith said. "I'm game for a search party. Arthur, you can come along and give us a list of her associates, the names of the low dives she frequents, and any aliases she may have used in the past."

"Of course." Stuart suppressed his irritation that McWraith should be the one to suggest this practical step, and that Arthur should respond to McWraith's style with a lack of apathy that, in Arthur, amounted to frenetic eagerness.

As Arthur jumped to the floor, he dislodged a metal trunk that McWraith caught in mid-air with surprising ease. Stuart recognized it as the trunk that held the manuscript of his unfinished play.

"I'd like to take that in with us," Stuart said, reaching to take his share of the load, but McWraith slung it to his own shoulder and trudged toward the house like a Viking with his booty.

They extracted a long list of Joan's friends from Arthur and determined which ones Gwyneth had already called. While she made sandwiches that no one but Arthur wanted, they began calling, spelling each other at the telephone. Everyone they reached was helpful, and the list of potential informants expanded with each call, but no one had seen her. Calm, even unconcerned at first, Stuart began to panic. The mechanical routine of dialing, introducing himself and asking his questions served as a hypnotic litany to raise monsters from his imagination. This man he was talking to now, this stranger—was he secretly laughing at him? Was his hand clamped over Joan's mouth as he spoke so civilly into the telephone? The telephonic network became a magic maze in which his daughter was imprisoned; only one number out of a billion possibilities could call her forth.

He had to go out and look them in the eye. Over Gwyneth's protests, with McWraith clucking at his heels, he rang every doorbell on their street, on the next, on the next after that. He became convinced that the householders who didn't respond had sinister reasons for lying low. It must have grown late, because he began waking people up, and he had no patience with their annoyance. McWraith finally dragged him back to his car and all but sat on him to keep him there.

"This isn't doing a bit of good," he kept saying until it had sunk in. "She's probably gone off somewhere—hitchhiked, as you say she's done before. Or even more likely, she's hiding with some friend for reasons of her own, whose parents don't know it. Arthur may have told us the truth, that she's trying to stiff him out of his pay. I'll bet he knows her better than you do."

Stuart at last let himself be driven home, even though he knew he wouldn't sleep. Tomorrow he would ring more doorbells, more telephones. He would look in ditches and abandoned refrigerators. . . .

He found himself alone in the kitchen, staring at his own refrigerator. McWraith must have said goodnight, and he hoped he'd thanked him, he must have walked up the path and through the house; but he could recall none of that. He could only remember, staring at the refrigerator, that he hadn't bothered to look for Joan's hors d'oeuvres at the party, or to ask her what substitute she'd made for *fea-falt*. The tears he had been holding back came at last.

The dusty trunk sat on the chair where McWraith had left it. To open it would be a well-deserved punishment. Like all writers whose works lie unfinished in trunks, he had sometimes blamed his failure on the times he lived in, on his lack of influential friends, on the fact that he didn't have a villa in the south of France or a garret in Greenwich Village; blamed it on his mother, his wife. And on his children. Opening the trunk and reading the callow fatuities he had written would be a proper mortification of his pride.

The kitchen held a drawer full of mysterious keys, but most of them were easily eliminated. The seventh key that he tried opened the trunk. He wished that it hadn't. The trunk stank. The stench was so vile that he ran to a window, holding his breath until he had flung it open. He leaned out for a moment, retching. A rat must have gnawed its way inside the trunk and died—of boredom, he added, having tried to read the play.

Having settled his stomach at last with some long, deep gulps of fresh air, he returned to the trunk, waving a towel before him and breathing solely through his mouth. The very worst of the odor had dissipated, but it still stank. On the top he found Chambers's book and some books on folklore; some helpful letters from Gwyneth on this subject; and notebooks crammed to bursting with ideas so jejune that he couldn't bear, after one or two peeks, to open them. Beneath all this he found the typescript of his *King in Yellow,* Act One.

And beneath that he found what must have been the source of the noxious odor. The rats apparently made a nest of matted straw in the trunk. He didn't know where they'd gotten it; certainly from nothing he'd packed here. He leaned down for a closer examination, unwilling to touch it. A note in what was surely his own handwriting lay among the brittle yellow strands. It read, "Act Two." He couldn't deny that he might have written those words on this piece of paper at one time, but he certainly hadn't stuck such a note in a dirty mop, or whatever this thing was.

He overcame his squeamishness and pulled it out. He had expected a weightless nest of straw, but this was large and heavy. Holding it up at arm's length, he let it revolve until he found himself staring into the muddy eye-whites and brown, putrefying flesh of Cassilda Oliphant's face.

CHAPTER NINE

Mattie Dreyfus was reading about the deranged emperor Commodus, who had used his power to impose his fantasies on the Roman public. Although it was one of Allison's favorite passages, she couldn't concentrate. Her orderly world, to which the balanced prose and lucid intellect of Edward Gibbon had once provided an underpinning, was disintegrating.

She interrupted the reading: "You have red hair, don't you?"

"Why, yes." Mattie hesitated. She glanced at the book in her lap as if wondering whether to continue. "Did someone tell you?"

"Your eyes are gray."

"That's true. Stuart must have—"

"Do you know anything about eidetic imagery? It

refers to a mental picture held so vividly that one can scan it for details. Few people visualize things so clearly."

"Blake saw his poems in letters of fire before he wrote them down."

She pressed on. "I've always had it to some extent. In the moments before sleep, pictures as bright and detailed as real life would rise before my eyes—faces, landscapes, rooms, some that I knew and some that were imaginary."

"Before—?"

"When I could see you, yes. With practice, I gained some control over these images and could summon them at any time by merely composing my mind. But I never mastered them completely until I was blinded and began painting imaginary pictures, as I was telling you at the party."

She would have liked to disclose her news by prudent degrees, but Mattie saw it coming and seized it: "Do you mean you can see me? Now?"

"Something like that, yes."

"What am I doing?"

"You've folded your arms."

Arms folded, Mattie gaped at her. "Why, that's wonderful! Do you think—"

"It's not *real!*" She spoke vehemently. She held her hands over the lenses of her dark glasses. "Do something. Very well. You've closed the book—with your

thumb at the top of the page to mark your place—and
you've crossed your legs." Mattie seemed frightened
and perplexed: so was Allison, although she had no
intention of showing it. "I can just imagine what Cassilda Oliphant would have made out of this. She'd
stuffed her head with nonsense about second sight."
When Mattie winced, she added, "That choice of
words was unfortunate."

Arriving this afternoon, Mattie had been the first
one to give her a clear account of the events early that
morning, when the police had arrived with sirens
wailing and tramped endlessly in and out of the
house. Stuart had considered the story of finding
Cassilda's relic unfit for her ears. She felt inclined to
repay Mattie's openness with trust. Up to a point.

"This demonstration isn't scientific," she said. "A
sensible doctor wouldn't accept it. He'd assume that
I'd once heard a description of you and forgotten it.
And that the rest was very good guesses, based on
data I might not be consciously aware of—slight
sounds, or minute changes of air pressure and temperature when you shift your position. Maybe he
would even discover that you're feeding me signals
without knowing it, with your tone of voice or inflec-
tion."

"That's harder to swallow than telepathy, or
magic," Mattie said, confirming her own opinion.

"Whatever it is, it's weird and marvelous."

"Weird, yes."

She couldn't tell Mattie everything. She couldn't tell her that they appeared to be sitting in the airy tower of a derelict castle, or that a warm summer breeze wafted through the unglazed embrasures in the yard-thick walls to dispel an odor of mold and corruption that was everywhere else pervasive. She was certain that Mattie wasn't wearing a gown more elaborate than one of Gwyneth's costumes, white satin trimmed with gold filigree; nor was the book across her lap an illuminated manuscript with thick iron hasps. But these fantastic details seemed as real to her as Mattie's red hair; as real as the nerve-racking boom of the waves against the deep foot of the outer wall.

She had come to feel at home in her dark world. She had known where everything was, she had been able to move with confidence. But that world had been steadily fading as the Castle, ever since the night of the party, had thrust itself forward in a vision more vivid and present than any of her memories.

The Castle hadn't surrounded her all the time. Often it would shimmer away into a comfortable darkness filled with the smells and touches and sounds of the real world. But this morning the real world had been struck like a carnival and the Castle had exploded upon her senses in all its arrogant substantiality. This moment, as she sat across from the elegantly

turned-out princess who called herself Mattie Dreyfus, was the most vivid of all. She could see the gold
sparkle of dust in the sunlight, the black sparkle of
pigmented flecks in Mattie's green eyes. The individual faces of the demons carved on the dark armoire
behind Mattie (the Doyle home held no such piece of
furniture) were more real to her than the remembered
faces of friends. She watched a white cloud divest itself of unraveling cloudlets as it sailed grandly beyond
the window in the tall summer sky.

Except for this bright tower, the Castle was a
dreary place. Damp twilight glowed in the lower
levels, fading to a blackness that was more than blindness lower still. A rainy Sunday afternoon in childhood, with nowhere to go and nothing to do, when
the cozy familiarity of her home and her toys and her
parents had worked on her soul like a rasp, had given
her an idea what hell must be like, an idea never su-
perseded until now. Here even Time was bored and
accelerated to hours a process of decay that should
have taken centuries. But no matter how many stones
tumbled at unnerving intervals from the battlements,
no matter how many swords and axes streaked with
dust and old blood clanged to the floor in the resonat-
ing distances, no matter how many tapestries collapsed in dust, no matter how many bones escaped
their rusted shackles as one or the other at long last
disintegrated, the process would never be complete,

she knew, for here dissolution was an eternal condition of existence.

She rose and looked out the window at the central courtyard far below. A forbidding, octagonal keep occupied the site of the playhouse. It was much larger than the playhouse, rising even above her tower. On this side of the keep lay an overgrown garden surrounded by a low wall. She saw unnaturally swollen and curiously colored fruit among the leaves of gnarled and twisted trees. This morning she thought she had caught a glimpse of the creature with the silver hair lurking in that garden. She now described his human semblance to Mattie.

"That's Dr. Woodling," she said promptly. "Were you able to see him at the party?"

"In a way." A man's distant singing distracted her. Like the lank lurker, like the walker with claws, this singer was, unlike Mattie, a creature of the Castle. She spoke a little too loudly to drown out the sound. "Tell me what you see out here in the yard."

"You . . . you're facing the wall, you know."

"Of course." She reached out and touched the sill of a Castle window. The hand she saw was strong and slim, as hers had once been; and as her body, clothed in black and burgundy brocade, now appeared to be. She was flustered by her inability to place the real window in the wall of the illusory tower, but she hoped that Mattie would give her a clue when she got up to look.

Mattie didn't. She went straight to the Castle window, forcing Allison to step aside. She put both hands on the sill and leaned out (impossible, for the real window was shut against a dank October day), lifting one foot daintily.

"I see some men in the lot next door. And a policeman with a dog, moving toward the woods."

"Looking for Joan, yes. They've been doing that all morning."

But they wouldn't find her. Joan was in the Castle. Last night, wanting to hear news of her granddaughter as soon as anyone, she hadn't taken a sleeping pill, and she had sunk into a fretful plane of consciousness swarming with insistent goblins. Sometimes drifting close to wakefulness, she would find herself in the Castle; and able to see. She would feel Joan snuggled beside her as she had always slept beside her before Gwyneth had come home to play at being mother and put a stop to it—or thought she had put a stop to it: until she was six, Joan would often wake at night and sneak upstairs to her grandmother's bed.

In her restless torpor, the knowledge that Joan lay safe beside her wouldn't, at first, seem unusual. Only by degrees would the awareness that her granddaughter was supposed to be missing act on her mind like a depth-charge, bringing her thrashing and gasping to the surface of consciousness. But on that surface lay only blindness and her familiar, solitary bed. To her waking mind, it would seem natural that Joan wasn't there. She had only been dreaming. But the dream had recurred until it had seemed more real than waking.

This morning she had waked fully, not to darkness and her room, but to light in the Castle tower, with the baronial bed disarranged beside her where Joan had slept. She had seen her since, wandering in the strange garden with a coronet of flowers on her hair. She had called as loudly as she had dared, but Joan had drifted out of sight without looking up. She supposed she hadn't called very loudly at all. She hadn't wanted to draw the attention of those in the real world.

But Joan was alive and well in the Castle. She seemed safe for the moment. The men with their dogs could search every inch of the Doyles' house and grounds, and they wouldn't find her. The searchers were like people trying to tune in a television program on a channel their sets couldn't receive. Only she, it seemed, could receive that channel. Perhaps the thing that called itself Woodling and appeared to everyone else as a normal human being had that power, too.

She wouldn't try to explain any of this to Mattie or anyone else. If she told them they would call a doctor, who would give her a shot and put her to bed. If she persisted in her belief next day, they would consider sending her where her belief would not be thought unusual. She remembered bitterly how she had humored Alan Braden's occult preoccupations, at first, and teased Cassilda's credulity. Humiliating though it was to admit, they both might have known a truth she hadn't suspected.

"Can you see the men with the dog?" Mattie plucked at her sleeve, seeming to draw her forward to the Castle window; but if she had been facing a real wall, Mattie must actually have drawn her to one side.

"I'm having trouble with . . . well, with seeing everything but you."

Mattie studied her closely. "You aren't pulling my leg, are you? I know you have a wicked sense of humor. If you're playing a joke, I'll laugh, honest."

"There's a ball of red wool—" she calculated the parallax of the real and the illusory and pointed— "there. Am I pointing at it?"

"Yes, but you must know—"

"I'm not finished. I want you to get it and, without any warning, toss it to me."

Mattie laughed, delighted with the experiment. The ball of wool, left over from knitting a sweater for Arthur, lay in a basket on top of a low bookcase. She knew this, although she could see neither wool nor basket nor bookcase. Mattie walked to the phantom armoire and stretched up on tiptoe. From the top of it she withdrew a massive and ornate silver dagger.

She forced herself to say nothing. It wasn't real. It wasn't a dagger, it was just a ball of red wool, just as the tall armoire was really a low bookcase. Mattie tossed it without a word and it spun end over end, flashing nastily in the sunlight. She would never be able to catch it right, she would grab the blade—but it has no blade, she told herself, it is a soft and weightless ball of yarn. She forced her fearful hands forward and somehow caught it by the hilt.

"I'm a believer!" Mattie cried, applauding. "Don't give me that air-temperature stuff. There's no way on earth you could have caught that without seeing it."

The hilt was formed by the figures of a nymph and a satyr, lubriciously intertwined. The satyr's bestial face leered and winked as if frozen in the moment of congratulating her on the success of her deception. She ran her finger along the sharp blade and found that it constituted the first mirror she had seen in the Castle. The reflected face was hers as it had been years ago. She felt a tear trickle on her cheek and turned away from Mattie's eager young face.

"Look there!" Allison cried. Turning, she had seen a girl in the garden: tossing a yellow ball in the air, now hurrying after it bounced toward the keep. She didn't dare point, to waste time by having Mattie tell her she was pointing at the wall. "Do you see—?"

"I saw—I thought I saw someone running around

the corner of the playhouse."

"A little girl."

"Maybe." She sounded unconvinced. "But it couldn't be Joan, not out there in the yard. The men—"

"Please go and look. Please? And hurry."

Mattie had apparently seen something, enough to send her quickly from the room without argument. Perhaps it was the simple conviction in Allison's voice, because she knew Joan was in the Castle. She had felt the warmth and weight of her sleeping body beside her last night, she had felt the trickle of her breath on her shoulder, she had heard her voice sleepily murmur, "Grandma?" when she had turned in her own restless half-sleep. And she had just now seen her in the garden, happily bouncing a ball.

The *tock-tock-tock* of Mattie's footsteps on stone receded until the echoes of that sound and its source blurred indistinguishably and faded together. She knew that she should have walked down through the Castle and into the garden herself, but she was afraid to leave her tower. One hesitant and incomplete trip into the depths, into the blackness that was more than blindness, had been enough for her. Unable to see what she could see, Mattie was safe.

She returned to her chair, a backless, ornately carved "U" that, she reflected wryly, wouldn't have accommodated her true girth. She ran her finger lightly over the fangs and claws of the carved gargoyles that were the arms, shuddering at the exact correspondence of illusory touch to illusory sight. The arms of her real chair were of smooth leather.

Like her real room, her imagination was furnished with sleeker and cleaner objects than any in this vision. If she were imagining things, she told herself, she would have been imagining things quite different from these. During the years when Joseph had been recreating the era of William Morris around her, she had often retreated to an imaginary penthouse with white, wall-to-wall carpeting, white leather chairs and sofas with a few black pillows, accessories of chrome and glass, many mirrors; perhaps one austere statement of color by Burgoyne Diller on the white wall opposite the terrace. If she had been convinced now that she was occupying that penthouse, she might have been more willing to accept madness as the explanation: the hallucination would have been hers, not somebody else's.

Perhaps hell wasn't a child's Sunday afternoon; nor, necessarily, an endlessly rotting Castle; perhaps it was decreed that the sinner would spend eternity trapped in the dream of his victim. Gwyneth, in her medieval dresses, or Stuart and Cassilda, in their medieval superstitions, might have provided her with this vision, but none of them was her victim in the sense that Alan had been; and she suspected that this Castle was his.

Alan's stories about Sebastian Gowdie had amused her at first, and she'd suspected that he made them up to amuse her. His tone had always been light and detached, no more involved than Gwyneth's would be as she related some three-hundred-year-old gossip about Beaumont and Fletcher at a cocktail party; certainly there had been no hint of the fanatical disciple when he spoke of Gowdie.

According to Alan, Gowdie believed that he had inherited occult powers from an ancestor who was burned as a witch in seventeenth-century Scotland. The artist was convinced that he had been put on earth to free the ancient demons imprisoned in the interstices of space and time by King Solomon, to usher in their eternal reign, and to fulfill the ghastly prophecy shrieked by his ancestor on her way to the stake:

"Waters shall waxe, and woods shall waine,
and Unman shall be Man, and Man shall be naine."

Gowdie confided his delusions of grandeur only to a few disciples; some of whom, after renouncing him, promptly met with bizarre and fatal accidents. To the world at large he projected an image of permissible bohemianism, although some people were profoundly repelled by him. In 1894, he met Arthur Machen at a dinner in London and reportedly told an anecdote on which the Welsh visionary later based one of his most disquieting tales of terror, *The White People*. Visibly shaken by the encounter, Machen was heard to murmur as he left the table early, "I have just broken bread with the Devil himself." Some rural preachers, although they were held up to ridicule in the centers of culture, denounced the Gowdie illustrations in popular children's books as inventions of Satan. In Hamlen, Ohio, Reverend Amos Flitt led a march on the public library, seized all the Gowdie books, and burned them on the lawn.

Oddly enough—so Alan claimed—the preachers had known what they were talking about. Gowdie designed his illustrations with the specific intention of corrupting children: not through any obvious means in theme or subject matter, but by the use of obscure symbols, mathematical proportions and color schemes of magical significance. Alan guided her through a volume of Grimm's fairy tales that Gowdie had illustrated and revealed its secrets to her, rather like those "Can You Find The Farmer?" pictures of barnyards that she remembered from childhood puzzle-books. Even when he had pointed them out to her, the various pentagrams and horned heads hadn't looked convincing; she suspected he was improvising these revelations as he went along and trying to sway her by the power of suggestion.

Gowdie had long known the reputation of the site of the Bloodstone House. Indians had always shunned it as the haunt of a nameless evil. Public hangings were held there in the 1670's, but the gallows was abruptly relocated after two years; a tourist from New York named Hager jocularly noted in a letter home that "ye Folk of Amworth complayne that ye Wretches whom they hang upon Hastur's Hill do not staye dead." Chancing to pass the site in 1842, unaware of its unsavory reputation, the celebrated psychic Margaret Fox fell down in a fit and remained unconscious for two days and nights. An orphanage built there in 1860 was abandoned because of "unsafe conditions" after only ten days of use. On the night before an official inspection of these "unsafe conditions" had been scheduled, the building was destroyed by fire.

Gowdie believed that the site was one of the three Ways mentioned by Arthur Lloyd Davis in his *Wonders of the Unknown Underworld,* paths between this world and another plane of existence. He was reluctant even to approach the site until he had made himself master of his inherited talents and of all sorcerous knowledge. In 1895, although he was only twenty-five years old, he believed he was ready.

He gained an introduction to Marcus Bloodstone and professed admiration for his house. Bloodstone was proud of the place and gave him a tour; during which Gowdie offered to decorate his daughter's playhouse. The price he named was so low, considering the popularity his work then enjoyed, that the wily old carpetbagger suspected a trick and said only that he would consider it. Besides, his daughter Melody refused even to open any of the Gowdie books she had received as gifts, saying that the pictures were "nasty."

Desperate, Gowdie said he would do the job for nothing, and that made his prospective patron even more suspicious; but after Bloodstone had discussed the matter with some knowledgeable people and gained Melody's grudging consent, and after he had let Gowdie stew for a few more days, he agreed to let him do the work for nothing, provided that he painted the murals to his daughter's liking.

Normally noted for the speed with which he could produce his clever works, Gowdie labored in the playhouse for weeks—not so much on the murals themselves as on the impressionable mind of Melody Bloodstone. He fulfilled her father's commission to paint what she wanted; but she came to want only what his evil influence suggested. He explored the secrets of her mind, dragged out her worst fears and most impermissible desires, and gave them form in his paintings. She became wholly his creature during this process, and in the end he used her in an obscene ceremony that permitted him to open the Way and pass into the Otherworld. He was surely never found in this one, despite an international manhunt that Bloodstone financed for almost twenty years in an effort to track down the murderer of his daughter.

That was the story Alan told her over the course of several evenings in the playhouse, and it seemed to be no more than what it patently was: a fairy-tale for summer nights, a line of patter to keep her mind off the surprising fact that he had persuaded her to pose nude for him; off the more surprising fact that they wanted each other, she and this ungainly juvenile.

Only later did it come out that he believed all the nonsense he'd been telling her. Because of certain calculations which he once tried to explain, even more complicated and silly than Cassilda's horoscopes, he believed that Gowdie was due to reappear on earth in 1965, and that he would effect his re-entry through the magical murals in the playhouse. Alan had come here and ingratiated himself with Joseph Doyle in order to be on the scene for the event, unknown on earth since the return from the Otherworld of Thomas Rymer in 1242.

Much as he wanted to witness this marvel, Alan feared it. When the Way opened, Gowdie might not be the only one who used it; and who could say what even Gowdie might have become during his absence from the world of men? Alan seemed to be working his way up from a neurotic fixation to a full-fledged psychosis as the appointed day drew nearer, a psychosis that might be precipitated when the day came and nothing happened. For of course, nothing would.

She believed that getting him away from the center of his obsession was essential, and at the last minute he agreed to go with her; just for the day, of course. As they drove, she had felt an almost irresistible tug of curiosity: what if Sebastian Gowdie really showed up? "You'll never in a million years guess what you missed," Joseph would say when she returned.

But she didn't return. She couldn't say how or when, but Alan Braden quietly took charge of her soul. The twitching neurotic she was rescuing from his appointment with disintegration became first masterful, then menacing. She began to live in a kind of dream, untouched by responsibility or the bonds of former affection, only now and then remembering her loved ones and wondering when she would love them again; wondering when she would wake up and deal with the fact that she was vegetating on a squalid houseboat in a swamp with a sadistic madman young enough to be her son.

Even when Alan raved of his intention to duplicate Gowdie's feat and began decorating the walls of the houseboat with his own unspeakable murals, she hadn't been stirred. By that time she'd seen and heard and endured too much. But when Stuart blundered into the situation and Alan gleefully whispered his

plan to make him assist in his scheme, when she saw
Alan talking with the blonde girl he intended to use in
the "Scarlet Ceremony" as a sacrifice . . .

She heard footsteps ascending to the tower, more
than one pair. She started forward to welcome Joan,
knowing that Mattie had found her, but she slowed to
a hesitant stop. Neither set was a child's footsteps.
Mattie might be returning with one of the others.

"Look who I found," Mattie said.

Allison looked away, unable to control completely
the release of her terror in laughter. Dressed in tights
and a sable-trimmed surcoat, a heavy chain of office
around his neck, Mattie's companion shouted, as one
would to the deaf, "It's I, Dr. Shaver."

Confident at last that she could keep a straight
face, Allison welcomed him. She wondered what she
appeared to them to be doing as she drove the blade
of her dagger into the arm of the chair and left it
there, quivering.

"I had hoped to see Um on a matter that's been
puzzling me, but it appears that I've come at a bad
time, as Miss Um has told me."

"It's *Mrs*. Um," Mattie giggled.

"You don't have to shout, Doctor, really. I'm not
deaf."

"Oh, of course. I see."

"Stuart has only just gone to bed." As Mattie

spoke, Allison turned toward her and hastily looked away in horror. "And I don't know exactly where Gwyneth is, I suppose she's out with the searchers."

Her hallucination had turned on her, and in just such a way that it explained itself fully; but whatever relief the explanation might have given her was negated by the frightfulness of what she saw.

One evening on the houseboat time had stopped, space had expanded, and the colors of the world around her had shone forth with the long-lost brilliance of Eden. As she had sat and observed in stunned silence, Alan told her that he had put LSD in her wine. It had been exhilarating until later, in darkness, when the slimy things had flopped out of the mephitic bay to invade the bedroom and fondle her. Alan had drugged her more than once, or said he had, and each time the initial layers of beauty had peeled away to disclose a core of loathesomeness. The Castle was a flashback to those acid nightmares. She could "see" because of the seemingly far-fetched reasons she'd adduced before; but she could see the Castle only because she had lapsed under the all-but-forgotten influence of Alan's drug.

No other reason could explain why Mattie talked so cheerfully when her formerly white gown was soaked with blood; why she could blithely ignore the fact that her skull had been split open, oozing gray pulp and red blood onto her chalk-white cheeks; why she could giggle at Shaver's asininity while her bulging eyes stared blindly at opposite quarters of the floor.

"You didn't find . . ." Even without looking at her, Allison couldn't address her without gagging. " . . . when you looked, that is. Would you mind looking again?"

"Not at all," Mattie said, sounding unenthusiastic, but she rose. Allison dared a glimpse at her. Her head rolled aimlessly on her shoulders as she left the room, her dress trailing a glistening red swathe on the floor. Allison looked up at the lofty, imaginary ceiling and breathed shallowly, trying to force down the sourness that rose to her mouth from her knotted stomach.

Dr. Shaver explored a repertoire of noises and gestures that were vaguely solicitous. His style of dress and his absurd white pageboy gave him an uncanny resemblance to some long-gone savant. Erasmus? Copernicus? She couldn't pin him down, but either would have been equally inappropriate. Focusing on his reassuringly familiar manner helped her win control of herself.

"I'm all right, thank you, Doctor."

"Yes—a bad time, I've gathered. I didn't know about your . . . um. Perhaps I should return another—"

"No!"

The vehemence of her interruption made him jump. More softly she said, "Please, don't go."

"Yes, of course not. Perhaps you could . . . I'd hoped to see Um, you see, your son? About a woman who . . . ah . . . approached me at the . . . ah . . . reception the other day. Was it Saturday? Why, yes, my word, it must have been, because . . . She demanded—she seemed to be attached to your household in some way, you see, I gathered that you would know her by sight—that he might know, you see—"

Allison was used to the "see" syndrome among sighted persons. Speaking with the blind, some try to avoid the word and suffer embarrassment when they use it inadvertently. But she had never encountered a case as bad as Shaver's. The embarrassment of her blindness had struck him dumb.

His silence was unfortunate: there were noises abroad now that she didn't want to hear. A gathering. An approach. Too loudly, she said, "Demanded *what?* Who was this woman? What did she look like?"

"Rather slatternly—but that's surely not the word, a member of your household—"

"Cassilda Oliphant."

"Why, yes! That name does ring a bell. Certainly. I have no idea why I couldn't recall it. Um, of course, Cass-um. She seemed to think that I owed her—or would have owed her—or should pay her—money, in the amount of one-hundred dollars. My memory for faces is not the best. My wife, for instance, became

quite exercised when I passed her brother without—
but I'm positive I'd never seen this person before,
much less been involved in any transaction or agree-
ment or . . . ah . . . promise."

The singing was coming closer. *Blood,* the voice
sang. *Doom.* She didn't want to hear the words—
Death—as the singer climbed the stairs, accompanied
by the skeletal scrabbling of the walker with claws.
*And then came out the bonny heart's bluid: there was
nae mair within.*

"She's no longer with us," Allison virtually
screamed. "You needn't worry about it—she was eccentric, whimsical. She was always having premoni-
tions. Second sight, she called it. 'Cassilda,' I would
say to her, 'Cassie, how do you expect me to understand second sight, when I'm deprived of first?' " She
knew from Dr. Shaver's expression that her laughter
was rising shrilly out of control, and she cut it short.
"And I would ask her—but we were children then, we
grew up together, you must make allowances for the
joke—if she'd heard of the two clairvoyants who fell
in love at second sight." Something metallic and heavy
and unmistakably deadly rasped ringingly against a
wall, quite near. The heavy breathing of a beast could
be heard even through the infernal singing. "At the
party—you called it a reception, didn't you, I suppose that's the more appropriate word, isn't it, even
though it did get quite out of hand, what with the

murder—I mean the *music*—she claimed she saw a man with a black aura. Are you at all familiar, Doctor—"

"Perhaps I really should go, I seem to have upset you in some way—"

When he made to rise, Allison's hand shot out to grip his wrist. He squeaked with surprise and subsided into his chair, where she held him.

"Who is Woodling, Doctor? Where did he come from? Who brought him here?"

"Didn't you ask me that very question at the party? Surely we've had this conversation before. Haven't we? You were concerned about the man with bells—"

"Yes, yes, yes, but you didn't *tell* me anything! A visiting celebrity, a writer-in-residence, surely he must come with the recommendation of some faculty member—"

"Why, yes, of course. He was highly recommended by Professor Um."

"You blithering idiot! You fool! His *name!*"

By his reaction, Allison knew that no one had ever spoken to President Edward Wheaton Shaver in just that tone or those words before; not even his wife, and that was a mystery to her. Shocked, even panic-stricken, he bleated the only thing that came to his mind, a rude student nickname she wouldn't have suspected he knew: "Barfing Bob."

"Professor McWraith?"

"I really must go. I don't know when I've ever been so—really! Madam, you—I must make allowances, of course, I see this isn't the time—domestic upheaval—considering the nature of this domicile and its inmates—and your son . . . Didn't you once set yourself up as a teacher of Japanese acrobatics? I had hoped to have a serious discussion with Um about the quality of his work lately—a jazz orgy to welcome a scholar, and on the day after a most untoward incident—but apparently he's passed out—"

The scream—but it wasn't a scream: it was like the far more urgent, far more chilling sound of a woman unable to scream, barely able to make any sound at all in the excess of her terror—cut through Shaver's words and silenced him. It was Mattie, she had no doubt of that, and the cry was followed by a sound like a butcher's cleaver hewing bone and meat.

"Good Lord," Shaver said, upsetting his chair and stumbling as he pulled free of Allison's grip.

"Don't go down—"

"I must! Surely Miss—Mrs. Um—she's in distress," he said, and he was gone, through the stone arch and down the stairs to the dank innards of the Castle.

She followed him, but only as far as the arch. She searched frantically for the invisible door of her bedroom, knowing that it was there, but her fingers scratched in vain against the rough stones of the doorless archway. She squeezed her eyes tight and willed the stone to change to the sturdy oak door that she could slam and bolt and barricade, but the Castle prevailed.

Below her she now heard Shaver screaming, screaming with the mindless desperation of a trapped animal, and a sound that she didn't want to try to identify as the singing went on:

"The gates they were locked
    Both outside and in,
But there was a wee hole
That let Lambkin creep in."

She struggled to pull the massive armoire ("It's only a cheap bookcase, I know I can move it!") in front of the arch, but it was far too heavy, too heavy even to topple from the other side. Fighting for breath, she sagged against it and faced the room. She doubted that she would have the courage not to fling herself from the window when the illusory demons at last came for her. Shaver was silent, and that sickening noise . . . a kind of grinding, wrenching . . . that noise had stopped, too.

The deadly iron boomed repeatedly against a door below, and the voice of the singer bellowed: "Come out, come out, Auld Catchy-Claw!"

The dagger caught her eye, poised where she had stuck it in the arm of her chair. She dashed for it and tried to pull it out. If she had let Alan have his way—it was absurd to think of such a thing now, fifteen years too late, but she couldn't shake the thought—none of this would have happened. He wouldn't be dead, she wouldn't be blind, she wouldn't be condemned to this nightmare from his imagination. The Otherworld that he had raved of was a place where blood— Mattie's blood, that she stood in now as she struggled with the dagger she'd driven with impossible force into the chair—where blood might be spilled before the axe struck.

"What in God's name is going on out here?"

That was James's voice, thick with sleep and irritation, but it wasn't his door she heard creaking open on ancient hinges. "Jamie!" she screamed as the knife came free at last. "Lock yourself—"

"Come away, wee Jamie!" boomed the singer, but his words were drowned in a bloodthirsty snarl.

She found herself racing down the spiral staircase with the dagger in her hand. With nothing but a ball of red wool in her hand, she tried to insist, but that now seemed insane, weighed against the sights and sounds engulfing her. What did James see around him? She heard him shouting for help, she heard the noise of a violent struggle, but these things gave her no clue to the reality he perceived.

At the bottom of the stairs she nearly tripped over Shaver's body. His face lay in a spreading pool of blood, and the handle of a tool that looked—but she didn't look too closely—like a giant's corkscrew protruded from the back of his head.

Mattie's body lay closer to the door where James fought a hairy shape that grappled with him in a way that made it seem almost like a man. Whatever it was, she drove the dagger into its back with all her strength. Its head whipped around and struck her like a club, and she was flung sprawling over Mattie's body. Another figure loomed over her, a bearded man with a crown and a double-bitted axe in his hands, but he and the Castle shimmered and dissolved like a broken reflection in a black lake.

CHAPTER TEN

Gwyneth had taken up the house-to-house inquiries where Stuart had left them in exhaustion this morning. Hobbling through the college's Rappaccini Arboretum at dusk, she found herself exhausted, too. She stumbled to a bench by the cinder path. Every bone in her body protested the change as she sat.

She heard a rustling in the leaves behind her. It wouldn't be unusual to meet someone taking a short-cut through the arboretum, but the sound—more precisely, the way the sound had been cut off so quickly when she'd turned—had been furtive. She stared into the gloom beneath the trees until a shadow congealed into a human form.

"Who is that?"

"I'm sorry. I shouldn't have followed you." He

inched closer, his white hair gathering what light remained. "I shouldn't talk to you."

"Suit yourself." Irritated, she turned her back on the Old Man Who Wouldn't Say His Prayers. After a moment she couldn't resist demanding: "You aren't my father, are you?"

"I have certain responsibility for you." He was creeping closer, but she refused to look at him. "In that way, I'm not unlike your father."

"In other words, you aren't, thank God. It must have given you a laugh when St. Stuart of Amworth invited you to come and stay with us."

"That would have been unthinkable."

He spoke with such fervor that she looked at him, and he took this as an invitation to slip onto the bench. He seemed even more ragged and unkempt than the only other time she'd seen him this closely, when he'd come to her house to announce his bogus identity.

"Why on earth did you tell me such a lie?"

"I could think of no other way to gain an audience. And I was sure you wouldn't remember your real father. As I said, I have a certain responsibility for you, and a long-standing affection."

"How could you be so sure? And what do you mean, a long-standing affection? How long? Did you know my father? Or my Aunt Isabel?"

"Do you know anything about Sebastian Gowdie?"

"My husband once knew someone who claimed to be him." The old man made a noise that might have been laughter. "Actually, he was killed in an air raid, wasn't he, in the First World War?"

"No. He disappeared from the world of men in 1895."

"The year he painted our playhouse?"

He said, "Your playhouse," with such odd emphasis that she was struck by the thought that this old faker might be scheming somehow to dispute the title to their home. He added, "That was where he disappeared."

"I looked him up once, but all I found were brief references that didn't even give his dates."

"He would have been pleased."

She didn't care for the faint sneer in his voice. Like other mad people she'd known, he seemed to believe that he was in possession of an incommunicable truth that exalted him above the herd.

"It's delightful to sit here in the cold and chat about obscure Victorian illustrators, but my daughter is lost. I have to look for her."

She wasn't yet ready to try walking. She hoped her sarcasm would drive him away, but it didn't. He said softly, "You won't find her."

"Do you know where she is?" Perhaps that was

just another mad opinion, but it had sounded sincere. "Did you take her?"

"No, I didn't." Meeting her eyes for the first time, he looked sane; and oddly dependable. But when she asked if he knew who had taken Joan, his answer outraged her: "The man who said he was Gowdie, for one."

"Talk sense. That man has been dead for fifteen years."

Unable to abide another minute of this conversation, she rose to leave, but she found that her blisters had gotten worse. She sat down quickly and tried to ignore Kemper as she gingerly worked her shoes from her feet.

But she couldn't leave the subject alone. "This is a silly discussion. The man I'm thinking about was named—Braden, I think. He died when a houseboat exploded. My husband was there, and so was his mother."

As if their conversation had never taken that weird turn, he said: "Sebastian Gowdie knew a great deal about those things which are currently dismissed as folklore."

"Dismissed," she grumbled, uncertain whether he was trying to insult her. The soles of her feet didn't look nearly as bad as they felt. She might be able to walk without her shoes, but she was unwilling to attempt it just yet.

"People no longer believe in witches and fairies and enchantments, but he did. Unfortunately for him, he was cursed with the ability to glimpse the workings of the Otherworld in this one. As a child, it was feared that he might be mad, until he learned to dissemble, to ignore the existence of certain things that others couldn't see, to accept the testimony of others' senses over his own. He painted, however, what he saw."

"He believed he *saw* those horrors in the play-house?"

"The influences prowling around your playhouse overwhelmed him. It was all the more unnerving because his psychic power had been steadily fading since childhood. He was forty-seven years old when he came to the Bloodstone house, and he hadn't experienced a vision in a long time, but . . ."

His fists clenched on his knees, his eyes bored into the darkness as if he himself were experiencing a most unnerving vision. The urge she felt to prompt him made her realize that he had hooked her, by the intensity of his manner more than his story, and it annoyed her.

At length he went on, in a calmer tone, "Sebastian Gowdie had a fatal fault: he was proud as Lucifer. He believed himself the equal, if not the superior, of Raphael.

"His opinion went unshared. The dimwit in the street thought his commercial work childish, his serious painting obscene. The critic called the one too *literary,* the other too *fanciful*—God! He painted what he saw!" It took him a moment to stop growling to himself and continue: "And of course the younger painter thought both aspects of his work old-fashioned and academic, because he had mastered the elements of draftsmanship and knew the difference between his canvas and his cleaning-rag. If he could have foreseen—"

"Starved for the approval of men, he found himself flattered by the silvery whispers of nymphs and demigods as he worked on the playhouse murals. To any mortal eye, it would have seemed that only the little girl watched him as he worked, but he knew that he was painting before an audience of immortals who applauded every stroke, who encouraged him to embody their mystical symbols and magical proportions in his work—for reasons of their own." He turned to pierce her with a feral eye. "You have to be on guard against your dreams. These unspeakable creatures delight in making them come true."

Remembering her recent dreams, remembering that damned policeman and his damned daughter, Gwyneth found it difficult to breathe. Gripping her arm, he said, "Get out of that house, get as far from it as you can. Better still, go now, and don't return to it. They want you. They want you all."

She jerked her arm free. "Don't be foolish. I can't

leave while my daughter . . ."

Her own words startled her. Had she just confessed a desire—even a resolution—to leave Stuart and the Haggworm and that horrid house, once and for all?

"I am perhaps the only man on earth who can find her and bring her back," he said with his familiar, lunatic certainty. "I've done that sort of thing before."

"If you have any real information about my daughter," she said, trying to keep her voice firm and businesslike, "tell me. But if you keep teasing me with these damned riddles, I'll go to the police."

He ignored her threat and resumed his story. She told herself this was proof that he knew nothing about Joan, or about her own past; but she was unconvinced.

"Despite his weakness for flattery, Gowdie was neither stupid nor ignorant. He eventually saw that the true object of their interest was Melody Bloodstone, and that they had merely been using him to cast the appropriate geometric patterns that would open the Way between the worlds. As you know, a mortal sometimes strikes their fancy, and she—a bright child, a pretty child, a rather spoiled child, no different from thousands of others—had done so. Sometimes I think they see our world as a kind of pet-shop, and once a sparkling eye or a frisky manner has caught their notice, no other pet will do.

Let them have her, he thought, when they at last

reached for her, *save yourself,* but when he looked into her face . . . those eyes, pleading with him for help . . . when he saw the true form of the Eldritch King, nothing at all like a human being or any other creature of this universe—he took the child and fled. In his confusion, he fled with her into the Otherworld, where they are the masters, but where not even they are omnipotent."

A most discomfiting suspicion was thrust upon her by these ravings: Kemper admired Gowdie, who had apparently done something nasty to a little girl—Young and Tragic, probably; and so Kemper, emulating his hero . . . but she refused to follow logic any further.

"Trying to explain to you what happened next," he said, "would be like trying to explain chess to a dog."

"Thank you very much!" she rasped, springing to her feet. He tugged her down hard to the bench.

"I meant no offense," he said mildly, though he still held her. "Utter chaos, it's been said, is a world where magic works; and by definition, chaos defies description or explanation. Depending upon the whim of the enchanter, *up* would not always be the opposite of *down;* effect might not follow cause; tomorrow might precede yesterday."

"And it would take all the running you could do to keep in the same place," she murmured mockingly.

He surprised her: not only did he recognize her allusion, but he was delighted by it. He laughed, releasing her to clap his hands. Now was her chance to run, but she was too curious to take it.

"You know, of course, that the author you quoted was a brilliant mathematician, one who might have anticipated Einstein if he'd spent less time on fairy tales. And isn't it suggestive that imaginative children, who know more about the Otherworld than you might suppose, are often scared out of their wits by his books?"

"He also had a thing for little girls," she said coldly. "If you don't—"

"They spent a very long time in the Otherworld—a long time as reckoned in earthly years, but time means nothing there. Gowdie was clever at divining their rules and using their limitations against them, and he was able to escape with her by the way they had come. The foulest of the King's servants, known in this world as the Pallid Mask, or sometimes as Sylvestris Tenebrion, was sent to reclaim her. As earthly years are counted, he passed through the Way six years after his quarry.

"He found her easily enough. Gowdie had left her to her own devices—honestly, he didn't do that through cowardice. They work on you through your affections, through your human attachments. Proud of his home, a man might be driven to glorify it by fire; desiring to protect his children, he might put them safely in the grave; lustful of a woman's flesh, he might devour it. So Gowdie left her, with instructions to flee the place where they had passed through, but she was too frightened or confused—or perhaps too willful—to obey him, and the Pallid Mask found her.

"But the Mask is a notoriously unreliable servant of the Eldritch King. He had a score to settle with your future husband and his mother, an unpaid debt from three centuries ago in another country. In his eagerness to settle it, he underestimated them, and he was blasted back into the Chaos he had seeped from."

"Are you by any chance talking about my mother-in-law's old boyfriend? This is insanity!"

"She was held in thrall. She was lost, body and soul, because she'd unwittingly made love to that . . . obscenity."

" 'If I should kiss your red, red lips, your days would not be long.' "

"But of course, you know all this even better than I do. You know how to recognize them. You know what things to avoid. You know how to destroy them, or at least how to send them back. It would be amusing if it weren't so damned dangerous to you and those you love. You're like a physicist who refuses to believe in nuclear fission, who even sits smugly at Ground Zero to prove his skepticism."

"If Allison was lost, why is she still with us?"

"Coming from you, that's a stupid question. The spell was broken by fire. You can also drown them or kill them with iron. What you kill, of course, is only their projection into this world, only the screen necessary for their magic-lantern show. When the time and place are right, another show begins."

"So when the Elfin Knight was blown up by the gas-stove, what happened to Young and Tragic? And where's Gowdie?"

She thought her sarcasm had drawn blood, since he was silent for such a long time. When he at last spoke he did so very softly, very sadly; and very effectively, for he sent a cold hand to touch her heart: "And who do you suppose we are, my dear, you and I?"

It was absurd. But even such an absurdity, whispered in the darkness of an autumnal grove by the creepiest old man she'd ever met, choked her attempt at laughter.

"Why do you think you've always been fascinated by the Otherworld? What drew you to study it, to write your doctoral dissertation on it, to make it your life's work? And let me ask you this: do you recall having been locked in the Bloodstone playhouse as a child? Do you recall anything of your childhood before that moment?"

"You're lying, you're mad! My Aunt Isabel—"

"—was a frustrated old maid who felt cheated because she'd never had a child. When she found one who had apparently dropped into her life through a time-warp, she assumed that God had taken extraordinary steps to grant her heart's desire. She wasn't about to question divine intervention or announce her good fortune to the local paper. As principal of the grammar school, she was in an ideal position to falsify your records and give you an identity. Whatever story she told you must have been an obvious tissue of lies, since you were so ready to accept me as your father."

"This is—"

"You believed me because, however dimly, you remembered me. As I told you, we spent a long time together."

"Once upon a time." Gwyneth found that she could feign a convincing laugh. "I know it would be kind to humor you," she said, getting up and trying not to limp as she walked away, "but I simply can't stomach any more of this nonsense. You're crazy as a bedbug."

When he followed her, she couldn't walk fast enough to escape him. "If I'm mad, Melody, let me make a mad guess about your past. When Isabel Underhill—she was the first person I came upon passing in the street, and I drew her attention to your cries—when she freed you from the playhouse, you were ravenously hungry, were you not? But you were unable to eat. You couldn't eat for weeks, you very nearly died."

"'God damn you, you found that out the same place you found out all the other gossip about me and my family! I suffered from *anorexia nervosa*—"

" 'For he on honey-dew hath fed. And drunk the milk of Paradise.' Because you had eaten in the Otherworld, you couldn't touch mortal food."

"God damn you!" she screamed. A branch came to hand in the path, not the rock she wanted, but she hurled it at him. He fended it off.

"Melody—"

"Don't call me that, you nut! Pervert! Liar!"

"Forgive me—Melody. I brought all of this on you through my vanity, but I tried to help you. I tried to save you." He had stopped following, so she slowed her pace, watching him. "But now you must save yourself—get away from that house. I'll find your daughter, don't worry about her."

"And bring her back safe and sound to 1895, no doubt," she cried, but her own sarcasm chilled her. At last she stumbled over a suitable rock and threw it, but she missed.

"Guard your dreams!" he called.

For the first time in her life, she directly faced her memory of being locked in the playhouse and tried to see beyond it. There was nothing beyond it. She might

have been born there, aged twelve. Her Aunt Isabel
. . . ("Who are you, Ma'am?" "I'm your Aunt Isabel, dear." Was that exchange a genuine memory, or
was it the power of Kemper's suggestion at work?)
Her aunt, she was sure, had said something about her
clothing when she'd let her out. She'd said . . . it was
old. Or had she said it was *old-fashioned?* She remembered that it had been promptly replaced, but
she couldn't recall what it had looked like.

Her next clear memory was a disagreeable one of
trying to eat chocolate cake and drink a glass of milk.
("Child, you're so *thin!*") She'd been so sick that
she'd never dared to touch chocolate again, and she
still felt uneasy about milk. After that she had refused
to eat anything, despite her aunt's pleas and warnings.
She remembered being in a hospital, her arm swollen
up like a thick red sausage, so sore from intravenous
feeding that a current of air on her skin was agony.
She was eventually able to eat, but she'd never developed a normal appetite. Eating was just a necessary
nuisance. People who could carry on at length about
gastronomic pleasures—like Allison—baffled her.
They seemed sincere, but she couldn't help feeling
that their zest for food was a foolish affection. She'd
gotten so angry at Kemper just now because Aunt Isabel had forever been teasing her with those lines from
Coleridge about honey-dew and Paradise. *Weave a
circle round him thrice. And close your eyes with holy*

dread, Aunt Isabel would chant when she picked at her food. Had she known—nonsense! There was nothing to know.

Kemper had said she knew enough to identify the Others when she saw them. But she wasn't mad, she'd never gone around with a checklist, testing her friends. They were fond of green. As was Tomlin Woodling. They liked music, they liked silver bells, they loved to dance. As did Tom.

And she'd made love to him.

If the folk-tales were true, if Kemper's claims were true, if Tom were a visitor from the Otherworld, then she was lost. Unless she killed him with fire or water or iron.

God, could she seriously be thinking these thoughts? She wasn't a thirteenth-century peasant, she was a twentieth-century American with a doctorate from Columbia. She'd chosen that university because her father, Marcus Bloodstone . . .

She chose to concentrate on the pain of her blisters and on her surroundings for the next few minutes. She was on her street, a few houses from her own. Reverend Maturin lived in this house, Mrs. Radcliffe . . . But that was horribly wrong. No such people lived in these houses now, she'd never had neighbors with such names. Not in this century.

"Gowdie is insane," she said aloud. "Gowdie is a madman, and he's infected me with his madness, but I can resist it . . ."

That made her feel better until she realized by what name she had just called the Old Man Who Wouldn't Say His Prayers.

The door stood open. Stuart and the Haggworm sat in the living room with a bottle of gin between them. A single lamp only emphasized the gloom.

"I was looking—" she began.

"Malkin's dead. Shaver's dead. Sterling's dead."

"Who is Malkin?"

"A demon, a specter, a cat, a slut."

"This is a lousy time to get drunk, Stuart."

"As Barfing Bob would say, there's no such thing. Do you know, the police have a theory that Sterling was hiding here all the time. Were you concealing him under 'Axe murderers' in your filing cabinet? Myself—" he sloshed gin into his glass and sat up straight—"I don't believe that. They're just excusing their stupidity for failing to have found him someplace else."

The Haggworm, who never drank but a glass or two of wine, astounded her by enunciating slowly and carefully, "I don't think he's really grunk, Dwyneth. His nerves have been under a terrible strain."

"Have they." She went to the kitchen for a glass and ice cubes. She floated an ice cube each in Stuart's and his mother's tumblers of gin and poured a small amount over ice for herself. "Now, about Sterling—"

"Mom stabbed him. Look at this." He pulled his shirt open to reveal taped and bandaged ribs. "The son of a bitch *bit* me. I staggered out of my room half-awake, and I thought at first it was a bear. He did a great animal impression, growling and snarling like a cageful of God knows what."

"Allison stabbed him? How?"

He released an alarming giggle. "With a ball of wool. Tell her, Mom."

"I was confused, naturally. Obviously, I had a knife, probably one from Joseph's tool-chest. But I lost it in the confusion."

"So when the police asked her to hand over the weapon, she hands over this ball of wool. They thought she'd gone nuts, and that I was concealing evidence to protect her. But she performed a public service by snuffing the little bastard, and what with the bodies sprawling in their gore all over the hall, there was no question that it wasn't self-defense."

"Stuart. I think we should get out of here. I think we should get in the car and go to . . . I don't know, *Tucson*. And arrange to sell this place when we get there, or burn it down before we go."

He laughed at her. "All our problems are solved. We are going to live happily ever after, believe it or not. Sterling is dead. Shaver is dead, too. I don't have to worry about getting fired, although I think I'll probably quit. Malkin is dead . . ." He began to cry.

"I agree with Gwyneth. I agree one-hundred percent," Allison said.

Gwyneth was thankful for the unexpected support. She had never seen her mother-in-law so subdued, so timid-seeming. She would have liked to hear more of her opinion, but one question remained unanswered: "Who is Malkin?"

By a visible effort of will, he stopped sobbing and composed himself. He pretended he hadn't broken down as he said briskly, "It's odd. McWraith was telling me this fantasy about Woodling—Woody the Termite—boring a hole in Shaver's head. And that's how Sterling did it, he held the poor fool down and took a brace and bit from my father's toolbox—"

"James," Allison said quietly, "James, please shut up."

"And he killed Mattie with the axe he used on Cassilda, they finally did find that."

"Oh, no. Mattie Dreyfus?"

"Oh, yes. Oh, yes." He swallowed an enormous amount of gin in one gulp. "Oh, yes."

"You were fond of her, I know."

"No, I wasn't. That's why I feel so rotten. I wish Sterling were alive again, I'd—I'd bite him back."

In a flash she understood the pet name and the cause of this maudlin exhibition. The world had changed as drastically as the popular trompe l'oeil of the Victorian beauty gazing into her vanity mirror that in the next instant becomes a grinning skull. None of the horrors she had passed through in dreams or waking life had defeated her, because she had drawn strength from Stuart's integrity. But her lighthouse had just burned out.

Unwilling either to confront her pain or show it, she began to talk: about her dreams, about Kemper's warnings, about the Otherworld and its agents in this one. She knew even as she spoke that she wasn't being persuasive or even coherent, but the effect of her words was extraordinary: not on Stuart, who laughed and snorted and gestured impatiently under the torrent of words, but on Allison, who listened in a respectful, even an awed silence.

She could see that Stuart wanted to air his opinions, but she didn't dare stop talking now, because remembrance had begun to leak like a deadly gas from the door that sealed her earliest memories. If she stopped talking and faced that door, she would find it wide open; and she didn't want to. But in the back of her mind the phantom of a little girl flickered through the Bloodstone house as it had once been, a little girl wildly exhilarated because the artist who had painted the pictures in her favorite books was coming to paint her very own pictures . . .

She told them about her dream of vampirism, but she couldn't bring herself to describe all the details that might have convinced them. She saw exasperation on Stuart's face, and the first uneasy signs of skepticism on Allison's. But as she blundered through the expurgated version, a memory rose that she couldn't blot out or deny, one that might have given rise to her later fantasy. Her little brother Kenneth had been born defective. He never cried. At an age when he should have been crawling and babbling, he lay listless in his crib; in the room that was now Joan's. One day when she was five or six, staring down at him, she'd been overcome by a powerful emotion. It had probably been a mixture of pity and resentment and a desire to get him working like a proper little brother. She'd reached down and pinched him hard. He hadn't reacted. A week later he died. Unable to confess to anyone what she'd done, she could only accept and suffer the horror that her touch could kill.

She faltered in her fright and confusion, and Stuart at last shouted her down 'Gwyneth, this is nonsense! Can't you hear yourself? Dreams, vampires, fairies, time-travelers—this is the stuff of your own ballads, stirred up by an overwrought mind, with a dash of Kemper's lunacy added. Sterling was responsible for the things, the *real* things, that have happened. Your friend Woodling is just a harmless twerp, and he wasn't even here this afternoon. I think Mom can spare you one of her sleeping pills, and after you've had a good night's rest—"

A dim shape, a child's form, moved in the gloom behind him, and Gwyneth shot to her feet with an involuntary cry. But it wasn't one of her long-dead brothers; it was only Arthur in his nightshirt. The relief left her shaking.

"We must get away tonight," she insisted. "They twist our dreams into something foul, they hate us just for being human, and they mock us with our own desires. I think Gowdie can handle them, but meanwhile we have to—"

"You're in no condition to go anywhere but to bed."

"Then be damned!" she screamed at his smug, sneering faithless face. "Allison, will you go with me?"

"Gwyneth, for reasons of my own, I don't entirely disbelieve some of the things you've said. Maybe you should go away for a while, if you feel this strongly about it. But I can't leave while Joan is still . . . lost."

"Get your clothes on, Arthur, we—"

"Like hell I will!" Arthur cried, shocking her by shielding behind Stuart's chair and putting his arms about his neck. Perhaps even more surprised, Stuart raised a tentatively reassuring hand to his son's. "I never heard such a crazy load of bullshit in my life. And if it is true, I'm not going to run off and leave Grandma."

Beyond the feeble lamplight she sensed the presence of old-fashioned furnishings that no longer belonged here. If she stayed here another minute she would see them, and she would hear voices that no one now living should have remembered, the voices of her mother and father.

Before Stuart could react and detain her, she dashed for the door. She grabbed her raincoat in the hall and fumbled in the pockets; her car keys were there. She heard Stuart call. He sounded more peevish than concerned. Maybe he would be safe; his faith might protect him, or Gowdie might succeed. She had to save herself.

She roared into the night. Beyond the town limits she opened up the powerful engine. In the gale of her passage, her raincoat-collar buffeted her cheek painfully.

She took her eyes from the road for a moment to adjust it.

CHAPTER ELEVEN

Stuart was relieved to find lights still burning in the leaded casements of Enoch Soames House, the mock-Tudor cottage where Amworth lodged its writer-in-residence, but his feelings were mixed that Gwyneth's car wasn't there. Considering her distraught state, he ought to be looking for her—but he recognized this as a lame excuse to shirk an unpleasant duty, and he knocked at the door before he could think of a more persuasive one. Almost immediately, Woodling flung the door open and cried: "Doyle! I'm so glad you knocked me up. Give me your watch."

"What?" But he had understood, and when Woodling made fretful gestures he took off his wristwatch and handed it to him. Laughing, Stuart said, "Do you know, that used to mean *tired?*"

"I beg your pardon. I'm afraid I don't follow you at all. I've sat on my syrinx."

He had vaguely expected a silk smoking jacket and an ascot, but Woodling was dressed like every other teacher at Amworth, in tennis shoes without socks, torn jeans, and a turtleneck sweater. As he entered, Stuart said, "To be knocked up used to mean *fatigued,* in American slang." Then he said, "You sat on what?"

Woodling flourished the wooden Pan-pipes in his right hand. "The instructions with the glue dictate that I hold it together for five minutes, and I was counting the seconds until you so happily arrived. How much time has this badinage taken, do you suppose? Two minutes?" He squinted at the watch in his other hand. "There's brandy on the sideboard, pour us each a glass."

Accustomed though he was to untidy scholars, Stuart had never seen a room this disorderly, with the possible exception of Kemper's shack. Half-disgorged reels of recording tape lay underfoot with books, papers, and discarded clothing, and there was no way to reach the sideboard—invisible beneath a pile of the same litter—without stepping on them. A bright little fire on the hearth gave this rat's-nest an incongruously homey touch.

"Now, of course, to be knocked up—in America, that is—means to be made pregnant," Stuart said as he picked his way on tiptoe.

"So I've been advised more than once. Old habits die hard." Most annoyingly, since Stuart was scissored to his limit as he searched for the next clear patch, he added, "Mind where you step."

Stuart surprised himself with his next words. He was sure he didn't mean to threaten, although his dislike for the man was growing by the minute. He meant merely to jolt him out of his patronizing air, to demonstrate that he wasn't overmatched by one who could open a conversation with the announcement that he'd sat on his syrinx. He said, "I killed the man who told me what *knocked-up* used to mean."

"Drastic, surely. I shall take care not to enhance your store of trivia in any way." He tootled merrily on his pipes. "I believe that's done it."

Stuart could find nothing but clutter on the sideboard, and Woodling came forward with no attempt to avoid stepping on his things. He returned Stuart's watch and rooted until he produced a bottle and two ponies that looked unexpectedly clean.

The effect of his words had fallen flat, and Stuart tried to relieve his embarrassment by explaining, "I didn't kill him for that reason. It may even have been an accident, everyone seemed to think so. But if there are no accidents—"

"Once a Jesuit, eh?" Woodling laughed. He upended a chair to empty it and gestured for Stuart to sit.

"I suppose Gwyneth told you that."

"Most people would be content to call it an accident, but you seem determined to shoulder responsibility. But at the same time you deny yourself absolution. She tells me you haven't been to church in years."

"She seems to have told you a lot." He thought of refusing the brandy that was now proffered, but he took it. "Would you suggest I go to confession?"

"Not at all. I'm merely curious about a man who believes in sin and its consequences but refuses to take steps to escape them." He dumped another chair for himself and coiled his bony body into it. "You may have invented a new heresy."

"Not a heresy, just the old-fashioned sin of sloth—which in theological terms means despair more than laziness. Despair of changing anything, especially myself." He was surprised to find that the brandy, not his drink of choice, tasted remarkably good.

"You felt differently about it at one time," Woodling said, reaching out to refill his glass.

"Oh, yes. Hell, yes. I wanted to be just like Jesus Christ. That's who you're supposed to imitate, of course, but I took the imitation with dreary earnestness. And when I saw how far short I was falling of my goal, I said to hell with it. Basically my vacation was a childish one. If I can't win all the marbles, I won't play."

It was odd that he should talk so much about things he no longer thought about, especially with Woodling. Perhaps drinking was a mistake, after the gin he'd consumed at home, but this insight didn't prevent him from accepting a third glass.

He couldn't help adding, "And I lacked faith. Transubstantiation—that the bread and wine are changed into the actual, physical body of Christ—I couldn't accept that, for instance."

"Your altar would have been rather a mess, eh, if you'd succeeded?" Woodling began to divert himself with random notes on his pipes.

Stuart regretted every word he'd spoken and resolved to discharge his duty without further delay. "I came to warn you that your life may be in danger."

"Oh?"

"Gwyneth's father, a man named Philip Kemper . . . well, he's crazy. He seems to have convinced her that you're some kind of evil, non-human creature. I know how absurd all this sounds, but I believe he's capable of anything. And Gwyneth. . . ."

Woodling suddenly jerked himself upright and said sharply: "Oh, please do stop this idiotic charade and come to the point! One dislikes concealing these things."

"What things?"

"Gwyneth and I, of course. An unkempt, red-faced husband reeking of gin knocks one up—forgive me, I can't seem to adapt to your dialect—knocks one up after midnight for one reason alone, certainly not for theological discussion. I must say you have a refreshing approach, though, warning me off lest *she* do me an injury. Tell me, dear friend—" here he released a startling bray of laughter—"have I knocked her up?"

He began to suspect that Woodling was even drunker than he was. His errand had been merely embarrassing, and now he felt humiliated. The emotion began to slide into a rage so intense that he knew he must leave now without speaking, without listening to another word from this posturing jackass.

"Surely," Woodling continued, "any method of birth control that we might have used would have offended your puerile religious scruples."

"You. . . ." Stuart rose, unable to speak. He flung his brandy glass at the fireplace. It shattered satisfactorily and the flame roared dramatically, but this did nothing to relieve his anger.

"Think nothing of it, old fellow," Woodling said, and in a parody of the well-mannered host, flung his own glass at the fire with the same result. "If you fear that I have any intention whatever of making off with your charming wife, be at ease. You see, she is—I do hope I've mastered this bit of your argot, please correct me if I'm wrong—she is a truly lousy lay."

Stuart lunged and yanked him out of his chair by the armpits. Either Woodling was even less substantial than he looked, or else fury had lent Stuart strength, for he found himself holding his tormentor off the floor.

Woodling didn't seem at all alarmed to be in this position. He sneered down at Stuart. "You filthy little swine," he said. "Merely because your wife is a whore, and rather an inept one—"

"I'll kill you both!" Stuart threw him down and kicked him in the ribs. Woodling tumbled through the firescreen, upsetting it. A burning log rolled out and ignited the mess on the floor. Stamping out the small fire and nudging the log back with his toe consumed minutes. When he looked back at Woodling, he lay just where he had fallen. The room was unbearably silent. He stared stupidly for several more minutes before kneeling beside Woodling.

"I'm sorry," he said. "Hey."

Reluctantly he took his shoulder and shook him. Woodling rolled limply. His head flopped to one side at an angle no living man's head could have achieved. His eyes glittered at the fire. Stuart saw now that the back of his head, where it had struck the andiron, was a concave mess; it seemed as if his skull could have been no stronger than an eggshell.

"Oh, shit." He knew this was inadequate, but he

said it again. He began to tremble uncontrollably. He sat back on the scorched litter and hugged himself. Bewildered, he said to the dead man, "Why did you ask for it?"

Is that the excuse he would give the police? "He asked for it, officer." But he had. It was as if Woodling had goaded him to murder. Why had he gloated, why had he spoken such detestable words? Or was he himself so drunk, so consumed by unacknowledged jealousy, that he had imagined the words and their tone, imagined the final sneer on that hateful face? He knew now that he was terribly drunk indeed, but he reached for the brandy bottle and took a long pull from it.

Even in death Woodling could annoy him. In an uncontrollable fit of whimsy, his late host had replaced the commercial label on the murky green bottle with a tag that read simply: "DRINK ME." He took a handkerchief from his pocket and wiped the bottle clean. But it occurred to him that a perfectly clean bottle would arouse suspicion, so he forced himself to press it against Woodling's dead fingers. The police might conclude that he had been drunk enough to fall down without assistance.

Shards of two glasses remained, however, and the police might get a fingerprint from them. He began to crush the bits of broken glass under his feet, but he was soon overcome with despair. He surveyed the disorderly room. If he wanted to make sure of getting them all, he would have to clean the room and vacuum it.

His frantic calculations were interrupted by a brisk sound of sizzling. The pool of blood under his victim's head had spread to the fire. Overcome by nausea, he dashed to the front door and tore it open. Deep drafts of chilly air helped him regain control of his stomach.

As he wiped the cold sweat from his eyes, sanity returned, but it gave no comfort. What had he come to? By what long, devious and unnoticed process had he degenerated so far from the ideal of his youth? And what in God's name did he think he was doing by rearranging evidence like a private eye in a novel?

He returned to the living room with the intention of finding a phone and calling the police. But he saw that it was unnecessary. He was the victim of a practical joke. Woodling's jeans and sweater and shoes lay by the fire, but they were empty. The man wasn't there.

"Very funny," he said loudly. He was more relieved than angry, but his anger was growing, for the joke had put him through hell.

He knelt beside the fireplace. He found no sign of the blood he had not only seen, but had heard and smelled burning as well. Nor, even more remarkably, did the hearth look as if it had been wiped clean. It was hard to believe, but Woodling must have hypnotized him, perhaps with the aid of drugged brandy. The only other explanation, that he had hallucinated the interview and spent all this time conversing with a pile of old clothes beside the fireplace, he found even less acceptable.

Examining the clothing, he disturbed a quantity of dry, translucent scales like the fragmented and discarded husks of a swarm of cicadas; but they were even more fragile and brittle, crumbling at the slightest touch.

"Not only do you have a juvenile sense of humor," he shouted, "you have the worst case of dandruff I've ever seen."

When that provoked no response, he searched the house, snapping on lights and shouting Woodling's name. In surprising contrast to the living room, the rest of the house looked as if it had never been lived in. There was no food in the refrigerator or the cabinets, no garbage in the pail beneath the sink, no razor or soap or pills in the bathroom; and a fine film of dust covered everything, even the toilet-seat.

Stuart loitered outside his own home for a long time, because Gwyneth's car stood in the drive and he had no idea how he should deal with her. It seemed only sensible, if she persisted in her fantasies, to have her confined somewhere. But however sensible that might be, he couldn't shake the thought that he would be acting from the basest of motives: to punish her for her affair with Woodling.

Thinking about her infidelity hurt him more than he would have imagined possible. He thought he had been prepared for it by his suspicions, but nothing could have prepared him for Woodling's words. He wanted to relieve his pain by lashing out at someone. But he had already done that; he could never do it again.

He concluded that the best course would be to suspend any action until he could think clearly. He'd had only one hour's sleep in the past forty-two, a fitful nap before Sterling Fairchild had burst upon him. He hoped Gwyneth had gone to bed and he wouldn't have to face her at all.

But she sat on the couch in the living room; and her appearance dazzled him. Part of the effect was her gown, which he had never seen before. He had never seen anything like it before; in fact, it seemed to have been spun from cobwebs and dewdrops. He couldn't have named its color, which shifted subtly with each slight change of his or her position.

But the true bedazzlement was Gwyneth herself. The gown was less concealing than the shadow of a cloud, and her body seemed as lithe and young as when he had first seen it in the tower fifteen years ago. He hadn't noticed that she had changed with the years, not until now, when he saw her looking eighteen again. It must have been a trick of the light, the deception of her dress; or, more plausibly, the liquor he'd consumed.

"Good Lord," he breathed. "Are you off to Prince Charming's ball?" He glanced at his watch, but he saw that it had stopped at midnight. "Or have you already been?"

"I thought I owed it to you to look my best."

"Owed it to me? For what?"

"For all I've put you through these past weeks. I don't know what came over me. The strain, perhaps, the shock of all the awful things that have happened. And Kemper's influence, of course. I promise you, Stuart, I swear to you, that I'm myself." She laughed lightly. "And by that, I don't mean that I'm Melody Bloodstone." She stood up. She seldom wore high heels, which made her marginally taller than he, but she was apparently wearing them now, since she gazed levelly into his eyes. He took her into his arms, but before he could kiss her, she said, "And Joan's back, Stuart, isn't that marvelous? That was enough, that in itself, to bring me to my senses."

"What! Where was she? Where is she?" He was already dashing for the stairs.

"In her bed, of course. Don't wake her. She went off on a lark, as you suggested. She's perfectly all right, just slightly knocked-up."

"What did you say?"

"Stuart, can't I tease you anymore? You yourself told me what that phrase used to mean."

It was too great a coincidence, that she should spontaneously produce the phrase he'd explained to Woodling; who could have called her and told her everything while he had been dawdling home. But he refused to let anything mar his happiness.

It seemed to take a far longer time to run up the stairs than it should have, and he was thoroughly winded when he reached the second floor. He experienced a singular disorientation that he ascribed to his shortness of breath: he couldn't immediately locate Joan's room. When he did, he saw her lying in her bed as Gwyneth had told him. He stooped beneath the canopy—but that was absurd, her bed had no canopy, and when he looked up he saw that he was right, despite a strong initial feeling to the contrary.

It took an effort not to cry out and gather his sleeping daughter in his arms; but Gwyneth was right, of course, she needed her rest. He looked down at her for a long time. She had acquired a crown of flowers for her hair, and she looked like a sleeping princess in a fairy tale.

Stealing from the room, he glimpsed the reflection of firelight on the wall. Alarmed, he turned to look for its source, but there was no fire. He saw only the usual electric light in the hall. The phenomenon persisted as he went to the stairs. It was as if the hall were lit by torches, but every time he looked at the source of the light, it proved to be only the electric bulb. He assumed there must be some fluctuation in the power, although the bulb seemed to burn steadily when he looked at it directly.

When he entered the living room, he saw that Gwyneth's feet were bare. The high-heeled shoes she must have been wearing were nowhere to be seen. He took his watch off and wound it thoughtfully. Holding it to his ear, he found that it still refused to run.

"I suppose you spoke to Tom," he said as casually as he could manage.

"Tom? When? What about?" Her guileless smile suggested that she was anticipating the punch-line of a joke.

"Your lover, Tomlin Woodling, damn you." He turned away. He'd intended to say nothing like that, but her extraordinary beauty had twisted the knife in his heart.

"That's absurd! My lover? I never—"

"He told me—"

"Then he *lied!*" she screamed. "He's a liar, Stuart, a chronic liar and a troublemaker. If he told you such a thing, it was because it appealed to his perverted sense of humor."

And indeed, Stuart thought, why wouldn't a man who pretended to be dead as a joke pretend to be his wife's lover? Another joke. That made sense, but he found it hard to believe.

"I love only you, I've never loved anyone but you, I've always been faithful to you and I always will," Gwyneth said; and in a gesture that was a bit melodramatic even for her, she slid from the couch to her knees, her hands extended imploringly. "If you believe otherwise, then kill me now. I couldn't stand to go on living if you doubted me."

The operatic intensity of her emotion embarrassed him. "I've bagged my quota for the night," he said with a nervous laugh.

"It would be the ultimate act of love, wouldn't it," she murmured in a dreamy voice, rising and swaying toward him, "a sacrament of love, if you were to take my life with your hands. It would be the ultimate act of penetration—"

"Gwyneth, please don't talk like that. Please. You said you were yourself—"

"Oh, I am, Stuart. I am. Didn't you feel closer to Tomlin when you killed him? Have you ever felt so inextricably bound to another person as you did in that instant?"

He stared at her, yearning for her. This confirmation that she had compared notes with Woodling now seemed strangely irrelevant. Her words carried an unthinkable temptation, one that he had never before imagined. He wanted her, but sex hardly seemed enough to satisfy the nature of that want. He wanted to possess her entirely, to devour her.

There was no graceless unzipping or unfastening; it was as if she merely flicked her wrists and her gown dissolved to the floor. He had never seen, he had never dreamed of a more desirable woman. He was drawn to her. In her bare feet, she was marginally taller than he.

"I have. . . ." He closed his eyes and breathed deeply. "I have the strangest feeling that you are not Gwyneth."

"Stuart, I can't help the way I am," she whispered in his ear as she embraced him, her body writhing invitation. "I'm your wife, your love, now and forever, and I want you to possess me utterly."

He wrenched free from the suffocating temptations of her undulant flesh. "Damn you, what have you done with her?"

Laughing in his face, she lilted:

"Are you a witch, or are you a fairy,
Or are you the wife—"

He flung her down and tore his clothes off. He fell on her and entered her brutally, but she responded with an ardor that was nothing less than ferocious. The twin pythons of her thighs strove to crush his ribs, her heels battered his spine, her hips pummeled his like deadly machinery. He heard her teeth click together through his lip, and he tasted the salt of his own blood.

"Taste my blood, Stuart, drink it—*consecrate* it," she moaned, offering her snowy throat with its shadowy blue veins.

She became a pure white altar-cloth spread before him. The flames of candles burned in her eyes. Her breath was incense. *"Introibo ad altare Dei,"* he intoned, and her voice was the response of a choir. He went through the ritual motions that he had never actually performed before with total confidence, with perfect grace, with certain knowledge that it was all true, that it was all holy.

And when he came to the moment of the transubstantiation, he knew beyond any shadow of a doubt that the miracle had occurred: that he was eating human flesh and drinking human blood.

CHAPTER TWELVE

At first Stuart had ignored the noise at the door, but as ringing had become rapping and rapping, pounding, he had been forced to endure it like a toothache. Now it burst on him like a revelation that he could pry himself from his corner, go to the door, and tell whoever it was to go away.

First he had to open his eyes and cross the room to the hall, and it was easier to think about these actions than to take them. The hammering persisted, it grew even louder. At last he found the will to move. Quickly. Not even daring to look up at the ceiling, for even there blood had spattered.

Without stopping to think what he must look like, he opened the door; and a policeman stood outside. Stuart edged back into the shadows and wiped his mouth on his sleeve.

"I'm sorry I woke you, Mr. Doyle." he paused, but Stuart couldn't speak. "I'm damned sorry I have to be here at all. It's your wife."

"Yes," he said at last, "of course. She's in here."

"No, you don't understand." The policeman tried to detain him at the door but was forced to follow him into the slaughterhouse. "She's had an accident."

Stuart couldn't understand it. The room looked as it always had. There was no blood. Gwyneth's body was gone. He examined his hands and arms, but there was no blood on them.

"She isn't dead," Stuart whispered.

"I'm afraid she is. Maybe you'd better sit—"

"You're crazy. She isn't here. I didn't kill her!"

The policeman forced him to a chair. "You were dreaming, I guess. Are you awake now? Do you understand me?"

"It was a dream," Stuart said, but only because he saw it was expected of him. He searched the policeman's face. "I know you, don't I?"

"Officer Jackson, yes. I was here when you reported your daughter missing. She hasn't turned up yet, has she?"

"Yes. No. I don't know."

"Is there someone else in the house now, Mr. Doyle, someone I could talk to?"

"I'm sorry. I'm still not quite awake yet. I dreamed

that my daughter came home." He tried hard to look alert, to say the things he should, but he couldn't wait to get rid of this intruder and see if Joan was still asleep in her bed. "What's all this about my wife?"

"This is terrible, all this at one time . . . I'm really sorry. Mrs. Doyle sideswiped a rig and went off the road at high speed. She was killed instantly, the doctor said. If that's any consolation. I'm afraid you'll have to identify her. It can wait until morning, of course. She's at Bradbury's."

Obviously thinking that Stuart was a mental case who might do something irrational when he left, Officer Jackson planted himself in a chair and talked for what seemed hours. He described the accident scene, the amount of time it had taken to free Gwyneth's body. Despite his genuine sympathy, he couldn't entirely conceal a certain professional delight in the details of the crash, viewed simply as a crash; it was the worst he'd seen in thirty years of small-town police work.

She hadn't felt a thing, he kept assuring Stuart, her spine had been severed at once. Miraculously, since the car looked like a "wad of tinfoil," her body was virtually unmarked. He told of finding a religious medal and of calling a Father Summers, for which Stuart thanked him; although he knew Gwyneth wouldn't have thanked him. When Jackson started talking about his home life and his brilliant daughter's ambitions, Stuart managed to pull himself together and eased him out of the house.

The minute he was gone, Stuart dashed upstairs to find Joan's bed empty and undisturbed. He sat on it for a long time and tried unsuccessfully to make sense of what was happening to him. He had killed Woodling, and Woodling had disappeared; he had killed Gwyneth, and Gwyneth had disappeared. But now Gwyneth was dead. Was Woodling dead, too?

He went to his own bedroom and got the number from Information. He found that Woodling's phone—as Braden's phone surely would have been—was out of order.

Come to think of it, he had killed Braden, and Braden had disappeared.

He knew it was a bad idea, but he went down to the kitchen as the windows were glowing gray and poured himself a drink. It proved a worse idea than he had thought. It was difficult to swallow the gin and impossible to keep it down. He brewed coffee, but his reaction to the smell of it convinced him not to try it. He felt unaccountably calm. It was as if his mind had not yet acknowledged the emotions ravaging his stomach.

He sat at the bare table and tried to feel the grief he should have felt for Gwyneth. The problem was, he couldn't believe she was dead. The garrulous policeman had seemed less real than anything he'd experienced last night. He was certain now that the woman he'd killed hadn't been Gwyneth. What had she been? Dreams didn't feel like that, or smell like that. Or bleed like that. Or taste—

Arthur appeared at the kitchen door. With unerring instinct he asked the hardest question: "Where's Mom?"

He hadn't even foreseen the difficulty of breaking the news to Arthur. "You were here when she said she was leaving—"

"But she came back. I saw her."

Stuart saw fear in his son's eyes. Maybe they only mirrored his own. "I was told . . ."

He was unable to continue from such a bad beginning, and Arthur demanded: "Where is she?" And then, "What did you do to her?"

He blurted. "She's dead."

Arthur flung himself on him. "You killed her, you son of a bitch! You killed her!"

Stuart suddenly found himself convinced that she was dead. It was hard to fend off Arthur's kicks and punches while he was crying.

When he presented himself at the funeral home, Stuart learned that identifying the body would be no quick and easy formality. The police had sealed off the place. He was shunted from one cop to another until Officer Jackson recognized him and led him inside.

"Look, they haven't had time to do anything with her."

"Do what? She's dead, isn't she?" Stuart had reached the limit of his patience. "What more can they do to her? I want to get this over with."

"Here, talk to Father Summers for a minute. I'll see what I can do."

"Would you care to pray with me?"

"No, I wouldn't, thank you." The thought of any religious observance made him shudder; and so did Father Summers. With his lank hair, shallow skin, and bad teeth, he looked unhealthy, even unclean. When he smelled the priest's breath, he tried to stroll away casually, as if he had business in the first room off the hall, but he was followed.

"The Bradburys' youngest son was murdered in his bed last night by an intruder. It was terrible, truly a horrendous crime. So sad, too, after the death of their older boy."

Stuart had to turn away from the pursuing, weasely eyes. He had remembered Gwyneth's reaction to the older boy's death and remembered how it had annoyed him. She couldn't annoy him anymore. As he wiped his tears, he was startled to see a rouged, wax mask of President Shaver before him; he was looking down into his coffin.

"I was called to give your wife the last rites," Father Summers said as Stuart fled past him, "but it was too late."

"She wasn't a Catholic."

"She was a lovely woman."

He hadn't yet decided how to react to that inappropriate observation when Jackson returned with a mortuary assistant, who also protested that nothing had been done with Gwyneth, but Stuart overrode them and was led to a tiled basement where she lay on a marble slab. He saw what they had meant. He had naively expected a body at perfect peace, but the white sheet tucked at her neck covered the angular irregularities of a form contorted and frozen in rigor mortis. Her lips were stretched back from her teeth in a sneer. Her green eyes, focused on nothing, glinted milkily, and one of them was half-closed in a salacious wink.

"Jesus Christ," he breathed.

"We don't like to—" the assistant began.

"It's all right, forget it." He stepped forward and tried to close her eyes with his shaking fingers, but the lids wouldn't stay down. It seemed a challenge that had to be met. He kept trying until Jackson finally drew him away. He knew that he would never get the chill of her eyelids off his fingertips. "That's her. That's my wife."

He discovered that he could pray when he went

home, and it gave him more comfort than he would have imagined. The blasphemous visions he'd experienced on the night of Gwyneth's death had shocked him back into the faith he'd strayed from. Those visions could have come from nowhere but hell, and it would be absurd to accept proof of Satan's power without accepting it as proof as well of God's love and mercy. He would have liked to go to mass and communion, but he was strangely unwilling to risk seeing Father Summers again. He told himself that this was uncharitable. He prayed to root out the fault, and he was able to go to confession at last.

He found it difficult to keep up the appearance of mourning. He was filled with exuberance from morning till night. He couldn't determine the cause. He felt that the real cause must be in the immediate future, that he was pregnant with some truth of such grandeur and beauty that it would transfigure not just him, but the whole world.

Woodling didn't come to the funeral. Kemper did. Stuart avoided meeting his eyes over the grave, although he knew Kemper was staring at him. As they returned to the cars, the old man grabbed him by the sleeve.

"Please go away. Leave me alone."

"Who is it?" Allison demanded.

"The Old Man Who Wouldn't Say His Prayers," Arthur said.

"Let me see you." Allison seized him and touched his face. "Who are you, and what more do you want from us?"

"I have to talk to your son."

"He's Gwyneth's father," Stuart said.

"No, I'm not. It was just a story I told her. I think you ought to have this."

He shoved into Stuart's hands the framed sketch of Gwyneth from his shack. It was an even better work than Stuart remembered. Through springy curls beneath an ornate bonnet, her sidelong glance was mischievous.

"Go ahead home, Mom. I'll talk with him."

She grumbled and fretted, but she went back to the chauffeured car with Arthur. The workmen were already shoveling dirt into the grave, and Stuart walked away from them as he studied the picture. He laughed when he noticed the signature. "Gowdie," he said.

"This was a portrait I did of Melody Bloodstone. The woman you've buried was born nearly a hundred years ago."

"It's a good forgery. The signature, I mean. I'm not an art expert. May I keep it?"

"Yes. But it's no forgery. Believe what you will about it, but you must believe me when I say you're in danger."

He looked hard into Kemper's crazy black eyes and tried to love him. Jesus wouldn't have hated him; he would have cast out his devils. He passionately wished he could do so. He rested his hand on Kemper's frail shoulder.

"I think you convinced Gwyneth of a lot of pernicious nonsense before she died. It had upset her so much when she ran from the house that night . . ."

Looking beyond Kemper, he saw that Bob McWraith had remained by the grave. Silhouetted against a tumultuous sky of bruised pearl, he stood in the attitude of a man stunned by grief. He would have preferred sharing real memories of Gwyneth with him instead of absurd fantasies about her with Kemper. But he still felt a responsibility for the old man.

"I think you're a danger to others, even though you don't know it. You need help. I'd be willing to pay—"

"You supercilious, sanctimonious boob!" Kemper screamed, virtually dancing with anger. "You have twice—*twice!*—slung Sylvestris Tenebrion howling back into the Otherworld, and you don't even have the vaguest notion of what it is you've done! In the names of your foolish little trio of gods, flee from your mother and your son as if you were death yourself. Forget about them. Never give them another thought, kindly or otherwise."

"I don't know what you're talking about."

"I'm talking about the safety of your loved ones,"

he said, struggling to suppress his fury. "I loved Melody, I felt a duty to her, but they use such feelings to work our destruction. So I stayed away from her, until, in my pride and folly, I thought myself strong enough to fight them. Until I deluded myself—or they deluded me—that they had forgotten me."

"They?"

"The Pallid Mask. The Eldritch King. Others, who knows how many, the demigods of myth, the fairies and goblins of folklore, intruders from the Otherworld. They prey on us through our dreams and fantasies. Each of us harbors repressed hatred, unspeakable desires, unknown wishes toward those we think we love the most. They will make your dreams come true."

"And your defense was to cut your connections with the human race, sneaking out every month or so to take a peek at Gwyneth, scuttling away if she saw you."

"I didn't cut my connections drastically enough." Kemper's anger had turned inward. "I should have cut my throat."

"And why me? What makes you think they can work through me? Or should everybody kiss everybody else goodbye and go hide someplace? The woods would get damned crowded."

"Oh, you fool, they *own* you! I can see it in your face, I can hear it in your voice. You've visited the

Otherworld, you've seen signs and wonders—perhaps you've even lain with one of them. Tell me, when did you eat or drink last?"

"I haven't had much appetite since Gwyneth—"

"The fact is you can't eat mortal food, you blind idiot, nor can you drink the water of this earth. I couldn't when I returned, nor could Melody. You must go somewhere by yourself and struggle to retain what tenuous grasp you have left on this world."

Stuart saw that the limousine still waited for him. He walked toward it, with Kemper tagging along. He looked inside his heart and found no hatred, no unknown wishes, no unspeakable desires; not even toward Kemper, much less toward Allison or Arthur. He found it brimming with God's grace.

"What you say is true," he admitted. "It was no dream, they sent me a woman like Gwyneth, and I sinned with her. And I killed her."

"If you believe—"

"My soul was darkened with impure thoughts and carnal desires. But I've prayed to our Lord Jesus Christ, who died for my sins, and for yours, to lighten my darkness. I've been absolved, I'm in a state of grace. Your fairies can't touch me, Kemper."

"*Horseshit!*" Kemper howled.

Not even this blasphemy could make Stuart hate the old man. He forgave him: not through some superior feeling of pity, but because he loved him, just as he loved the gravediggers trudging now from their task.

His exultant pregnancy was over; the truth had been made flesh. He had at last been granted the gift of perfect faith. It was not merely passive acceptance, it was a positive force whose existence he had never even imagined in his former blindness. It seemed as if it ought to be crackling visibly from his hair and his eyes and his fingertips. It united him in a torrent of raw power that connected the worms in the earth with the majestic cycles of the galaxies. The glory of God blazed forth in the angry sky and the dead leaves, in his heart and even in Kemper's mockery. He knew now what it meant, the faith that could move mountains. He could move them.

Kemper was right: the creatures of the Otherworld could make our dreams come true. But their power was neither good nor evil, and our dreams were our own responsibility. Through prayer and perfect faith he had made certain that he could no longer be an instrument of evil. Even though he knew this interpretation was correct, he had to give proof to Kemper.

With the old man still babbling his foolish warnings, Stuart went to the limousine and opened the door on his mother's side.

"I waited in case you decided . . . James, what are you doing?"

He didn't speak as he removed her dark glasses and pocketed them. He reached down for some graveyard earth, spat on it, and worked it into a paste with his fingers. Then he rubbed it on her eyelids.

"Is that you, James?" she cried, striking his hands away. "Who are you?"

"It's him, all right," Arthur said. "He's finally flipped, too."

"Go, wash in the pool . . ." he began to say, for they were the right words, but then he saw there was no Pool of Siloam. An ornate memorial fountain stood across the path, however. He pulled her from the car and forced her to walk to it.

"What are you doing, James? Do you know what you're doing? Speak to me—*please.*"

"As long as I am in the world," he said, "I am the light of the world."

"Oh, no," she groaned, beginning to resist, but they had reached the fountain. It had been turned off for the coming winter, but the basin before them was filled with black-green water under a mat of leaves. He directed her hand into the water, and she splashed it on her eyes.

He waited, exultant. She braced both hands on the stone rim and leaned over the black water. He looked at her image in the pool. Her eyes shifted to meet his reflected eyes. She saw him. It didn't mar his exultation that her look was one of pure terror.

"How . . .?" She straightened to stare at him directly, her lips quivering, her face streaked with mud.

"Go home. I must work the works of him that sent me while it is day, for the night cometh."

"James, I can't deny that you've worked a miracle," she said somewhat peevishly as she scoured her face with a handkerchief. "I can see. But this attitude of yours . . . those words . . . I think you ought to come home, too, and rest."

Across the path, Arthur goggled at them and Kemper seethed with rage. "She can see, and you're blind," he snarled. "You haven't read your damned collection of goatherds' ravings well enough, you fool. Your Lord said that many would work wonders and prophesy in his name, and cast out devils. And he said he would tell them, 'Depart from me, ye that work iniquity. I never knew you.' "

Allison stared at him, and at Arthur, at the black chauffeur who had stepped out to gawk, at the bare trees around them and the gravestones across the way. She couldn't entirely hold back a flickering smile that struggled to break free. Suddenly sobbing, she ran awkwardly across the path and hugged her grandson.

"Go home," Stuart said. "I have work to do."

He watched the limousine out of sight before he strode purposefully forward. Kemper tried to bar his way.

"Leave her alone!" he shouted, guessing Stuart's

purpose and trying to push him back. "You've got no right! She's escaped them at last, leave her in peace!"

He saw no point in arguing. He was doing good; his holy acts would speak for themselves.

"You maniac! Do you know what she is? She's been eviscerated and stuffed with cotton, her veins have been pumped full of formaldehyde, her body is basted with undertaker's stiches! Her back is broken!"

"O ye of little faith," Stuart said gently, while Kemper frothed at the mouth and pounded him with innocuous fists.

McWraith still stood alone by the grave with a bundle wrapped in canvas under his arm. At first Stuart thought it a trick of the mutable autumn light, but a nimbus in constant, confusing pulsation hung behind McWraith's head. It was not merely black, as Cassilda had described it. It was like a Black Hole, dimming the light around it.

"A truly remarkable demonstration," McWraith said. "What's next on your agenda, Stuart?"

"Gwyneth. Malkin. Cassilda. Shaver. The coeds whom Sterling killed. And even Sterling himself. If he can be made to accept me—to accept Christ as his Lord and Saviour, he, too, can enter the kingdom of heaven."

"Oh, my. Why not everyone?" He laughed and

gestured expansively at the waste of headstones around them.

Stuart smiled lovingly at him. He forgave him his mockery. He turned to the fresh earth of Gwyneth's grave to concentrate all of his powers, but now Kemper rushed at him. In his hands, poised like a bayonet, he held a shovel left by the gravediggers.

"I'll kill you first!" he screamed.

"Give the lad a chance," McWraith said, seizing the old man and restraining him.

Stuart ignored them. The power he had felt was now increased a thousandfold. A thunderstorm of pure energy raged in the frail confines of his mortal body. His veins and nerves and bones sang with it as it discharged into the earth from his outstretched hand. "Gwyneth!" he cried. *"Come forth!"*

He felt utterly drained. He heard nothing but the wind soughing through brown grass and naked branches. McWraith freed Kemper, who fell to his knees and pressed his ear to the earth. At length he rolled a crazed, bloodshot eye on Stuart and whispered, his voice choked with loathing, "You wretched man, you've done it. She's pounding . . . down there."

"Well, then!" McWraith sang jovially, flinging his bundle down jangling beside Kemper. "There remains but one thing to be done. You'll find everything you need there, Mr. Gowdie." He came forward and grasped Stuart firmly around the shoulders. "Sorry about the crown of thorns, the scourging and all that, but one can't have everything. And as for your resurrection after three days, well ....."

Stuart was too shattered to resist. His feelings had been a deception, a trap. He was only a man. No matter how hard he concentrated, no matter how fervently he prayed in silence, the power of his confident faith was gone. He saw that the bundle Kemper had unwrapped contained a sledgehammer and iron spikes.

"Nor a proper cross, either," McWraith said, leading him down the hill. "But here's on oak tree that will do nicely."

"Wait! For God's sake, Bob, we have to dig her out—she's buried!"

"And as Mr. Gowdie so astutely pointed out, she's a thoroughly horrid mess. But once she begins to rot away in earnest, she won't feel much. We'd be obliged, Jamie, if you forgot about 'Bob.' You know who I am."

He twisted his head to stare into McWraith's eyes. They held the same utter blackness as his aura, which now looked like nothing so much as an elaborate crown. As he looked he began to feel an excruciating pain in his right hand. He thought that McWraith might be crushing it, but he saw that it was free. Before his eyes, the fingers twisted into a splayed arch from which he could not move them.

Despite the pain, he began to laugh. This was a dream, surely the most extraordinary and vivid nightmare that anyone had ever dreamed. McWraith as the Eldritch King. Kemper as Sebastian Gowdie. Himself as Jesus Christ, and now as Auld Catchy-Claw. All the mad turmoil of the past weeks had caught up with him in his grief and exhaustion to produce a vision he could scare his grandchildren with. He would, of course, presently wake up in his bed to find that he had rolled over to lie on his right hand.

He cried out as McWraith flung him against the tree a foot or so from the ground and held him there. Kemper reached up to seize his withered hand and centered the point of a spike against his palm.

"For a life-long pagan, Mr. Gowdie, your ignorance of Roman customs is deplorable. Drive it through the wrist, between the radius and ulna, or it will just tear the tendons and slip free."

"It's my dream," Stuart said, "and if I'm going to be crucified . . ."

"This is no dream," said McWraith, and when the hammer drove the spike through his wrist, Stuart knew that for a fact.

He at last began to scream and struggle, but it was too late. The spike pinned one arm, McWraith held the other, and Gowdie was already hammering in the second spike with a vengeance. Although his legs were free, his kicks had no leverage. Each attempt twisted his hands and left him breathless with pain.

"Gowdie!" he screamed. "You have the iron. For God's sake, strike *him!*"

"Now that sounds more like the Bailie of Glenwearie I once knew! But you forgot that Mr. Gowdie is living out his own dream. And he forgot that the strongest of all human attachments is hatred. His defense against love may have worked, but he wallowed in his loathing for you, Jamie, and he's mine."

"And my daughter—?"

"A suitable replacement for dear Melody. Pierce the side now, Mr. Gowdie. I'd love to leave you to hang for the appropriate time, but I've wasted enough time on you." He restrained Gowdie, who was convulsed with impatience, as he asked, "Tell me, Jamie, do you forgive us, for we know not what we do?"

"Oh, God, send him back to hell!" Stuart screamed.

The first thrust of Gowdie's shovel only broke Stuart's ribs. The Eldritch King advised him how to thrust upward, beneath the rib-cage, and he did.

CHAPTER THIRTEEN

"They're nothing but lurid cartoons," Allison said with mild surprise. "I remembered them as being much more impressive."

"*I* like them," Arthur said, but she knew that his taste had been shaped by the ghastly comic books she had learned about only recently.

She recalled now that her last viewing of the Gowdie murals had been imperfect. On the hot summer evenings she had spent here with Alan Braden, the walls had been carelessly draped with old blankets that had revealed only random fragments. Eyes had stared with singular intensity, hands had reached from the walls. Often the fragments would seem to have changed while her attention was elsewhere. A fanciful person might have imagined that the figures were restless behind the makeshift hangings. Now they seemed flat and faded and harmless in a submarine twilight reflected from snow outside the door.

Turning to the Hansel and Gretel mural, she started violently. In the ambiguous light it had seemed for a moment that she saw a woman with ravaged eyes fleeing a fire. But it was only the witch beside her flaming oven, her face streaked by leakage from the roof.

"What's that doing here?" She had seized on the first distraction to present itself. "It looks brand-new."

"The safety switch is broke."

"Broken."

"Mom thought we'd cremate ourselves." Arthur climbed on some boxes to reach the microwave oven and bring it down. "Or even if it worked right, she was afraid we'd all grow six toes."

Arthur was too tough for his own good. The deaths of his parents had seemed to break him. Less than two months ago he had become hysterical on a visit to their graves, insisting that he could hear his mother's cries from the earth. But his shell had grown back harder than before, and now he could joke about Gwyneth's whims.

"I used to be clever with electricity," she said as she gave the device a preliminary examination.

"I know, you wired the whole house."

The pride in his voice was so evident that she wondered if he hadn't taken her for his model. When she'd been blind, he was the only one who'd appreciated her jokes about it. They had merely upset Joan, and James and Gwyneth had deplored her taste for gallows humor. And now Arthur must know—how could he not?—that their house couldn't have been more dangerous if it had been on fire; yet, like her, he refused to show fear.

She had seen nothing of the Castle since she'd stabbed James's attacker and been stunned by the thrashing of its inhuman head. She had no evidence to contradict Gwyneth's theory that Tomlin Woodling had been at the root of their troubles; and he had decamped, merely following—or so it was generally believed—in the footsteps of several previous celebrities—in-residence at Amworth. No one had suggested that he might have been there when that old man had murdered James, or that he had fled town only afterwards. The old man had said nothing about it, nor was it likely that he would, for he had neither spoken a word nor voluntarily moved a muscle since they had found him with the body.

Nevertheless she felt like a prisoner living on a tenuous reprieve. Just as Gowdie's murals looked disingenuously lifeless, so the stillness of the house seemed deliberate, its emptiness a transparent sham. She sometimes caught herself tiptoeing through the silent rooms like a knowing guest of honor at a surprise party, straining her ears for a whisper or a giggle from concealed pranksters; who had not come to give gifts, but to claim them. More than anything, she feared that the miraculous restoration of her sight was a joke they would eventually tire of.

She hoped Arthur didn't know it, but she had spent the two months since James's death building up her courage for this visit to the playhouse, which seemed the very center of the evil vortex; but it was into this vortex that Joan had vanished.

"I'd like to try plugging it in . . ."

Before Arthur could climb to take down the socket of the extension-cord, she impulsively restrained him. Changing anything from the way it had been—for who knew what rules applied?—might destroy Joan's chances of returning. She saw that her grandson's eyes were on her, that his face—so like James's at that age—registered amused scorn. She released his sleeve.

"I read the book, too," he said. "It didn't say a thing about light-cords."

Unexpectedly, and to her intense relief, it was at last all out in the open. There was no need to conceal from Arthur the fact that they had been—and might still be—besieged by the legions of the Otherworld. It was even more of a relief to know that they wouldn't have to discuss it, or discuss the need for staying in the vile house until Joan's return. He knew it all already. He had read the book: *The Myth of the Otherworld in the English and Scottish Ballads,* by Gwyneth Underhill, that she had read and re-read with growing exasperation, for it wasn't the instruction manual she needed. It contained no sure answers, only maddening hints.

She had just mated the plug with the socket when she heard the crunch of snow under heavy feet. "Ho-ho-ho!" boomed a deep voice. "Merry Christmas!"

She laughed with pleasure at the familiar voice and went to the door to greet McWraith; but as he straightened up within the low doorway, the sight of his figure looming above her alarmed her obscurely.

"Sorry to startle you," he said when she took a backward step. "And I'm even sorrier not to have called on you before now, but the pressure of my new duties—good Lord, what a fool I am! I'm Bob McWraith, Mrs. Doyle. I'd forgotten that you've never seen me."

"I know you, of course." She firmly put aside her irrational fright. "But are you sure I've never seen you . . . years ago?"

He took a seat on the dilapidated couch where Alan had often sulked. Well-worn lines of merriment creased his face as he beamed at her and Arthur; but in his scarlet coat with white fur trim, with gaily wrapped packages in his arms, he looked less like Santa Claus than he did some Cossack who had pillaged a Christmas tree. And he looked damnably familiar.

"You were quite blind when I first met you, ten years ago, and I haven't seen you since your miraculous recovery. Tell me—"

She had tried to conceal the suspect miracle, but the undertaker's chauffeur had told the story, with imaginative embellishments, all over town. She had managed to dissuade the newspaperman who called her from printing anything on the grounds that her blindness had obviously been hysterical in origin; but her explanation had been gossiped about, too, and she felt that it had made her a laughing-stock. So she interrupted brusquely: "I guess congratulations are in order."

"Not at all. The trustees named me acting president only until they can find someone able to fill his mouth with President Shaver's shoes. Here you go, Arthur, you young devil, merry Christmas!"

Even though she had refused to be frightened without specific cause, she found herself unwilling to move far from the open door while he was in the room; and it fretted her that Arthur's path to the door was blocked by the couch. Now McWraith extended one of the packages to him, but Arthur stood out of reach with his hands determinedly at his sides. Whatever bothered her about the man, it bothered her grandson, too.

"We had planned not to observe Christmas this year," she said.

"So like his father, isn't he." McWraith thumped his gifts down beside him with no visible dilution of his high spirits. "You'll save them for Easter, then, won't you? A far more joyous festival, you can't ignore the day that gives the lie to all mourning. I've often wondered what our Lord will think when he comes back to find his resurrection celebrated with colored eggs and chocolate bunnies. A chocolate cockroach would be much more suitable, don't you think, they're impossible to kill. I'd venture to say that even crucifying one and piercing his little side would have no more effect than it had on our Galilean jack-in-the-box."

Could he really have forgotten for the moment the manner of her son's death? Rather than remind him, she turned to Arthur and said sharply, "Don't tinker with that!"

"These remarkable murals!" he cried. "Poor old Gowdie would have been shocked speechless to see what's become of them. Have you thought of selling them, or better still, donating them to our Arthur D. Pickman Museum?"

"I plan to sell the house. Eventually."

"It would certainly enhance the price if you had them spruced up. I've used my exalted position to invite a celebrity to Amworth who might help you, an artist named Schalken, who's a great fan of Gowdie's. Between your charm and my bullying, we may get him to do the job for nothing."

"Woodling's replacement?"

"Who could replace that nonpareil? It cost half our buildings and grounds budget to clean up the mess he left in his quarters."

"Before he died, President Shaver told me that you had recommended . . ."

She saw it coming and might have stopped it, but for no clear reason she let it happen as if she were watching a movie. While McWraith listened with polite attention, a smile touching his face as he prepared his no doubt witty response, Arthur, wobbling slightly from the weight of it, approached him from behind with the microwave oven in his arms. Even before he raised it higher she knew what he intended. But still she said nothing, nor did she betray him with her expression.

". . . Woodling," she concluded, and Arthur dropped the open oven on McWraith's head, then flung himself on top of it to hold it down.

"Grab him, Grandma! Hold him!" When she didn't move, he cried, "He gave Joan candy before she disappeared—if we kill him she'll come back and all his spells will be broken!"

She thought that she had come to believe the truth of Gwyneth's book; but when that belief was weighed against the reality of her grandson's attempt at assassination, it seemed insane. She must have been the victim of a contagious hysteria generated by Gwyneth and James. This shocking sight had finally restored her to her senses.

Before she could act on this flash of insight and help McWraith, he gave a frightening display of strength by rising to his feet with Arthur and the oven on his shoulders. He gripped the appliance with both hands and tried to raise it from his head. It seemed he must succeed, but the oven stuck. He roared like a very dangerous animal in a very flimsy snare, and in that instant her momentary reversion to faith in a rational universe was overturned: for his voice was that of the distant singer in the Castle, the voice she had heard summoning James on the day she killed Sterling Fairchild; and she knew that his was the figure with the axe that towered over her.

"Grandma!" Arthur began to slip from his tossing perch as McWraith blundered about the room, striking out savagely at the junk in his path, smashing sturdy boxes with his fists.

Still she held back. No matter what she believed, it seemed far too drastic a step to assist in a murder because of the intuitive impulse of a boy and the ravings of his deranged mother; and because of her own Castle experiences, which any impartial person would have dismissed as hallucinations. It would be so much easier to stand by and let the situation develop.

But now McWraith—who had survived the microwave bombardment far longer, it seemed to her, than any mortal man could have—overcame his panic and acted with intelligent purpose: he seized the line-cord and began reeling it in. The plug and socket would soon be in his hands.

Arthur slid from the oven and seized his arm. McWraith flung his arm back, and Arthur hit the wall with a thud that churned Allison's stomach. McWraith had momentarily lost the cord. As he fumbled to retrieve it, she acted. She kicked his legs from under him and sent him sprawling forward, then she fell on his back and seized his right arm in a hold that would dislocate his shoulder if he struggled too vigorously.

She couldn't say exactly why she found it odd to be holding a gift-wrapped package in her hands. She turned it this way and that, examining it in bewilderment. She had a vague picture of a ruddy Santa Claus bearing gifts . . .

But that was nonsense. It wasn't Christmas, it was Jamie's twelfth birthday. She had hesitated in the act of bringing her gift—Kipling's *Jungle Book*—into the dining room, where his friends were gathered around the cake.

She walked briskly onward with the intention of

putting the book with the other presents. But something was wrong. Jamie's guests sat at the table like perfect little ladies and gentlemen. Their attention was riveted on her. Their breathing suspended as she started to put down the book.

A perverse impulse made her withdraw the gift and clutch it to her breast. But it was more than an impulse: it was as if her life depended on retaining it. The book had become much heavier, almost as if it were trying to pull itself out of her hands. She tightened her grip.

Jamie looked into her eyes, and for a moment he reminded her of a boy much closer to her . . . more nonsense, surely; he was her only son. He looked far more upset than her action would seem to warrant.

"Put the book down, Mom. Look, the wax is dripping onto the cake. Sit down while I blow out the candles."

"Put the book down," the other children repeated, tugging at her dress. She noticed what extraordinarily beautiful children they were, how elegantly dressed; and she wondered why she could match none of them with a name. Beautiful or not, the picking of their pale little hands was vaguely distressing, and she pulled out of their reach.

"How do you know it's a book?"

Realizing that she had sounded unintentionally harsh and suspicious, she put on a smile, but it was too late, for Jamie had burst into tears. Arthur would never—who the devil was Arthur? The name "Arthur Conan Doyle" glimmered in her mind, it seemed almost as if she knew a child so impertinently christened. Trying to puzzle this out, she started thoughtlessly to put the book aside. It alarmed her by trying to wriggle from her hand. She held it tight and scrutinized it once more, but it was only a wrapped gift.

"You're ruining my party," he sobbed. "I'll only have one twelfth birthday as long as I live, and I'll only live until you run away and leave me in the graveyard with Sebastian Gowdie. You are going to murder me when you grow old. Can't you try to make up for it by letting me be happy now?"

She knew somehow that he was telling the truth. She could not so much see into the future as feel the crushing guilt of a deed that was hurtling through the years to meet her. She knew that she would one day blame herself for her son's death.

"Murderess," the children hissed like pale, beautiful snakes as Jamie reached for his book.

"Grandma! Don't!" The cry was a tiny one, but it seized her attention as if it were a tiny needle entering her ear, and she twisted away from it. "Hold him, and Mom will be really dead at last!"

Jamie's chin melted into his neck as it elongated to become a swaying stalk. His eyes, now red coals, came within an inch of hers as he whispered, "And you will be *really blind!*"

She was in total darkness. The book had become soft and wet and unpleasantly warm. "Pass it on," a girl's voice whispered.

"What is it?" Allie Stuart whispered back.

"Her heart. The old witch's heart." Giggles and whispers swarmed in the darkness.

Allie clasped it in both hands. It wasn't at all like the hearts on valentines. It was large and heavy, irregular in shape, and altogether messy. She knew it was dripping on her dress, and she hoped Joseph Doyle had been thoughtful enough to use a prop that wouldn't stain. She had a sneaking, sickening suspicion that it was a real heart, a pig's or a lamb's.

"Here, take her head," said a voice on her left.

"Come on, Allie, pass her heart!"

"You're holding up the game, Allie," Joseph said from the opposite side of the room.

"She's choked up," a girl said. "Scaredy-cat! We took her apart, and you have her heart."

"I don't want to play this anymore." She stood up. Despite the hands that picked at her in the darkness and tried to take it, she held the heart to her own.

"Now, don't tease her," Joseph said. "We don't want anybody getting the heebie-jeebies. It's only a game. Turn on the lights."

Light crashed on. She was in Cassie's parlor. The

first thing she saw was the Silvertone radio that had scared them out of their wits just two Halloweens ago with Orson Welles's Martian invasion. That had been more fun than this dumb game.

Joseph grinned at her. He would look dreamy if he didn't slick his hair down and part it in the middle like a lounge lizard, but she couldn't make such a suggestion to a mature, sophisticated young man of seventeen. He might guess that she was sweet on him.

Her eyes lowered to the white bundle in his lap and she began to gag. It could only be a store-window mannequin, headless and limbless and smeared with ketchup. But she had seen unclothed mannequins. They didn't have nipples or pubic hair. They weren't so white, so ghastly limp, nor would they yield like dough, as this one did, to Joseph's busy knife.

Dizzy and sick, she scanned the room and the unexpectedly brilliant company. She knew them, and yet she didn't. Her friends would have had neither the imagination nor the money for such dazzling outfits, nor were her friends so uniformly beautiful. It was like the court of the Faerie Queen; but this beautiful girl had a severed foot, that handsome boy a red, ropy tangle of intestines. And the girl to her left, rising now, held up by its blonde ringlets the head of pretty young Cassie Castaldo.

But the horror around her was nothing against the bloody mass she held in her own two hands. Even as she recognized what she was holding, the heart began to beat with a strong pulse. She felt her hands slipping on its slimy, writhing surface. She wanted to throw it as far from her as she could, but an irresistible compulsion forced her to cling even more tightly.

"Pass it on," said a new and very familiar voice to her left. She looked. Cassie's head smiled and the eyes transfixed her with a fiendish intelligence.

Still she refused to release the heart, and the mummers simultaneously flew into a rage, as if guided by one mind. They hurled themselves on her, clawing and spitting, but oddly their fury had as little effect as a flock of angry butterflies. She shut her eyes and held on.

"Can't you take a joke?"

She wiped the sweat from her eyes on the back of Alan's shirt. She didn't have the heart to carry out her plan. But she couldn't release him, either. She felt him shifting slyly to the edge of the dock, where he might dunk them both in the greasy water and make his escape. She forced his pinned arm up until he cried out.

"Please, let go. Please. I'll leave you alone. Honest. Let me go, and I'll let you go home. Father Doyle's gone home, right? I can't hurt him. That girl. I was lying. That was just a girl I was talking to. I wouldn't hurt her. Let me go."

"You hurt me, you son of a bitch. You've done

nothing but hurt me. You've drugged me and tortured me and humiliated me and—God damn you, I don't believe a word you say! If I let you go you'll kill her, I know you will."

She knew that she could do it, after all. He lied, he lied all the time, but he never lied when he bragged about his evil, sadistic deeds. And he had bragged in detail about his plans for the little girl she had seen talking to him. He had boasted of his plans for Jamie, too. She hoped her son had taken her seriously and left Malneant this morning, but she couldn't be sure.

"Look. That stuff I told you. About Sebastian Gowdie. That was talk. I don't know a thing. About him, about sacrifices to the Fourth Dimension, that's just a lot of crap I picked up from reading H.P. Lovecraft. I was kidding you. Can't you take a joke?"

"The body was no joke."

"There was no body! Allison, I swear to God, you were having a bad trip! You were stoned!"

Two people had occupied the houseboat when they arrived, a man and a woman. She waited in the car while Alan went aboard. An hour later he called to her and she picked her way down the long, rotting dock to find Alan alone. No one, in the meantime, had left by way of the dock. He said they had left by boat. It was his houseboat, they'd been minding it. The man who owned the dock never questioned the story. Since this stagnant arm of the bay had silted up, the houseboat was his only customer, and his interest didn't go beyond collecting payment for the slip, the fresh water, and the electricity.

Two weeks later, under the influence of some vile potion Alan had put in her wine, she had gone out onto the rear deck to look at the Van Gogh stars. From the black depths where they were reflected a pallid blot had risen, breaking the surface to reveal itself as a great white balloon in the shape of a man, his face and extremities gone to feed the crabs.

If Alan could kill two people for this derelict, he would surely not stop at killing a little girl—as he'd said his hero, Gowdie, had done—for a glimpse of the Otherworld.

As she forced him the last few steps to the deck of the houseboat, she was struck by a frivolous qualm: she wasn't dressed for this. Tabloid starlets were found dead in black bikinis, not she or anyone she wanted to know. She wished she had a plain white dress for her immolation scene.

"You won't die, you fool," Alan snarled. "You won't die at all, you'll live for years to come with your eyes burned out. And I'll make certain you won't grow used to it, for in fifteen years I'll restore your sight and give you one more chance to *let me go!*"

There was no way he could know that she had bared the electric wires and crossed them in the bilges, which she'd flooded with gasoline. And yet what he said was true: if she carried out her plan, she knew she would be blinded. And not just now, but in some future time when her sight would have been restored.

"Help!"

She had been on the verge of releasing him in her fear and confusion when the little girl had cried out. She renewed her grip as she turned to look. It wasn't the blonde girl she had seen with him. This one was younger, and dark, and she looked hauntingly familiar. Of course: she looked like Gwyneth Underhill, the weird girl from Amworth who wore those bizarre dresses. Gwyneth was too young to be her mother, nor did she have any sisters, but the resemblance was uncanny.

What was far more uncanny, the little girl was running toward the houseboat across the water. The water was shallow toward the shore, it was just possible she might wade in it, but she wasn't wading. The water didn't even splash beneath her running feet. Beneath her it appeared dazzlingly white, as if it were not water but snow.

"Help me, Grandma! Hold him!"

"Don't listen to her!" Alan screamed in sudden panic. "She's not real! She's not here! Let me go!"

"Grandma," Allison laughed, shoving him through the door. With her free hand she stabbed at the lightswitch. "I'll never live that long."

She saw the brightest light she had ever seen. Then she saw nothing.

She scrabbled on a cold floor among discarded clothing of fur and wool for something she desperately needed to hold. Arthur was laughing beside her in a way that sounded perilously close to hysteria. She couldn't see him.

"Stop it, Arthur!" she shouted.

"We did it! Feel it! Feel!" he laughed or sobbed as he pressed some brittle shreds into her hand. They crumbled even as she touched them. "That's Barfing Bob! And she's back! Oh, God, the little rat is back!"

"Will you two please stop rolling around on the floor and tell me how the ground got covered with snow while I was walking between here and the house?"

"Joan! Joan!" Allison cried. "I can't see you!"

"You never could," Joan blurted in surprise. She recovered by turning brusquely on Arthur: "I'm not paying you a dollar an hour to play with a Santa Claus suit, Arthur. You'll be sorry when I die young and tragically and you haven't cleaned this place out yet."